FORKING AROUND

HOT CAKES BOOK TWO

ERIN NICHOLAS

ISBN: 978-1-952280-04-7

Editor: Lindsey Faber

Cover design: Angela Waters

Cover Photography: Lindee Robinson

Models: Kelly Marie & David Turner

PROLOGUE

He could watch this woman eat cake all night.

That was a weird fetish he hadn't been aware of until now, but he was totally okay with it. As fetishes went, this one seemed on the tamer end of the spectrum.

The curvy redhead put her third cake pop in her mouth. The mouth he was now going to have major fantasies about. She had full lips that matched the pink icing on the vanilla cake pops, and every time she ran her tongue over that bottom lip, his body tightened. And she was running her tongue over her lip a lot with all the cake eating she was doing.

She'd eaten the first two in a couple of bites each. But she'd just stuck the entire third cake pop in her mouth. The girl liked cake. Man, he loved people who were enthusiastically open about the things they enjoyed.

People should never apologize for loving what they loved. Especially if they were gorgeous redheads who loved putting balls in their mouths. He grinned. He was totally going to use that line. It was just the right amount of immature and dirty and playful that he appreciated.

He definitely knew there were times when lines like that

were inappropriate. Knowing that wouldn't keep him from using the line, of course, but he did know he couldn't expect an equally playful, good-natured response from just everyone. That was why it was perfect. It was a great way to find out if he was talking to someone he could have fun with or not.

He definitely needed to talk to her.

"Excuse me."

He'd moved around the table so he was slightly behind her now, but he saw how she froze. Then she started chewing faster, then swallowed, wiped her mouth, and turned to face him.

"Um, hi."

He chuckled. "How's the red velvet?" he asked. She had a few red-velvet crumbs on the front of her dress, the red pieces standing out against the teal fabric.

"Um." She swallowed again. "Great. They're all great."

"I guess I'll have to take your word for it. Since you took the last one," Dax said, looking pointedly at the now empty tray with the tiny sign next to it that read RED VELVET.

She glanced down and knocked the sign over. "Sorry."

"I don't think you are. You ate two of the last three and have the third in your hand." He gave her a grin.

She looked startled for a second. She probably hadn't been expecting him to have been keeping track of her cake-pop consumption.

"Sorry is just the polite thing to say." She swiped her thumb over her bottom lip. "I don't mean it."

He lifted an eyebrow. "I'm going to assume that means you're not going to share the strawberry one you're holding either. It's the last one of those, too."

She lifted the strawberry cake pop to her mouth and took a bite. "Nope."

He definitely liked her. His let his mouth drop open in mock outrage. "Wow."

"I know. I'm the worst. You should definitely go find someone else to talk to."

There was absolutely no one else he wanted to talk to more than he wanted to talk to her. He also wanted to kiss her. But he'd wanted that even before he'd known she'd taste like red-velvet and strawberry cakes. He stepped forward.

She didn't even blink.

He lifted a hand and picked a crumb of cake from the front of her dress. It wasn't on her breast, exactly. It was just below the scooped neckline. It wasn't like he was feeling her up. But it was safe to say he hadn't missed the fact she had some very nice curves. Without them, those crumbs might not have gotten hung up during their fall to the floor.

He met her gaze as he lifted the cake crumb to his mouth. She watched as he licked the tip of his index finger.

"Mmm, the red velvet *is* good," he said.

She looked down to where he'd touched her. But she didn't slap him or shove him away. Her cheeks got a little pink. Then she stuffed the rest of the strawberry cake pop into her mouth, chewed, swallowed, and smiled. "They're all very good."

"Not the slightest bit apologetic?" he asked, incredibly amused and very drawn to her.

"Nope."

The strawberry cake pops were coated in white icing and she had a streak of it just to the side of her mouth.

He wanted to cover her in that icing.

He grinned. "Excellent. Never apologize for doing stuff that makes you feel good."

Her eyes widened slightly and for just an instant, her gaze dropped to his mouth.

He definitely made a note of that.

"So I'm going to go," she said, taking a half step away from the table.

"I'm Dax." He needed to know who she was.

Appleby, Iowa, the town where his best friends—and business partners—had decided to buy a snack cake factory, was tiny. It wouldn't take him long to find out who she was. But he wanted her to tell him. And give him her number. And agree to have dinner with him tomorrow. And eat cake pops in bed with him.

Not necessarily in that order. But giving him her name would be a great start.

"I'm... late," she said.

She grabbed one of the vanilla cake pops and started to slip around him. Then she paused, turned back, grabbed a chocolate, *then* slipped around him.

"Do you work for Hot Cakes?" he asked, watching her go with a grin.

She turned back and met his eyes. But didn't say anything.

For nearly thirty seconds.

She just... looked at him.

Finally, he asked, "Are you okay?"

She blinked, seeming to realize she'd been staring. She nodded. "Um, yes."

She didn't sound entirely convinced.

"You're sure?"

"Yes."

"You don't need another cake pop, then?" he asked, eyeing the four she held. "If I go for one, I'm not going to lose a finger or hand?"

He really wanted her to smile again, instead of the way she'd been looking at him as if she'd gotten lost in her thoughts. Thoughts that weren't especially happy.

He wanted her to be happy. That was a strange instinct. He didn't know this woman at all. He loved her curves, and her lips were going to star in some of his dreams, he was sure. He was newly addicted to cake pops because of her. But the urge to

4

make sure she was actually, legitimately happy was a little out there.

Sure, in general, he liked hanging out with happy people. His friends were, for the most part, optimistic, driven, happy guys.

Dax worked hard to make their company—Fluke Inc.—an upbeat, positive, relaxed place to work. He also refused to do work that didn't fulfill him.

But a lot of his... penchant for fun... was about proving to his father that you didn't have to be an overbearing, micro-managing, superficial asshole to be successful. You could laugh and enjoy your work and make the world a better place and still make money. Lots of it. Dax and his friends had proven that repeatedly over the past nine years.

"Nope, you're safe." The redhead finally gave him a smile. But it was clearly forced.

She did, however, take a bite out of the chocolate cake pop she now held.

He picked one up. Also chocolate. "So do you work for Hot Cakes?" he repeated.

He really needed to know who she was. If this woman worked for his new company, Dax could easily see her again.

This party was step one in their plan to make Hot Cakes bigger and better than it had ever been. They'd had a huge town hall meeting where they'd introduced themselves to the employees and the town at large. They'd presented their new ideas, taken questions, and rolled out some new benefits programs. Then they'd given everyone cake and champagne.

Judging by the smiles and laughter—and the need to open the second case of champagne—it was going well. That, or everyone had just decided to drink their worries away. Either way, the guys were determined to make this work, and Dax's specialty was making things better.

He'd never met a situation he couldn't make more fun. Not

that he knew anything about factory work, but they made *cake*. They literally dealt in sugar and chocolate and frosting. It was, if he did say so himself, a sweet gig.

Hot Cakes snack cakes were sold in grocery stores and convenience stores throughout the Midwest. There were very few people who hadn't had a Peanut Butter Pinwheel or a Strawberry Swirl, or the original and best-known Butter Sticks, in their lives. Mass produced, individually packaged, available anywhere chips and beef jerky were sold, Hot Cakes was a multimillion-dollar business.

And he, Aiden, Cam, Grant, and Ollie were going to make it even better.

"I'm... a friend of Whitney's," his cake-pop goddess finally said.

Whitney was Whitney Lancaster, the granddaughter of the founders of Hot Cakes who had served as the vice president of marketing for the past nine years. She was thankfully staying on to work with the guys now that they'd taken over.

"Oh, Whitney's great," Dax said, finishing off the chocolate cake pop and reaching for another. Damn, these were amazing. He would have eaten four hundred brussels sprouts if it kept this woman here talking to him though. And that was saying something. He was incredibly grateful he didn't have to prove his devotion via brussels sprouts.

Zoe, Aiden's girlfriend, and the owner of the town bakery, Buttered Up, had made the cake pops for the event. Apparently, Buttered Up and Hot Cakes were longtime rivals. The grand-mothers, Didi Lancaster and Letty McCaffery, who had started each business, had been best friends at one time. Until Didi allegedly stole the recipe from Letty that would go on to become the beginnings of Hot Cakes.

For over fifty years, the two women had hated each other, and the town's loyalties had been divided. Now, with Aiden taking over Hot Cakes, and he and Zoe falling in love, things were starting to heal.

Hopefully.

At least, that was the plan.

"Whitney *is* wonderful," the cake-pop goddess nodded. "So... it was nice to meet you. I need to go."

"You know if you don't tell me your name I'm going to have to refer to you as Red," he told her.

She rolled her eyes. "Real original." She shook her head, her thick, wavy red hair swishing against her mid-back.

"Because of the red-velvet cake, of course," he said. Though, damn, he loved her hair. It was a deep, rich medley of gold and auburn and copper and crimson. And that was pretty damned poetic for a video game designer who loved Ping-Pong and gummy bears.

She actually laughed. "Oh, of course."

"Just one little crumb, and it's all I can think about." He wasn't talking about the cake. She'd given him a few little crumbs of flirtation and humor, but he was already addicted.

"Zoe can totally hook you up with as much as you want," she told him.

He didn't want anything from Zoe.

Okay, not true. He suddenly fucking loved Zoe's cake pops.

But everything else he needed in this moment, he needed from Red.

Yeah, that wasn't original at all. He was going to have to come up with something else.

"You're really not going to share that last one with me, are you?" he asked.

She glanced down. "Um..." She looked up at him. "No."

"Not even if I say please?" He leaned in a little.

"There are maybe two things in the *world* that could get me to part with a red-velvet cake pop from Buttered Up," she told him. "And hot millionaires with sexy smiles are *not* one of them."

Ha. He felt victorious in that moment. She'd called him hot and said his smile was sexy. She'd also called him a millionaire. That meant she knew who he was. Maybe not from his YouTube videos like his millions of adoring fans did. Those were mostly boys between the ages of ten and twenty-five who were crazy about *Warriors of Easton*, the video game he and his friends had developed in college and that had accidentally turned into the biggest online gaming phenomenon of the past decade. But she knew who he was, and she was still here flirting—kind of—with him.

"So what *can* hot millionaires with sexy smiles get you to do?" he asked. "Because I'm thinking that cake pop may not be the most interesting thing you can give me." He really wanted her name and phone number.

Her eyes widened. She actually looked shocked. And maybe mildly amused. But mostly shocked.

"Are you seriously thinking I might give you a blow job?" she asked.

Dax's eyes widened as well. They were now talking about blow jobs? How had that happened?

"Does that happen a lot?" she asked. "You just meet a woman, know her for like five minutes, and she ends up on her knees?"

He sucked in a quick breath that made him cough. Holy shit. "That is... damn... that's *not* what I was thinking."

Once in a while... okay, more often than he could even believe... he got blatant offers very quickly at Comic Con. The ladies—not *all* his fans were boys between ten and twenty-five—who played *Warriors of Easton* were also big admirers of the game's creator.

Red rolled her eyes. "It's a blow job. Guys think about those like twenty-seven times a day."

He half laughed, half choked again. "Wow, who are you hanging out with?"

"You *don't* think about blow jobs twenty-seven times a day?" she asked.

He actually thought about her question. He was sure he saw the corner of her mouth twitch as if she was fighting a smile.

"No," he finally said, shaking his head. "Maybe fifteen. I mean, if we're talking averages anyway."

"That's it?"

"Blow jobs, yes. But there's all the sweet stuff I like to put in *my* mouth to think about too."

It wasn't a quip about her putting balls in her mouth, but it still checked all the boxes—a little dirty kind of funny would definitely reveal what kind of sense of humor she had.

He was rewarded for it when she lost the fight to not smile and grinned.

She held up the red-velvet cake pop toward him.

"Oh, I couldn't."

"Honestly, you have to now," she said. "You *have* to add these to that list of things you like to put in your mouth. You'll definitely be thinking about these tomorrow."

She was rolling with it. Awesome. His grin huge, he took the cake pop from her. "Yeah, I've definitely got a couple of new things to add to those daydreams."

She took a deep breath. "And *now* I need to go."

He bit into the red-velvet cake pop then ran his tongue over his bottom lip.

She watched and his body heated.

"Still no name?" he asked.

"Definitely not."

Huh, that was very adamant. Now he really needed to figure out who she was.

"I don't think it will be that hard to find out in Appleby," he told her. "Gorgeous redhead with a big sweet tooth. It will probably take me two minutes."

"You don't need to know. Zoe can keep your mouth full of all the sweet stuff you could possibly want."

"Yeah, I don't think so," he said, his voice a little husky and his gaze on her mouth. Aiden would kill him for thinking the things he was thinking right now if they were about Zoe.

But the redhead started to turn, then stopped again, quickly grabbed another cake pop, and *then* headed for the doors.

Grinning, he just watched her go. This time.

He *was* going to find her again.

Later, on his way out to his car, he saw a chocolate cake ball on one of the steps leading from the main doors to the sidewalk. He stopped and picked it up.

It had to be hers.

He smiled as he studied the little bite taken out of it.

Well, it wasn't midnight, and this wasn't a glass slipper, but he was feeling the urge to comb the town to find this girl.

He could probably even rent a white horse.

Move over, Prince Charming.

Of course, he didn't need the ladies of the village "trying on" any cake pops. He'd recognize her immediately. He'd never mistake another woman for the redhead with the flashing blue eyes and the full lips he wanted to see curve into a sexy, mischievous smile almost as much as he wanted to taste them.

He really thought there was some mischief in her. He really thought he was the one who could bring it out.

He pulled his phone out and started to search for white horse rentals in the area. Then he sighed. Dammit, he could hear a voice in his head telling him he should probably start by asking Zoe who she was. That was a lot less fun, but it might be faster. And God forbid, more practical.

That voice definitely sounded like Grant's. The bastard.

Still, Dax was grinning as he headed for his very impractical 1960 MGA Roadster in Old English White with black leather interior and classic silver wire wheels. It wasn't a terrible replacement for a white horse.

He plopped his dark gray felt Frank Sinatra fedora on his head—the thing had seriously been worn by Frank in the movie *The First Deadly Sin*—and headed for his hotel.

Practical wasn't his strong suit, it was true. But maybe the cake-pop goddess could use a little more impracticality in her life. In his experience, that was true for about 96 percent of the adult population in the United States.

He was just the guy to help.

1

"Is that a bouquet of cake pops?"

Jane was staring at the small silver metal bucket that had a dozen sticks poking out from it. Each stick had a red or white ball on the end. She felt a mix of resignation, amusement, and horror.

It was, indeed, a bouquet of cake pops.

Dammit.

"Seems to be," she agreed with her friend and coworker, Max.

Max plucked one out of the bunch—they were close enough friends that he felt safe touching her sweets without permission—and bit into it. "Damn, these are good. Must be Zoe's." He grinned and took another. He popped the whole thing into his mouth.

"I found that putting a whole one in your mouth at once makes it hard to talk," she said absently, thinking back to three nights ago.

She should probably be sick of cake pops by now, but she wasn't. She so wasn't. That was in part because her best friend

was magical in the kitchen. It was also because cake balls now
made her think of flirty, charming millionaires.

Max grinned around the cake. "When you've got a ball in
your mouth, talking shouldn't be your first priority."

Jane snorted. She should have been expecting that. She
clearly wasn't fully focused this morning. "Well, you know
more about having balls in your mouth than I do. It's been a
while."

Max swallowed and wiped a hand over his beard to brush
away any crumbs. "Yeah, well, I've gotta drive to find balls. *You*
could have a set just by walking down the street."

Being an openly gay man in a small Iowa town did have its
drawbacks. Primarily that Max was in a *very* small minority.

Jane loved him like a brother. She did, sometimes, wish he
had more of a filter though. He had an active, fun sex life he
enjoyed immensely. And told her about in great detail. Which
made her incredibly jealous. She loved sex. She wanted to have
more of it. She just needed no-strings-attached sex and *that* was
as hard to find in her small Iowa hometown as openly gay men.

The guys here who were her age wanted to settle down.
They wanted wives and kids. Most of them already had jobs
they were going to hold until they retired. They had homes.
Many of them had farms and livestock, and a social life, and
support network made up of family and friends they'd had
since grade school. They just needed a wife to plug into the
equation.

That's what people did here. They settled down. Made lives.
Raised families. Jane had no desire for that. She was plenty
settled down with her father's illness and trying to help her
little sister not follow in the footsteps of their stepmother and
stepsister. She didn't need a husband. She definitely didn't need
children. She needed no more people who needed her.

But sex? Yeah, she kind of needed that.

Okay, she very much needed that.

"I want to go with you next time you drive to find balls," she said to Max. "I need long-distance balls. The local balls, while plentiful, are way too serious."

Max eyed the cake-pop display. "Did you send yourself this bouquet?"

Jane's mouth dropped open. "I wouldn't do that!" But her protest lacked conviction. She would do that. She'd just never thought of it.

"You've been substituting sugar for sex for a while now," Max said. "Thought maybe you'd graduated to substituting cake balls for real balls, since we're on the topic."

She started to protest again but then looked at the cake pops. It wasn't a terrible idea.

"No," Max said. He grabbed the container of cake pops and held it out of her reach. "That's a terrible idea."

It was annoying how he could read her mind at times. A lot of the time, actually.

"Is it?" she asked. She started to reach for one. "I'm not so sure."

"It is," he said.

"You're just afraid I'll put on weight," she said.

He looked her up and down. "Lady, I love your curves. Every man who meets you loves your curves. I'm not one bit worried about that."

She smiled. She'd never been skinny. Or even thin. She had boobs and a butt and hips and, well, a deep and abiding love for baked goods. She'd never been apologetic about it either. She ran but not for her weight—though it did give her more wiggle room for treats—but because she was scared of getting sick like her dad.

The doctors assured her his progressive neurological condition, which they didn't even have a specific name for, was most likely caused by pesticides and other environmental factors rather than genetics. But she couldn't shake the anxiety around it. Or the idea that while she didn't work directly with the chemicals like he had, she'd grown up in the area where they used those chemicals on the fields and knew they were in the air and probably in the water.

Exercise and eating well and all that seemed like a good idea whether his illness was because of genes or environment. So she ran. And ate vegetables. And then didn't feel one iota of guilt about her daily dose of sugar and fat from Buttered Up.

"I'm more worried you're going to forget how great the endorphins from sex feel," Max was saying, pulling her away from her thoughts and back to the topic at hand. "And you're going to be content with the sugar high instead."

She nodded. "The sugar high is nice."

"It's nothing like the high that comes from a good hard fucking," Max told her bluntly.

Jane sighed. It was true. She had vague memories of that being true anyway.

"So yes, I'll take you with me next time," he said. "But if you didn't send yourself these cake pops, who did? Zoe? Please tell me it wasn't Zoe. She does *not* need to be supporting this addiction."

"She's thrilled Hot Cakes employees can now buy from her," Jane said. Maybe Zoe *had* sent them. That actually made a little sense. "Maybe this is a little advertising gimmick. Send these over so everyone here sees them, and a few people sample them and talk about how amazing they are." That was actually a great idea.

"Oh, okay," Max said, putting the bouquet back down on the break room table. "But that means you can't eat them all. You should leave them here for other people to taste. It would be good for her business." Max even put the second cake pop he'd grabbed back into the bouquet.

Because of the rivalry between the Lancaster and the McCaffery families, Hot Cakes employees had been banned from buying from Buttered Up, the local bakery. Wedding, birthday, and other special occasion cakes, along with muffins, scones, and other everyday bakery items had to be purchased in the next town. And they were nowhere near as good. But Hot Cakes was now under new management.

The new owners had rescued the company from closing its doors, had saved over three hundred jobs, and were, more or less, considered heroes in the town. Two of them were also hometown boys. One was Zoe's brother, Cam. The other was the man she was madly in love with, Aiden.

It had been a rocky few weeks.

Now, though, the bakery ban had been lifted, and things were starting to improve. The guys really seemed intent on making things at Hot Cakes better. Not just business-wise, but also for the employees.

As Zoe's best friend, Jane had Aiden's ear and she'd been taking advantage of that. Now they just had to wait to see if the guys could pull off this big makeover.

Considering they had, more or less, accidentally become millionaires and learned all about business management as they went along, Jane had her doubts.

But she was keeping those to herself.

Mostly.

"Though," Max mused, "it seems she should have sent a sampling of all her cake pops, right?"

Jane frowned. "What do you mean?"

"I mean, if Zoe wanted to use this to advertise, why not send a bunch of different flavors? Why are they all red velvet?"

Jane's gaze flew to the bouquet, and her heart flipped in her chest. "They're all red velvet?"

"Yep." Max picked another one out of the bunch and bit into it, then held it up.

It was definitely a deep-red cake, surrounded by a white icing coating. Jane groaned. Those were not from Zoe.

Dax Marshall had figured out who she was.

It wasn't like it would have been hard to find out or would have taken long at all.

She just hadn't been convinced he'd care enough to try.

Or what he'd do with the information once he had it.

The cake-pop bouquet was nice. And funny. She felt her mouth tipping up at the corner.

"Is there a note or anything?" she asked.

Max turned the bouquet and then reached into the middle. Jane felt her heart rate pick up as he withdrew a card.

"See you in my office at one. Looking forward to—dot, dot, dot—working with you." Max lifted his gaze. "What the hell is that about?"

"There's actually a dot, dot, dot before working?" Jane asked.

"Yep." Max turned the card to face her.

Why did that ellipsis make her feel a little warmer?

"You're going to Aiden's office at one?" Max asked. "You should tell him the dot, dot, dot thing makes that seem dirty. I'm sure he didn't mean it that way, but that's definitely how I read it."

Jane did too. She snatched the card from Max's hand. "It's not from Aiden."

She wasn't sure she should share that information, even with her best work friend. Dax was their boss, but he was here temporarily just to get things with their new ownership smoothed out. He'd be going back to Chicago. He was a computer geek. A game designer. He went to Comic-Con on behalf of their gaming company. He was originally from California. He owned a fedora that had once been worn by Frank Sinatra in a movie.

Yes, okay, she'd looked him up after their tête-á-tête at the party.

So he was her boss, but he hadn't done anything *wrong* she

supposed. Him being a little flirty with her was okay as long as *she* was okay with it.

Which she was. She definitely was.

He was not in possession of local balls. He wasn't going to be taking her to Sunday dinner with his mom and grandma on date three. Yes, that had happened to her. He also wouldn't consider a tailgate party and hometown football game a date. That had also happened to her. Nor would he think they should roll out of bed on Saturday morning after a night of not-too-terrible sex to do farm chores. She wasn't above getting a little muddy or feeding chickens. It wasn't that. It was that she'd really just been in it for the sex and maybe some pancakes in the morning. Feeding chickens together seemed, stupidly, more serious than pancakes.

Dating guys she'd known forever in her hometown was tough.

Dax Marshall was… none of the above.

And she didn't want to date him. At all.

But she wouldn't mind eating cake pops in bed with him.

"Who's it from?" Max asked.

"Dax Marshall."

Max lifted a brow. "Oh."

Of course he knew who Dax was. Dax had been at the town hall that preceded the party the other night.

"He's hot," Max said, nodding.

Jane sighed. He was. "And funny and charming," she added.

"And he knows about your cake addiction?"

"He does."

"You're in huge trouble," Max decided.

Yeah, that's what she figured.

But maybe Dax Marshall could be the kind of trouble she needed. Fun trouble. Sexy trouble.

And most importantly, *temporary* trouble.

———

At one, Jane stopped at the desk outside the suite of executive offices. There were six. The Lancasters had been all about big, fancy offices. She had no idea which one Dax was using.

There was a new woman standing behind the reception desk today. She was watering the plant that sat on the tall filing cabinet just to the side of the receptionist's desk, and Jane actually stopped in her tracks as she took the woman in.

The woman was stunning. She had long, dark hair and curves like crazy. And she was *celebrating* those curves. She was dressed in a fitted white sweater with tiny pearl buttons that started just below a not-inappropriate-but-very-tantalizing glimpse of cleavage. She had a thick black belt cinching her waist above a pink skirt that flared out, hitting just below her knees. On her feet were pink wedge heels with a huge white bow above the toes. Most interestingly, her long hair—which had to hang nearly to her butt when let loose—was up in a high pony tail with a pink scarf wrapped around her head and tied in a huge bow. She also wore horn-rimmed glasses. In pink.

For a second, Jane felt like she'd possibly stepped into the 1940s.

The woman looked over just then. "Oh, hi! You must be Jane." She gave Jane a big smile, setting the watering can down.

Jane blinked and made herself cross the space to the receptionist desk. "Yes. Hi."

"I'm Piper." She extended her hand.

"Hi. Jane. Obviously." Jane took her hand, feeling stupid. She wasn't used to going to executive offices or introducing herself by handshake.

That just wasn't necessary when you knew everyone you worked with and had worked in the same place since you'd been sixteen. She'd been hired by filling out online paperwork, showing up at the factory one day after school, saying "sure" when Bruce, the then foreman, had asked if she could work every day from four to eight, and then going to the women's locker room to change into her Hot Cakes polo shirt with her jeans. She'd trained on the job for about a week, and then she'd been a full, regular employee.

"I work with the guys in Chicago," Piper explained. "I was technically hired to be Ollie's executive assistant, but I help all the guys. Between you and me, I keep things organized and on schedule."

Jane gave her a little smile. "It's nice to meet you. Did you replace Sandra?" she asked of the former receptionist.

"Oh no." Piper waved that away. "Sandra is in her own office." She pointed at one of the doors. "She's doing everything she normally does. She's still working closely with Whitney and is helping a lot with the transition. I'm here to... keep the guys in line," she said. Her pink lips curved into a warm, sincere smile. "No one else should have to deal with them. Especially when they're in this state."

"This state?" Jane asked.

"All excited and wound up about a new project," Piper said. "They're brilliant, and they all have big hearts and mean well, but honestly, when they get together on something like this, they're like a bunch of twelve-year-olds with too much sugar and too much allowance money." Her expression was a mix of affection and exasperation. "They do big things. And to do big things, they have to think big and be willing to take risks. But someone"—she pointed to herself—"has to say things like, 'That's going to take three weeks even if we pay triple and call in favors,' and 'You tried that four years ago and it was horrible,' and 'If you do that, I'm quitting.'" She lifted a shoulder. "I'm the voice of reason."

Jane laughed. She liked Piper. The woman obviously knew the guys well and cared about them. But she was also clearly under no illusion that these handsome, charming, rich men were perfect.

"So Sandra's job is very intact. My job responsibilities are very specific—babysit the hot millionaires and keep Oliver's feet on the ground. At least some of the time."

"Oliver is the biggest problem?" Jane asked, entertained and intrigued.

"Oliver is definitely the biggest problem," Piper said. "He's the dreamer, and he hates the words 'no' and 'can't.' The rest of them are at least slightly reasonable."

Jane couldn't help herself. This woman clearly knew these guys well, and if she was going to get a scoop, this was the perfect opportunity. She opened her mouth to ask, "Dax too?"

But before she could say it, Piper added, "Well, except Dax, I guess."

Jane snapped her mouth shut. She should not be this interested in Dax Marshall. She just shouldn't. Maybe it was because Piper had just filled her in on Ollie a little, and Jane already knew Aiden and Cam.

Of course, she knew nothing about Grant.

And she definitely hadn't been Googling Grant or Oliver last night. Nope, her searches had all been about Dax.

"Dax—Mr. Marshall—isn't reasonable?" Jane asked, really hoping she sounded even one tiny bit casual. She didn't think she did. She was pretty sure she sounded as casual as a little girl bouncing on her toes and asking Santa, "You brought me a puppy? For *reeeeal*?"

Piper gave a little laugh. "No, that's not a word I'd use for Dax." Again, her smile was clearly affectionate. "Dax is an enabler of the first order for Ollie. He loves big ideas. He loves big plans and adventures. All Oliver has to do is say is, 'Hey, do you wanna...' and before he's done asking, Dax is saying, 'Hell, yes!'"

Jane smiled. Then frowned. "So he's a flake?"

Piper looked surprised by Jane's comment. "No. That's not the right word. He's... fun. Spontaneous. Always up for something new. And he makes sure the other guys have fun and don't work all the time."

"Ah," Jane said. "He's the life of the party."

Piper smiled. "Yes." Then she frowned, clearly realizing Jane hadn't meant that as a compliment. "Dax is the one who makes sure things stay balanced. The guys work really hard. They're very driven. Without him, they'd all have ulcers and insomnia and no personal lives."

Jane nodded. Uh-huh. Sure. Dax was their personal party coach.

That was fine. Whatever worked for them. She certainly couldn't argue with their success. She wasn't the one he was nagging about working too hard and taking things too seriously. But this was good to know. She couldn't hang out with a guy who thought life was just one big happy hour. Happy hour was supposed to be just that. *One* hour. Compared to the *eight* —or more—hours people spent at work.

"I feel like I've given you the wrong impression of Dax," Piper said, worrying her bottom lip.

Jane met the other woman's gaze. "Have you?" she asked seriously.

Piper's brow creased. Then she sighed. "I mean... not really. He is definitely the fun one. But he works..." It was clear she *wanted* to say that he worked hard. But was unable to.

"He works. He does his part," Jane filled in.

"For sure," Piper said adamantly. "I mean, he's the heart of Fluke. Without him, we wouldn't have a game at all. The idea and story for *Warriors of Easton* were mostly Oliver's," she went on. "But Dax made it all actually happen. He's designed every part of it and oversees the team of designers now."

Jane nodded. She believed all that. Hell, she knew most of it from her online search from last night. "But he doesn't have to really work at it," she said. "That's all really easy and natural for him, right?"

Piper looked like she regretted getting into this, but she nodded. "His greatest gifts are having fun and thinking outside the box and being big and over the top."

Jane couldn't judge him for that. Dax had found Oliver, and they'd been given the chance to do something big, and it had turned out amazing.

"So, um... the guys are just finishing up a call with Grant, but it shouldn't be too much longer," Piper said. She was maybe feeling the sooner she and Jane stopped talking, the sooner she'd stop saying things that made Dax look bad.

"Okay, I can wait. I guess." Jane shrugged. "They're my bosses now. I suppose they can't yell if I'm not down on the floor."

"Well, I'll cut them off in another few minutes if they keep going," Piper said. "In my experience, they can stay on track and be productive for about forty-five minutes. We're at..." She glanced at her computer. "Thirty-three. So they're going to veer off into crazy territory if it goes much longer,"

Piper said with a totally straight face, and Jane, again, found herself mildly intrigued by the way this company worked and the way the people in it kept it going smoothly.

"Do you want to sit and wait? Do you want coffee or anything?" Piper asked.

"Um..." Jane looked around and noticed a sitting area along the far wall across from the desk. There was a couch and two chairs around a coffee table. "No. I'm fine. I think."

She honestly had no idea how she was.

She'd been surprised for only about five seconds that Dax had found out who she was and wanted to see her again. Then her imagination had definitely wandered into dirty fantasies about bosses and suits and desks. There had been a spark between them the other night. She hadn't wanted it. Or so she'd thought. But she hadn't been able to forget it.

Then all it had taken was a bouquet of cake pops to get her thinking that seeing him again was a *great* idea.

And now she was sitting outside his office, talking with his assistant, and realizing they had *nothing* in common.

Jane made her way over to the couch and took a seat on the leather couch that probably cost more than all her living room furniture combined. Hell, she could throw her kitchen table and chairs into that total too. She looked around.

She'd never been up to these offices until two weeks ago when all her coworkers had been freaking out about the new owners. She'd worked with some of these people for twelve years, and they'd been terrified of things changing. They were working moms and dads, grandparents, people supporting their families. Some of them had sick kids, or disabled spouses, or were just regular people who lived paycheck to paycheck. None of them had loved the Lancasters, but they'd known what to expect from the family that had owned Hot Cakes as long as it had been in business. The idea of change had sent a wave of panic through the workforce.

So before she'd realized that two guys she'd gone to high school with and knew pretty well were their new bosses, Jane had stomped into the CEO's office and confronted Oliver Caprinelli. She'd demanded to know what was going on and what their plans were and when they intended to tell the workers about what was going to happen with the transition process.

He hadn't had any answers.

That was when she'd gotten riled up herself. She'd been a little anxious before. It wasn't like she had any other true skills, and she hadn't gone to college. Her dad had been sick before she'd even graduated high school, and her stepmother had been horrible and had been trying to control Jane's little sister,

Kelsey, even before that. Jane hadn't felt like her family would be safe if she left, honestly.

Hot Cakes had always been fine. It hadn't been something she'd been all that excited about, but she hadn't dreaded going to work either. It had been... work. It had been exactly what she wanted it to be—a paycheck. And benefits. Those she definitely needed. But otherwise, it was just a place she showed up to for a few hours, did work that was pretty easy with people she generally liked being around, and then she went home. She didn't have to think about anything too hard. She didn't have to *do* anything that was too hard. She didn't have to really get too invested. It wasn't dramatic or emotional. Which was fantastic, and she didn't apologize for it because, good Lord, things were plenty dramatic and emotional *outside* of work.

The door to one of the offices swung open, and Aiden stuck his head out. "Hey, Piper—" He spotted Jane and straightened. "Jane. Hi." He stepped fully out the door. "Everything okay?"

Jane got to her feet. "I have no idea." Well, she had an *idea*, but she wasn't going to tell Aiden she was here so Dax could ask her out.

"Dax requested a meeting with Jane," Piper said smoothly, handing Aiden a folder.

He glanced down at it, read the front, then looked at Piper. "How did you know this was what I needed?"

She smiled. "You guys are so cute when you forget how good I am at my job."

She rose and came around the other side of the desk as Aiden continued to stand there looking impressed.

"Right in here, Jane." She took Jane by the elbow and steered her around Aiden and toward the door to the office he'd just emerged from.

"Huh." Piper paused just outside the doorway. "Dax is wearing his lip tie today." She said it almost thoughtfully as if something was just occurring to her. "He might have decided this should be a surprise to everyone."

Jane felt something that was a very weird mix of dread and excitement flutter through her stomach. "This?" she repeated, her voice a little squeaky.

Piper nodded. "Whatever he's got in mind."

That didn't make Jane feel calmer. Even before she'd realized that Dax was probably the one voted Most Likely to Take a Stupid Road Trip on Ten Minutes' Notice *and* Most Likely to Blow Four Million Dollars on an Idea Written on a Bar Napkin, she'd had an inkling that Dax Marshall would be a handful.

But the idea of him being a temporary handful—and being a *literal* handful—involving cake and icing and mouths and dirty talk and *nothing else*, had been okay. More than okay. Enticing. Tempting. Doable.

This... whatever this was... was going to be too much. She could feel it.

"'Mornin,' Red." Dax rose from the bright red beanbag chair he'd been lounging in.

She was distracted for a moment by that beanbag chair. The thing was huge. More like a chair than the type of kids' beanbag she typically thought of. But it was still... a beanbag chair.

Then she was distracted by the rest of the office.

The big desk had been pushed to the far end of the room with the swivel leather chair, and the beanbags had been grouped in the middle of the office.

The whiteboard on the wall was covered in words and a few diagrams done in multicolored marker. Then she looked closer. Some of the words and numbers looked like official business, but on the one edge there was definitely a completed game of hangman.

She looked back at Dax and realized he'd called her Red.

That immediately gave her the surge of *hell no* she needed. She narrowed her eyes. "No," she told him.

He just grinned. "Ms. Kemper?" he asked.

"How about in between? It's just Jane," she said.

"Jane," he repeated, his smile still in place but softer now. Less teasing. "It's nice to see you again."

She took him in as he came toward her. He was in black dress slacks, a black button-down shirt and a white tie with red lip prints all over it as if a woman wearing bright red lipstick had kissed her way up and down the length of the tie—from the base of his throat, down his chest and abs, to the middle of his belt buckle.

Jane felt herself grow a little warmer. She didn't have red lipstick like that, but she suddenly wanted to buy some.

"Hi," she finally managed when he stopped in front of her.

"Thanks for coming up."

"I didn't realize I had a choice."

One corner of his mouth kicked up. "Of course you did."

"The cake pops would suggest otherwise."

"You'd do anything for a dozen cake pops?" he asked, one eyebrow going up in a way she found sexy, distracting, and annoying all at the same time.

"In my world, a dozen cake pops are a serious gesture. Someone must really need my attention to send those."

"Duly noted."

He hadn't expected her to show up here? Right. "I don't remember the note with the one o'clock meeting on it including a question mark," she said dryly.

"I'll admit I'm not used to people not wanting to spend time with me," he said in a flirty, self-deprecating way she was sure he thought was adorably sexy.

He was kind of right.

"Well, here I am, so I guess your ego can pretend that your record is intact," she said. "For now."

His grinned at her add-on. "For some reason I have no question that my ego will always know exactly where it stands with you around."

"I think that's a fair assumption," she admitted.

"Want to share what's going on with the rest of the class?" Oliver asked, coming up next to Dax.

She'd been vaguely aware that he'd been sitting in the green beanbag. But honestly, Dax—and the presence of beanbags in the first place—had sidetracked her from many of the other details of the room. Like other people.

And like the narrow table that was sitting under the window along the west wall. The table that held a collection of glass jars that were full of what appeared to be gummy bears and M&Ms.

"I have a sweet tooth," Dax said, noticing her gaze.

"I remember," she said before she thought better of it.

He gave her a sexy grin.

Ollie interrupted, extending his hand. "Hello, again."

"Hello, Mr. Caprinelli." She took his hand a bit sheepishly. The last time she'd talked to him, she hadn't been especially friendly. Or professional.

"Good God, call him Oliver. Or Ollie," Dax said. "When I hear Caprinelli, I look around for his grandmother and a plate of cannoli. Then I'm disappointed when I realize someone is talking about the guy who thinks Hamburger Helper can technically be considered pasta."

"It can be," Ollie insisted. "It's got pasta in it."

"How do you even face your grandparents?" Dax asked him. "How do you not feel your Italian ancestors stabbing your soul with their ravioli cutters from their graves?"

"Ravioli cutters aren't really appropriate for stabbing," Oliver said. "They've got rollers and they're for cutting ravioli out of rolled out sheets of pasta."

"Are there special forks for making pasta? Or for eating

pasta?" Dax asked. "Because they'd be stabbing you with those."

"We always just used regular forks," Oliver told him.

Dax shook his head as if disappointed. "Well, at least I know you used a spoon with the forks to twirl the spaghetti." He looked at Jane. "His grandmother taught me how to do that." Then he looked back at Oliver. "Your ancestors' spirits are stabbing you with regular forks."

"Weird, I don't feel a thing," Oliver said.

"Is Hamburger Helper a pasta?" Dax suddenly asked Jane. "And be honest. You don't have to worry about hurting his feelings."

Jane had been watching and listening to this exchange with a mix of amusement and a touch of they-can't-be-serious. But they'd seemed serious.

"Uh..." She looked at both men then decided to actually think about what they were asking. Finally, she shrugged and answered honestly. "Yeah, I guess I would have classified it as a pasta dish. I mean, most of them have noodles or something in them."

Dax's eyes widened and he slowly shook his head. "Wow. I almost don't want to sleep with you as much now."

Jane felt her mouth drop open. That was... kind of funny. She was definitely realizing that thinking she knew what to expect from this guy was a big miscalculation. "Almost?" she finally said.

"Well, now I have to make you pasta and show just how far from the real thing Hamburger Helper is," Dax said.

"What does that have to do with us sleeping together?" she asked. Probably stupidly.

"Once you've had my homemade pasta, you're going to be all over me," he said very matter-of-factly. "And I won't be able to resist you offering to do all the dirty things with those cake pops."

She felt warmth flood through her. It was maybe because she hadn't pegged him for the type of guy to make homemade pasta. It was probably because the charm and confidence just dripped from him like the sugary syrup that dripped out of the icing machine downstairs. It was definitely *not* because he kept surprising her. She didn't want to hang out with a guy who kept her on her toes. Her toes were very tired from all the time she spent on them.

"The cake pops you sent are going to get very stale," she said. Unless he wanted to make her that pasta tonight...

"Well, obviously you'll have to bring new ones over when you come to dinner." He gave her a wink. "It's the least you can do when I'm making you dinner and rocking your world."

Yeah, that confidence was *oozing*.

She looked at Ollie, who had been standing there just watching the entire exchange. "Isn't this sexual harassment or something?" she asked.

He looked at Dax. "Do you feel harassed?"

"Not a bit."

"I meant *me*," she said, fighting a smile.

"Oh." Ollie tried to look concerned. "Are you feeling harassed? I mean, you don't have to do a single thing he says, and if you knee him in the balls, all I'm going to need is a little warning, so I can get my phone out to record it, but if you're feeling harassed I'll... do something about it."

She shook her head. She could not smile about this. She was definitely not feeling harassed, and she had a feeling pasta and cake pops were in her and Dax's future—she'd worry about what that meant later—but she couldn't pass up this opportunity to make a point.

"You should probably figure out what you would do if someone came to you with an actual sexual harassment complaint," she said.

Ollie nodded and went to the door and pulled it open. "Piper?"

"Yeah?" Jane heard the other woman answer.

"Do we have a sexual harassment policy?"

"We do," she said. "It's don't sexually harass people."

Ollie looked back at Jane. She shook her head. "More."

"We need more than that," he told Piper.

"No shit," Piper retorted. "It's in the file on your computer."

"Which file?"

"The one labeled Sexual Harassment Policy," she said, her tone long suffering. "I apologize for hiding it like that."

Oliver grinned. "Want to go over it with me at lunch?"

"You mean, read it to you while you eat?" Piper asked.

He glanced over at Jane and winked. "That would be great. I'd love a chicken salad sandwich."

"You bet, boss."

He shut the door and turned back.

"Wow," Jane said. "She's very... patient."

Oliver chuckled. "Well, I'm sure I'm getting ham and cheese. Or a salad. Likely with kale. And when she reads it to me it will be with embellishments like '... and if some dumbass thinks he can touch your ass while at work, you have every right to stab him in the back of the hand with a letter opener,' but it will be far more entertaining than reading through it myself."

"Ollie is basically a huge child, and he doesn't like to work alone at his desk," Dax said.

"Oh, hey, pot, I'm kettle," Ollie said.

Dax just shrugged.

Jane wondered how Piper managed to not stab both of them with letter openers.

"So... can we get on with... whatever this is?" she asked. After witnessing all this, she wasn't at all surprised Dax would be asking her out in front of Ollie. "I really do have work to do downstairs."

Aiden came into the room just then. "So what's going on with this meeting with Jane?" he asked.

"Just waiting for you," Dax said.

They'd been waiting for Aiden? Jane frowned. He wanted Aiden to witness this too? Dax definitely seemed like the grand-gesture type, but this was a little ridiculous.

"He hasn't been at all," Ollie told Aiden. "He's been sexually harassing Jane."

Aiden looked at Jane quickly. "What?" He frowned. "He has?" He turned his frown on Dax. "What the hell?"

"He hasn't," Jane said quickly. She was sure Aiden knew Dax well and surely wouldn't believe that of his friend, but she also knew Aiden would be protective of her.

Aiden was a good guy. And Dax was clearly... a goofball? That wasn't exactly the word she wanted to use. He was fun, as Piper had put it. He was playful and irreverent. Those were maybe more accurate. She also knew Aiden was trying very hard to make this new shift in management at Hot Cakes a good move for everyone, and he was taking it seriously. Someone like Dax could probably be annoying to someone who took things seriously and wanted to buckle down and just focus on work.

Or maybe that was just her.

Aiden looked at her. "Everything is fine?"

"Totally fine." Then she looked at Dax. "At least, so far." She still wasn't sure how she was going to handle Dax asking her out. She should turn him down. For sure. But she didn't really want to.

Aiden looked at Dax too. "So why is Jane here?"

Oliver also looked at Dax. "Yes, Dax, please fill us in."

"I invited Jane up to discuss an idea I had," Dax said.

Oh boy. Half of her was very nervous about this. The other

33

half really wanted to know *all* his ideas that involved the two of them. That was trouble.

Though she really wasn't sure she needed Oliver's and Aiden's input on any of those ideas.

He was a hot, charming millionaire who clearly got his way a lot of the time. What the hell was she doing even thinking about flirting with him? Not to mention *actually* flirting with him? Because she had been. A little. And entertaining the idea of pasta and cake pops.

Damn. Just an hour ago she'd been entertaining the idea of cake pops with him, even while knowing that was a bad idea, and now she'd added pasta to it all.

"What idea?" Jane asked when no one else did.

Really, wasn't that where Aiden or Oliver could have jumped in?

"I want *you* to be *my* boss for a week."

She lifted a brow. Was that an innuendo about the bedroom? He wanted her to be a dominatrix or something? Because she wasn't doing that. She had no energy for leather and whips and sex swings. "I don't think so."

"No, really, it's great," Dax insisted. "You show me up close and in personal how the factory works."

"The factory?" She frowned. "Wait, you want to *work* in the factory?"

"It's the best way to learn all about the company from the inside out," Dax said. "I need to get down there with the people who do it every day. Reading reports and listening to management can only get us so far."

"And you want *me* to be your boss on the factory floor?"

"Absolutely."

Yeah, he might not have meant it in a dominatrix way initially, but there was something flirtatious and innuendo-ish in his tone now.

But in regards to the factory, this was a terrible idea.

Well, it was a terrible idea in the leather-and-whips way too. Actually it was an even worse idea in the whip way. She *really* didn't have the energy for that.

She was pretty sure she didn't have the energy for Dax, period.

But she couldn't have him work in the factory with her. She wasn't anyone's boss. No one freaking listened to her. Not her father when she told him he had to go to physical therapy every day. Not her stepmother when Jane told her to lay off her little sister, Kelsey. Not Kelsey when Jane told her a C in English wasn't good enough. She didn't even try to boss anyone around at work.

"In other words, you're tired of sitting in an office and talking to only us all day," Aiden said to Dax.

"There's that too," Dax agreed, without looking the least bit sheepish.

"This isn't a terrible idea though," Oliver said, nodding thoughtfully.

Oh, it was a terrible idea.

"He's got a point," Ollie went on. "We do want to know how everything works. We know everything about Fluke because we built it from the ground up. Everything that happens is there because we made it happened as we went along."

"What's Fluke?" Jane inserted.

"Our company name is Fluke Inc.," Aiden told her. "That's the parent company our game and all the merchandising and everything falls under."

"We called it that because it was a total fluke that the game took off and that we were even remotely successful," Dax said with a grin.

"It's a constant reminder that we basically got lucky, and we still have to work to keep things going," Ollie added.

She liked that.

"Ollie's right," Dax said. "We know everything about Fluke because we created it. We need to know Hot Cakes that well."

"The Lancasters owned this company for fifty years, and they didn't know all the ins and outs," Jane said. "I can promise you Eric Lancaster has never pushed one button or pulled one lever in that factory or in the warehouse."

"Well, we want to be better than the Lancasters," Aiden said firmly. "We *will* be better." He looked at Dax. "This is a pretty good idea."

Oh, it *really* wasn't.

"I know," Dax said.

Jane gave a little snort and shook her head. He said it as if it was the most obvious thing that his idea was good.

"It is," Ollie said. "I wouldn't mind learning a few things about how the factory functions and getting to know some of our new employees."

"No," Dax said. "I've got this."

"Has to be you, huh?" Ollie asked. He was watching Dax thoughtfully.

Which made Jane look at Dax thoughtfully. He was watching *her*.

"Yes. I have a specialty that can help a lot in this area of the business, and a particular interest in this project, so my time would best spent in the factory," Dax said.

"You have a particular interest in the factory?" Aiden repeated.

Dax was still looking directly at her when he said, "Definitely."

Aiden nodded. "Ah." His tone indicated he suddenly understood everything.

Shit, Jane thought maybe she did too.

She looked at Aiden. "Do I want to know what his specialty is?"

"That's probably a no," Aiden told her.

"Oh, ask me anyway," Dax said, giving her a grin that was playful and sexy, heavy on the sexy.

She wet her lips and thought very hard about *not* asking him. She even pressed her lips together and shook her head.

He leaned in slightly. Not enough to come even close to any kind of potential sexual harassment—dammit anyway—and said, "Come on, ask me, Jane."

She swallowed. Ugh, she was dumb. She'd never been dumb about a guy before. This was uncomfortable. "What's your specialty?"

"Getting women to tell me all about what they want and need."

Yeah. She'd asked. And she was glad.

That was super dumb.

She stared at him and had the definite urge to tell him she needed *him* covered in strawberry pie filling.

She loved cake, but if they were going for what she *really* wanted, it would always be pie. Strawberry pie.

"Jesus," Ollie said, laughing. "I need to get Piper to fill me in on the sexual harassment policy and get me the forms over lunch today, for sure. I have a feeling we might be needing them soon."

Aiden looked from Jane to Dax and back to Jane. "I absolutely will keep him as far away from that factory floor as possible. Just say the word."

Jane studied Dax. Okay, so he was definitely flirting. But he was also serious about working in the factory. Was this was his way of... spending time with her or something?

This was definitely him being funny. He probably thought it would be hilarious to spend the week at the factory learning how the humongous mixers worked and how to set the machines to get the right coloring mixtures and how they sorted through the damaged products. Lord knew the tours of kids they brought through on a regular basis thought it was all pretty cool. Dax Marshall definitely had a kid-in-a-man's-body vibe.

A very hot, hard, leanly muscled, sexy-beard, piercing-green-eyes, big-hands body...

Jane shook herself. This was clearly a lark to him. He probably thought he got to eat free cake all day. And he did. That was one of the perks working here. Employees could eat as much of the products as they wanted whenever they were on shift. Everyone took huge advantage. For about three days. New workers, surrounded by sugar and vanilla and sweet smells and sights all day, gorged themselves with free treats on their breaks. Then most of them never wanted to put another Hot Cakes snack cake in their mouths ever again. Being around it every single day just almost made you numb to it.

But in the midst of feeling her very-neglected-for-far-too-long girl parts reacting to his flirty smiles and sexy innuendos and doesn't-make-sense attention, she was aware this could be a good thing.

The hot millionaire game designer thought it would be fun to make cake all day? Sure. She'd put a hair net on him and make him stand on his feet all day and show him how to work machines that would make his shoulders scream from the repetitive pulling for hours.

This really could be fun.

"Let's do it," she said.

If nothing else, he could report back to his friends, her other new bosses, what it was really like down in the factory.

"Yeah?" he asked, his eyes lighting up.

And maybe she could show the laid-back charmer that most people didn't get to coast through life on flukes. Raising his awareness of real life for real people could be a nice side effect to educating the new management about their workforce.

"Sure. Why not? We can always use some extra hands."

She was 1,000 percent positive his hands would be

completely worthless to them as far as their efficiency and productivity numbers, but hey, that would give her a chance to talk to Aiden and Oliver about those very measures and how they should actually look at what was going on in their factory.

"Great." Dax looked at Ollie and Aiden, clearly pleased with the decision.

Ollie was smiling too, seeming completely agreeable.

Aiden, on the other hand, looked slightly suspicious. Of her. But the look he was giving her was also amused. Because Aiden had known her since high school, and he knew that she might tolerate cockiness and charm, but she saw right through it.

Aiden was wondering what she had planned for Dax.

She gave him a wink. He should definitely be wondering about that.

2

———

"I *promise* everything is fine," Jane told her dad for the fifth time.

"Cassie j-j-just said K-K-Kelsey hadn't been home m-m-much," Jack said in his stilted speech.

"She's been working on a school project," Jane said, moving a stack of books and a pair of shoes so she could get his walker closer to his chair. "She's been over at friends' houses getting that done. Come on. Let's go for a walk."

"C-C-Cass thinks K-K-K doesn't like her."

He sometimes shortened their names to the first letter because it was easier to get out.

Jane put a hand on her hip and regarded her father. Jack had always been a strong man. He could do anything, in her eyes. Lift anything, fix anything, jerry-rig anything. He'd always been the one helping others, never the one needing help. She knew he hated it now. He often stalled when she was here and trying to get him to do something. He was fine if she'd just sit and chat, but if she wanted him to walk or show her his therapy exercises or even go out of his room, he balked and would try to distract her.

"If I confide something in you, will you stand up and walk out into the hall with me?" she asked him.

"B-br-bribery?"

"Yep."

"Okay."

She smiled. "Okay. I don't think Kelsey likes Cassie all the time, no."

She had to be honest with him. He would know if she was lying anyway, and the more sincere she was, the better the chances he'd follow through on his end of this bargain. The nurse said he hadn't walked more than a few steps to and from the toilet in the past three days. That was not okay. It was difficult, for sure. She understood that. But he had to do it.

"But," she went on. This was the part that was partially true and partially sugarcoated. "She's a teenage girl, and Cassie tells her to do things like clean up the kitchen and do her homework and to be home by curfew."

Jack thought about that then nodded. "M-makes sense."

Jane nodded. It did. Most teenage girls didn't like their parents all the time. Of course, she wasn't telling Jack the *whole* story.

The things she'd told him were all true, but she'd left out the part about how Kelsey was expected to clean up the kitchen *all* the time, no matter who had last dirtied it up. Or that the homework she was supposed to do was "tutoring" Aspen, their stepsister, in English *and* math, both of which Aspen was horrible at, though it was Kelsey who got blamed when Aspen's grades were poor. Or that the curfew was 9 p.m. whenever she went out with friends and didn't take Aspen along. Most of Kelsey's friends couldn't stand Aspen, for good reason in Jane's opinion, so that was almost all the time.

It wasn't the worst thing any kid had ever been through, that was for sure, but Kelsey was unhappy a lot of the time. Jane wasn't above taking Kelsey on a sister outing and then letting her go hang out with friends. Jane also helped with the chores around the house because there was too much, and it was ridiculous to expect Kelsey to pick up after Aspen. Jane had also talked to Cassie, repeatedly, about the tutoring. When she did, it would lighten up for a few weeks, but that didn't mean Cassie wasn't a complete bitch to Kelsey the whole time.

If Cassie wouldn't run straight to Jack and stress him out and make him miserable, Jane would move Kelsey out of there and into her apartment in a hot second. But Cassie knew Jane and Kelsey both worried about Jack, and she used that to get free housekeeping and to help her daughter get good grades and friends she couldn't get on her own.

Two more years, Jane thought to herself. *Just two more years...*

"Okay, come on. You promised me a stroll through the building." She held out her arms.

"Hallway," Jack corrected.

"But once we get to the hallway, we should keep going," Jane said.

Jack shook his head. "Too f-far."

"Dad." Jane sighed. "You know you need to do this."

He studied her for a moment. His body was failing him, and far too quickly, but his mind was there and finally he said, "We'll t-t-try."

Jane smiled. "Okay." She'd take what she could get.

Forty-five minutes later, which felt like five minutes and also like four hours at the same time, they were back in his room, watching his favorite police drama on TV, him in his recliner, her on the love seat, her feet tucked up under her.

She'd worn him out. He'd walked into the hallway, as promised, then to the end of the long corridor, but they'd needed one of the nursing aides to get his wheelchair as he'd been too tired and shaky to make the trip back. By the time they got to his room, he was ready to relax for the evening, and frankly, she was beat. She was happy to watch TV for a little while and just chat too.

She didn't like pushing him like that physically. It truly was one of the things about him being in the nursing home she was good with. *They* were supposed to make him do the hard stuff. It just didn't always work that way.

———

S he was nervous.

That was so stupid. She was showing a guy around the factory she'd worked in for as long as she'd been employed. That was it. It was something she'd done dozens of times before with new employees and with various tours. But she'd been thinking about this almost nonstop since leaving Dax's office.

Twice last night at dinner, Zoe had needed to repeat a question to her. Jane and Josie—Zoe's partner and Jane's other best friend—joined Zoe and her mom, dad, and little brother, and now Aiden, for dinner at the McCaffery house. It was a lot of fun, and Zoe's mom was a fantastic cook, so usually it was a highlight of Jane's single-girl-cooking-for-herself week.

But last night she'd been completely distracted by the guy who sat in beanbag chairs in his office and displayed gummy bears where most people in executive offices would have flower arrangements their assistants took care of or expensive art pieces a decorator picked out or leather-bound books they never actually read.

She had a feeling Dax definitely dipped into those candy jars and had to refill them regularly.

She'd waved off the questions about if she was okay, though, using her sister as an excuse for her clear preoccupation. Everyone around the table knew about Jane's chaotic personal life, so they accepted that excuse without question.

And she hadn't been totally lying either. Not that there had been anything specific going on with Kelsey at *that* moment, but it was only a matter of time.

After dinner, because she felt guilty for using Kelsey as an excuse when really it was a perpetually happy and flirty millionaire Jane couldn't stop thinking about, Jane had swung by her childhood home to see her little sister—and be sure she was studying for the chemistry exam she had the next day. Thankfully, Kelsey had been at a friend's studying, and Jane had been able to limit her time with her stepmother to a ten-minute conversation about Kelsey's bad attitude and how Jane needed to pick up some more toilet bowl cleaner before she came over tomorrow.

Yes, Jane cleaned the toilets at the house every week. Well, she *helped*. She helped Kelsey clean the whole house, mow the lawn, and do other basic chores and errands—replacing light bulbs, picking up the groceries Cassie ordered online, things like that.

Jane put up with it. It just made life, for everyone, easier. Kelsey had to live there for only two more years. The situation was complicated and not perfect, but Cassie was her legal guardian, and well, if Jane moved Kelsey in with her permanently, Cassie would throw a fit. The role of young woman who'd gotten out from an abusive relationship and fallen in love again only to have her new partner fall seriously ill and put her in the position of caregiver who was now raising two daughters alone, was one she played well for the community. She had the martyr thing down. Everyone thought Cassie was amazing. No one blamed her for finally moving Jack into the nursing home. She'd done her best. It tore her up. It was a horrible decision no one should have to make.

Yeah, Jane had heard all the bullshit.

She blamed Cassie for it. Kelsey blamed Cassie for it. But neither of them were in a position to do anything about it except support their father as much as they could and *not* let Cassie make his life miserable.

Which was why Jane helped Kelsey with her chores. It kept Cassie from complaining to Jack about having Kelsey living with her. The last thing Jack needed was any kind of stress. Stress and worry made his neurological symptoms worse, and the fact he couldn't be there for his family made things emotionally harder for him.

Kelsey and Jane doing those things to make Cassie's life easier also just kept the peace. Sort of. Mostly. At least, it was better than it would have been if, God forbid, Cassie had to scrub something or run out for more eggs.

Jane didn't know if Cassie would do anything truly horrible to Kelsey or Jack, or even what that would be exactly, but Cassie was a selfish bitch, so she wasn't going to take any chances.

And then there was Aspen. Cassie's daughter. She was only a year younger than Kelsey, and she was truly the epitome of a spoiled brat. She did nothing around the house and not only delighted in having Kelsey essentially be her servant, but made a point of making the biggest messes she could and always needing stupid crap from the store when Jane or Kelsey had just gotten home.

Aspen was a nightmare.

But it was only two more years. Two more years until Kelsey went off to college and could spend her breaks at Jane's, and neither of them had to ever see Cassie or Aspen again.

Okay, that probably wasn't realistic in Appleby. But they sure as hell wouldn't have to be friendly when they did.

Except that would probably stress Jack out.

Jane sighed. Hiding this from him was really the hardest part. It was in his best interest to believe his girls got along famously and were doing fine even though he couldn't be there.

Good God, she was probably going to have to keep having

Christmases with Cassie and Aspen for years. And pretending to be happy about it.

With that depressing thought, Jane turned around the corner that would take her to where she was meeting Dax this morning. Yeah, she *really* didn't need any beanbags and gummy bears in her life. She had progressive neurological disorders, toilet bowls, and a stepfamily she disliked intensely—not necessarily in that order—to worry about. Dax was... a lot. She so didn't need a lot.

"No, that one's a *white* mocha. Here, this one's chocolate."

She came up short as she came to the end of the hall where everyone gathered for their quick morning meeting around the time clocks.

Dax was already there. And in the middle of the cluster of people, seemingly holding court.

He saw her immediately. "Hey, Jane." He plucked a wrapped square from the cardboard cupholder, Jim, one of her coworkers, was holding and passed it to her. "I was going to get you coffee, too, but Josie told me not to bother, that *this* was what got you going in the morning."

Jane knew immediately what it was as she took it from him. A strawberry cream cheese bar. Her second favorite thing in the Buttered Up bakery.

Josie had given Dax ammunition. He thought she'd do anything for a dozen cake pops. That wasn't true. There were some restrictions.

There were no such limitations on what she would do for one of Zoe's strawberry-cream cheese bars.

She thought, for about a second and a half, about thrusting it back at him and refusing it. But she was simply not strong enough for that even on a good day. This was really not an especially good day.

"Thanks." She even said it sincerely. Because so what if he

religiously are enjoying introducing the younger people—some of the guys too—to the show. And then Maria and Adelina have a Spanish soap they want to watch and Lexi and Morgan are watching with them." Lexi and Morgan were two young moms in their twenties. "They took a bunch of Spanish in high school and say it's fun to practice what they learned that way. And then a couple of the high school girls have introduced a whole group to *The Bachelor*. Which is awful, of course, but Linda and Kevin and Terrell think it's hilarious." He paused. "It's amazing what you can find on the streaming services."

She said nothing.

"I've been wanting to ask you about something I've been thinking about."

"I know nothing about *The Bachelor*."

He gave her a smile. "If anyone asks, just say Amber. She's the one."

"So you're buying Ping-Pong tables and TVs and cappuccino machines to get out of doing actual work?" she asked. "I thought you wanted to know how the factory worked?"

"I've been working," he told her, mildly offended. "You haven't heard everyone gushing about me?"

She lifted a brow. "I guess not."

"Because you haven't been taking your breaks in here."

"I've been... busy over my breaks the last couple of days."

Dax started to say something about her avoiding him, but he looked more closely. She seemed to mean it. In fact, her lips were pulled tightly at the corners, and her eyes were filled with fatigue.

"Is it your dad?"

Startled, Jane's gaze met his. "My dad?"

"Max said he's sick."

She frowned. "You and Max have been talking about me?"

"Everyone talks about you," Dax said. He gave her a little

smile. "I fully intended to ask about you, but I didn't have to. People love you. And they know a lot about you."

She was still frowning when she said, "These people know me too well."

"And love you," he said again. He wanted to be sure she heard that part. They might not have been gushing to her about him, but they'd all had a million great things to say about her, and it seemed they were thrilled to have someone to say them to. Since everyone knew Jane so well, they probably didn't have reason to talk about how wonderful they thought she was.

"Yeah, well, they don't get out much. Their bar for greatness is pretty low," she said. She reached for his cup and took a drink of his cappuccino.

He grinned watching her. "Well, they haven't said great," he told her.

She looked up at him. "No?"

"Nope. Not one person has used the word great."

"What word have they used?" she asked. Her eyes were lit with something else now—sass, spunk, something other than exhaustion and the touch of sadness he'd thought he'd glimpsed too. This was much preferable.

She sat back in her chair, folded an arm over her stomach, propped her heel on the chair on the other side of her, and kept drinking his cappuccino.

He leaned in, pretending to think. "Let's see. I'm trying to remember if there were any specific adjectives."

"Hard working?" she asked.

"No." He shook his head. "I mean, it's clear you know everything there is to know about this place, but nothing they told me was about the factory."

She lifted a brow then lifted the cup. She was intrigued but trying to hide it. He was going to draw this out, not give her what she wanted right away. It would keep her with him longer. He'd felt like he'd missed her. It had only been two days, and he barely knew her, but he'd been disappointed to not see her over the past couple of days. Now it was bugging him that she'd clearly been dealing with something unpleasant.

He'd also noted she hadn't answered him about what that was and if it had to do with her father. No one had given him specifics, but knowing he was sick and in a local nursing home made Dax want to know everything.

She swallowed her drink and said, "So what did they tell you about if not the factory? All I really do is work and go home. I'm not interesting at all."

Uh-huh. He'd be the judge of that. She was very interesting if for no other reason than she was completely the opposite of the last several women he'd dated. She was a blue-collar worker from small-town Iowa where she'd spent her whole life. Her wardrobe, at least her daily work clothes, consisted of denim and t-shirts. She had gorgeous eyes and lips and skin and hair and not one bit of it was adorned with makeup or jewelry. She drove a forklift, for fuck's sake.

"Let's see, well, Alecia told me you came over and slept on her couch and took her two little girls to school for three days when her baby was sick with RSV and she was up all night with him."

Jane paused with the cup halfway to her lips. She looked at him with surprise. "She did?"

"Yep. And you puppy-sat for Daren and his wife when they took their first vacation in five years last summer. He said if you hadn't been willing to take their *three* dogs to your house for a week, they wouldn't have been able to go because no one else would take them, and they couldn't afford boarding, but you insisted they deserved to get away."

Jane set the cup back on the table and crossed her arms. "Well, they did."

He nodded. "And Marsha said you stayed an extra two hours every day for ten days, so you could give her a ride home after her shift when she was in a car accident, and it was taking the insurance company forever to get her the money to fix it."

"I got paid overtime," she muttered. But she was studying the cup on the table instead of looking at him.

"I guess that one was kind of about the factory," he said.

And it occurred to him that none of them had said they loved her; it had just been very clear.

"Other people do that stuff too," she said.

That was true. They'd told him those stories too. The stories about Jane had come up within conversations about how the factory workers felt like a little family and how they all helped each other out. He just homed in on her and what kind of person that clearly made her. Because he was incredibly attracted to her, and he'd never dated a woman who would have done any of those things he'd just talked about. Though to be fair to the women he'd dated, none of them worked with people who couldn't afford to board their dogs or get their cars fixed right away.

"I buy cappuccino machines and subscribe to streaming packages that have classic game shows on them to make people happy and feel a little lighter about their work," he finally said. "You actually *help* make things a little lighter for people."

Her gaze came back to his, and he felt the connection in his gut. He hadn't intended to say that, but it was true. He admired her. He took seriously his desire to make people happier and add some frivolity to life. Life was hard. It was serious no matter how hard you tried to have fun. So having moments, here and there, where it was *just* about fun and laughter were important. But Jane made people's lives a little easier by *doing* things, getting in there and sharing their loads, and he really fucking liked that about her.

"I think this cappuccino is pretty delicious," she finally said, her voice a little thick.

He smiled. Coming from her, that was huge. He'd take it.

"Can I ask you about an idea I had? I'd love your input," he said.

"I know nothing about air hockey."

He cocked his head. "What?"

"If you want to know what other tables to put in here, I'm not the right girl."

He laughed. "Not that." He paused. "And I think you are the right girl."

Their eyes locked again, and the moment seemed heavier somehow. The right girl for what? Yeah, that was a good question. One he kind of wanted the answer to. A lot.

She pressed her lips together, and Dax realized he really was obsessed with that part of her body. He'd thought maybe that had been about the cake—then the strawberry bar—but no, it was the lips. The strawberry bar had been something. She'd gone right in on it and he'd loved that. This woman might not think she was into all his shenanigans, but when she had something that made her feel good, she dove right in. Now to show her that not all those things had to have sugar...

Or maybe they did. He had some ideas about him and her and those bars and his silk sheets...

"What's your idea?" she asked.

He shook himself. Right, he wanted to ask her about... work. Something about Hot Cakes. And the employees. Something that had occurred to him over the past couple of days. But he bet her lips tasted like the strawberries she liked so much. And he did intend to find out.

"Right." He leaned in as the thoughts came flooding back. "I have an idea about employee scheduling and stuff."

Her eyebrows went up. "Oh."

Her surprise was fair. So far he'd been more the air-hockey-table type. Dax actually smiled at that. He *was* more the air-hockey-table type. But this was a great idea. He knew it.

"I was reading about companies where employees set their

own hours. They're given a base salary based on their type of work. Expectations are set about what they're going to produce in exchange for that salary. But how and when they do it is up to them. As long as the outcome is there, no one cares when they do the work."

Jane frowned and sat forward in her chair. But she didn't say anything.

"There's a lot of research behind employee happiness and satisfaction being tied to autonomy," Dax said, feeling the need to keep talking. "There's also *a lot* of research showing that happy employees are more productive and are more loyal to their companies and their output is higher quality."

Jane held up a hand. "Just give me a second," she said. "I need to switch gears. You're actually being serious here."

Now his eyebrows went up. "I can do that sometimes."

"I've seen zero evidence of that," she threw back.

He opened his mouth then shut it. That was fair. He *could* be serious, but he preferred to leave that to Grant and Aiden. They were a lot better at it, for one thing. But he couldn't deny it made him itch a little to know Jane had no clue that he could take things seriously when needed.

"You've been reading about this?" she asked.

"I *can* read," he said. That was a little more defensive than it needed to be. *Relax, man*, he told himself.

"Good to know Piper doesn't have to read things to you like she does Ollie," Jane commented dryly.

Dax grinned. "He only does that because Piper has the prettiest eye roll on the planet and her sarcasm is magical."

Jane actually smiled at that. "I can't imagine keeping you all in line."

"And she does it all without breaking a nail. Thank God. Because, holy shit, the one time she *did* break a nail... we heard about that for a month after. Do you have any idea how expensive manicures can be? She's written those into her employee benefits package."

Jane wiggled her fingers at him. Her nails were unpainted and short. "I actually have no idea."

He smiled. He'd never talked about factory work shifts with his past girlfriends, but he'd had a few conversations about manicures.

"I don't see how what you're talking about could work here," she said, switching gears back to the idea of self-scheduling and salaries. "In offices where people are doing marketing projects and things, maybe. But how would that work here? You need a certain number of people to complete a process. And we need to turn out a certain amount of the product every day for the bottom line. It's not an advertising campaign. There is actual inventory that needs to get loaded onto a truck and shipped out before people can buy it."

He nodded. "But the *concept* could work. I was thinking about it after Alecia and Marsha told me about you switching up your schedule to help them out."

Jane blinked at him again the way she had when they'd been talking about the game shows. "You were thinking about this because of me?"

"I was thinking about you, and then this idea came to me," he corrected.

"You were thinking about me?"

"I've been thinking about you since I saw you fit an entire cake ball in your mouth," he told her.

Her cheeks got pink but she snorted. "Not my finest moment."

"I disagree. That told me so much about you in one little action."

She arched an eyebrow. "All about my oral capacity and willingness to stick a lot in there?"

Surprise hit him in the chest, and he tried to suck in a breath while also saying *something* and he ended up coughing.

She grinned. He shook his head.

"You're... unexpected."

Her grin grew. "Good."

"What I *meant*," he said, shifting on his chair as his body was still responding to ideas about her sticking a lot in her mouth, "was that you were going for it because you wanted it and didn't care what anyone else thought."

"Well, if someone judges a grown-ass woman, who can clearly make her own decisions, for something as harmless as eating cake, that person is an asshole."

"Absolutely."

They just grinned at each other for a long moment.

"Tell me more about this idea," she finally said. "I don't think I'm getting how it can work here, but I'm listening."

Dax was shocked by how much that made him want to kiss her.

Eating cake pops? Licking frosting off her fingers and lips? Checking out his abs? Being sassy and sarcastic? Pitching in to help the people around her and then being surprised when someone thought that was really great? Driving a forklift? Sure, that all made sense. But her wanting to hear more about his idea? Taking it seriously enough to sit and listen? It made him want to kiss the hell out of her. And then impress her. With more than his tongue.

He cleared his throat. He had to talk first. Then kiss. Maybe. If he was lucky. "The people here know what they're doing. Hot Cakes is fortunate as hell to have a ton of people who have been here a long time. Even when new people come in, the current employees are very capable of training them and demanding good work."

"They've been demanding good work from you?" she asked. "Really?"

He nodded. "They have. They've been... deferential because, I guess, I'm kind of the boss, but yeah, they correct me and make me do things over if I mess it up."

She laughed. "You *are* the boss. Period. There's no guessing or kind of about it."

He sighed. "I don't feel like a boss."

"You're new here. This is all new," she said.

He shook his head. "Ever."

"You never feel like a boss?"

"I'd much rather just work *with* people. I'm only a boss because I have money. There are a lot of people who know more than I do, who are more talented than I am, who have better ideas than I do."

She gave him a funny look.

"What?"

"Yeah, you're not a very good boss."

He laughed.

"Seriously, that is not any kind of boss attitude I've ever seen before. You need to be full of yourself and certain that you know more and that you're always right."

"And certain that my farts smell like cookies?"

Her eyes widened. "Pardon me?"

He chuckled. "Cam says he doesn't believe that my farts smell like cookies, but that I walk around as if they do."

She narrowed her eyes. "But you walk around like that because you're trying to convince everyone that cookie farts are all you're really concerned about."

He narrowed his eyes back at her. "You think you've figured me out?"

She looked mildly surprised but she nodded. "You don't think of yourself as a boss because you don't want to be a boss because you think people don't like bosses."

Damn, she maybe *had* figured him out.

He liked the idea of her knowing him. Jane knowing him

67

made him think she could also help him be better at all the things he wanted to do. Which meant that maybe he was figuring her out too. She wouldn't put up with his bullshit.

She'd be like Grant. Except she had gorgeous lips and curves and he wanted to get naked with her.

Actually, she'd be better than Grant in another way too. Grant actually gave him a long leash at times. Grant told him when he was being a dumbass and definitely got pissed off at him, but Grant cleaned up his and Ollie's messes and just took care of things he didn't want them dealing with because they were business partners, and he had to keep Dax out there doing his thing.

Dax definitely liked the women who would show up in fairy or princess costumes to cosplay characters he'd created. That was huge for his ego, no question. He loved having fans. But in spite of the fact that he resented every time his father tried to get him to stop messing around, he knew he actually needed someone who would say, "Your farts do not and never will smell like cookies, so knock it off."

Jane wouldn't care about his ego staying big enough that he could entertain a crowd of thousands at Comic-Con. In fact, if things went well and progressed the way he'd like, they'd get to a place where she would prefer he *not* hang out with hot cosplaying princesses.

He'd also bet a million dollars she'd make him clean up his own messes.

"You think I need people to like me?" he asked. That wasn't exactly it.

"You brought coffee to *eighty* people your first day of work."

Fair enough. "Well, of course, I like when people like me. But actually, I want people to feel... better off because I'm around."

Her expression softened. "I think you're pulling that off."

He liked that. "Yeah?"

"Well, you're down here learning about how this place works and what the workers think even two days after realizing you're not going to be around me enough to *try* to seduce me. And you brought in a TV, not to win people over or help people kill time, but to help them actually interact with each other outside of what they're doing at work. And you appreciate the fact that these people are correcting what you're doing even though you *are* their boss."

He basked in that for a moment. He couldn't help it. Jane Kemper was a tough girl with a heart of gold, and her giving him five minutes of consideration—and deciding he wasn't a total fuck-up—was pretty damned great.

"Wow," he finally said softly, looking right into her eyes. "I am pretty awesome."

She blinked once. Then again. Then rolled those gorgeous eyes—Piper might not actually have the prettiest eye roll after all—and blew out a breath. "Okay, boss man, tell me the rest of this brilliant plan."

Boss man. Huh. Maybe he could be a boss. Maybe being a boss didn't mean being a hard-ass and someone people hated or were intimidated by. Maybe the things he did were boss-like.

"Okay," he said, filled with a confidence that was unlike the kind he was used to. This wasn't cocky confidence. This wasn't I-just-nailed-that-design confidence. This was this-could-*really*-matter confidence. He liked it. "The factory already works because the employees are divided up into various areas that specialize in certain parts of the production. There are managers and so on. But they have specific work hours, and people are paid based on how *much* they work, not *how* they work."

"Okay," Jane said. "Go on."

"But *how* they work and how they feel about their work matters. It shouldn't just be punching a time clock. It should be about being a part of a team. I get that we can only care so much about snack cakes," he said. "But we can care about the people around us, the people we're working with, and how they're working."

She nodded. "I think most of us already do."

"I do too. I've already seen it. Which means, this will be an easy adjustment and one people will embrace. It will reward them for what they're already doing. Working as a team." He scooted his chair forward, leaning in, excited the more he talked. "Each area becomes a team. There's no manager. There's no hierarchy. Everyone is the same. You work together to figure out when everyone works and what they do. Someone needs longer breaks because their carpal tunnel is flaring up? That person takes those breaks and works a longer day. You need shorter breaks more often? Take them. You need shorter days but want to work six days a week? Or longer days and work only four? You want to come in later on Fridays or earlier on Tuesdays? Great. Everyone knows what they need to get done and then they're in charge of making it happen."

She was frowning but she was listening. "But no one keeps track? How do they get paid?" Jane asked.

"The team is given a percent of the overall company earnings. Every piece of the factory is important. Equally so. We couldn't run without the mixing and baking area, but we also need packaging and shipping. We need the maintenance crew and the business office and... everyone. We all rise or fall based on how everyone else does."

She watched him, her wheels clearly turning. Finally she nodded. "Okay."

"Really?" He was a little surprised. "You think it's good?"

"I didn't say that." She pushed back from the table. "But it's not *bad*. As a *starting* point. It will never work exactly like that, but I like the thought you've put into it."

"Yeah?" She didn't think it would work, but she liked the

general idea. For some reason that made Dax feel downright triumphant.

She stood. "I think that you've really thought about this a lot and clearly researched some things, and obviously, you've been paying attention around here." She pushed her chair in. "And *that* is all great."

"I'm glad you think so."

"And I think you just need to do a lot more of it. Ask questions. Talk to people who have been doing this work for a long time. Don't assume anything."

He nodded. "Okay."

She started to turn away but then faced him again. "And... you made me realize something."

"I did?"

She nodded. "I've thought for a long time I could just come to work, put in my time, and then go home. I thought this was just a job and that's what I wanted because I have so much going on outside of work."

He nodded.

"But..." She paused, then went on. "Some of the guys built a ramp at my dad's house for his wheelchair when it got to the point he couldn't do the steps with his walker anymore. They just showed up one Saturday and did it. Just like that." She swallowed. "And when my sister needed her tonsils out last fall, they covered my hours, but then they went even further, and a bunch of people from my department brought her ice cream and magazines, and they didn't forget to bring me strawberry cobbler and wine."

He chuckled.

She took a breath. "I guess I do leave the work here when I leave, but I don't leave the people here. And neither do my coworkers. So..." She looked at him, her bottom lip between her teeth. "Thanks for pointing that out to me."

Then she did fully turn and walk away. Back to work.

Dax sat at the table by himself for a long time after she left. Thinking.

Dax almost never sat—or did anything alone anywhere—for any extended period of time.

But the true sign his world was tipping on its axis?

He didn't even really want to play Ping-Pong.

4
_____

Jane approached the door to the break room on Monday with trepidation. She'd avoided it Friday and had been off for the weekend. She was always glad to have the weekend off, but she'd welcomed the time away from Hot Cakes even more than usual. After her sit-down with Dax the day before that, she'd been shaken. By him. By his ideas and his sexy smile and his desire to make things better for everyone and the way he'd gotten her thinking about things.

The guy with the gummy bears in his office wasn't supposed to make her _think_ about things.

But today she was going in there. Because... she wanted a cappuccino.

No, that wasn't true. Entirely. Those were pretty damned good. Especially the way Dax put cinnamon on the top of his. But that wasn't what was drawing her toward the break room today.

She'd been at the nursing home yesterday, and the nurses had told her that her dad had been in his room and hadn't wanted to come out for the last couple of days. He wouldn't come out with her either. He said he had no interest in doing anything that was happening outside of his room, so why would he come out? Which was logical. Though sitting in his room all day wasn't great either. Jack's mind was fully functional except for the fogginess one of his medications caused at times. But he took that at night, so during the day, he was mentally functional. It was his body that was failing him. And none of his nurses danced around the fact. His condition wasn't going to get better. The best they could hope for was to treat the symptoms, like the tremors and muscle tightness, and hope the disease could be slowed. But all the experimental programs were happening in bigger cities, and they simply couldn't afford for Jack to participate in any. It was one of the truths of living in a rural area. Medical advancements didn't get here as quickly and specialists were spread thin.

Which left relatively young men, whose minds were still intact inside of failing bodies, living in nursing homes with people who could be their parents and who needed a different type of care.

Jack just didn't want to do the activities offered at the home a lot of the time.

Jane was so frustrated. She felt guilty he had to live there but knew she couldn't care for him herself. He'd be sitting in her apartment alone all day if he lived with her. And there'd be no one there to help him with even the simple things like getting up to the bathroom or eating. Things the tremors and muscle spasms made impossible for him to do on his own.

He needed another person to physically help him up and down, and as the psychologist had explained to them while they'd been dealing with the move to the nursing home, it really was easier for everyone most times if that person was a professional. Not only because they knew safe techniques for helping but also because helping your father use the toilet was just something that was difficult emotionally for both the child and the parent.

Still, when Jack said he spent his day reading and watching television for days on end, she felt terrible. She visited three tim̶ ̶̶ ̶̶ ̶̶t there more often. She ̶ ̶ ̶ ̶ ̶ friends and coworkers— ̶ ̶ ̶itting—that needed her ̶ ̶ ̶ ̶ ̶eeded time to sit in her ̶ ̶ ̶ ̶e time. She really did. ̶ ̶ ̶uld be different.

̶ ̶om and jerked her out of

̶ ̶ypically she would be out ̶ ̶ilence, just breathing, not

̶ ̶n front of the break room ̶ ̶hoping he could distract

̶ ̶e'd get really addicted to

She couldn't just ignore all the stuff going on in her life. She couldn't make a habit of letting Dax take her mind off everything. She needed to *deal* with everything. She should probably be on the phone with the nursing home administrator or Zoe and Josie, someone who could give her advice.

Instead, she wanted to drink cappuccino and flirt.

"Hey, you joining the tournament?" Gabe, one of the other guys in the shipping department asked, passing her on his way to the break room.

"The tournament?" she asked. She started after him. Now that someone had seen her in the hallway, she had to go in. Not going in would be silly.

Just today. Just this one time. Just one hour of distraction.

"The UNO tournament," Gabe said, pushing the door open. "It's Monday."

She assumed that was supposed to make sense. It didn't, exactly, but she knew Dax was behind it, and that was really all she needed to know to know it was something fun and popular.

Honestly, the employees really had been talking about him a lot. How funny he was. How enthusiastic he was to learn everything about the factory. How self-deprecating he was about getting a lot of it wrong. Apparently, the mixer had "somehow" gotten switched to high with very few ingredients inside and had sprayed runny pink batter everywhere yesterday. He'd been coated in it.

Jane was suspicious. She wouldn't put it past Dax to mess a few things up on purpose just to help everyone around him relax and to give them a good laugh at his expense.

But she wasn't going to ask him about it. It made her like him more, and if he confirmed it, she might have to admit she had a little crush.

The noise from inside the room rose as she and Gabe stepped inside and she took in the sight. The tables were full. Four to six people sat at each one and they were all playing cards. It looked like a poker tournament. Other than the brightly colored cards and lack of cigar smoke and bourbon, she supposed. Instead, they had glasses and cups beside them. She assumed those held soda and cappuccino. Bowls of pretzels and M&M's and chips sat around as well, and yes, gummy bears. Seeing those made her smile and she searched the room for Dax.

She found him lounging at a back table watching the whole thing. His chair was tipped back on two legs and he looked pleased. Happy. Almost proud. And looking at him just then, simply watching other people having fun, she realized this really was him. He really did like to make other people happy.

And if she'd had a crush on him, it would have grown a little then.

Or a lot.

She needed this. Just today. Just for this hour. Not for good. But yeah, for right now, this seemed like a great idea. Not the card game. She didn't want to play UNO. She wanted to talk to Dax though.

His gaze found her when she was halfway across the room. The front legs of his chair hit the floor with a thump and his grin grew. It made her heart thump hard in her chest. The last time someone had looked that happy to see her had been last night when her dad had seen her come through his door. But that thump had been accompanied by sadness and guilt and anger about how unfair the whole situation was.

This thump, the one Dax caused, was all about fun and anticipation and how good that Hot Cakes t-shirt looked on him.

"Well, hey there, Ms. Kemper."

"Hi, Boss Man," she returned.

He chuckled but shook his head. "See, I can think of some ways that could sound hot as hell, but not here and not like that."

She lifted an eyebrow. "That could sound hot as hell?"

He pushed out a chair at his table for her. "Sure. 'How can I help you today, Boss? What can I do for you, Boss? Would you like me to clear out the conference room, Boss?'"

Jane took the chair, avoiding his eyes so he wouldn't see she was actually unable to smile at any of that or come up with a sassy comeback. Because she was breathing a little faster, and she was afraid her fair skin would give away that she was a little hotter now than she'd been a few seconds ago.

"But no," he said, sitting forward and shaking his head. "I think it would be better with 'sir.' As in 'Yes, sir,' and 'Whatever you want, sir.'"

Dammit. How had she gone from "Oh, he's so fun and flirty and I could really use a diversion today?" on the other side of the room to "Holy hell, he's hot, and I really need to lose a few articles of clothing" now that she was sitting next to him?

"What do you think?" he asked.

She finally looked directly at him. "About?"

"Would you rather call me Boss or Sir?"

She swallowed. "Am I saying it sarcastically or seriously?" she asked.

He gave her that half grin that sometimes seemed very knowing. "Breathlessly."

Well, at least the diversion thing had been accomplished. All she could think about right now was how green his eyes were and how she wanted to run her hand over his beard and how big his hand was where it was wrapped around his cup.

"Probably Sir," she answered, deciding to be honest. Maybe it would at least throw him off his flirty game a little. "Boss reminds me that you're, you know, my *boss*."

And she might want to forget that once in a while.

That thought surprised and bothered her, but it was true.

His eyes flashed. "Sir, it is."

She nodded. "Thank you."

"For letting you call me Sir? Absolutely no problem."

"For distracting me."

"You need distracting?" His gaze dropped to her lips.

She pressed them together as they tingled. She nodded. "Lots on my mind."

"Stuff you don't want to talk about."

"Right."

"Want to play Ping-Pong?" he asked. "Best game for thinking things through. If you don't have a solution by the time we're done, I'll give you twenty bucks."

She laughed. "You and throwing money around."

He shrugged. "I'm good at it."

She couldn't argue with that. "I don't play Ping-Pong."

He slapped a hand over his heart. "And I thought you were the perfect woman."

Hardly. She was a woman juggling a bunch of balls that were starting to fall and bounce around all over the place. "Ping-Pong requires another person. I need something I can do alone."

"Some of the best things in life require another person," he said.

She narrowed her eyes. Oh yeah, he'd meant that dirty. She wasn't just making it sound that way in her head.

"But all those things can be done by yourself too, and not dealing with another person can be worth it sometimes."

"So you want to scoot the Ping-Pong table against a wall and play by yourself?" he asked, pretending to be confused, but one corner of his mouth was definitely curving up.

She actually chuckled. "Figuratively."

He studied her for a second then pushed back from the table. "Stay here. I have an idea."

Jane didn't stay there though. She headed for the cappuccino machine. By the time she'd returned with her cup—topped with a sprinkle of cinnamon—Dax was there. With two coloring books.

"Seriously?" she asked as she took her seat.

"Yep." He pushed one toward her along with a pack of colored pencils.

She looked at it. And grinned. "A coloring book of swear words."

"Well, of course," he said as if that should have been obvious. He reached for the book in front of her and flipped it open. "Nothing is quite as good for the soul as coloring a page that says *This Is Horseshit* surrounded by beautiful flowers."

She laughed. "I have to say, the idea has merit."

"So dive in."

He opened the book in front of him as well. Hers was called *Fuck Off, I'm Coloring.* His was *Chill The Fuck Out,* and his page was a squirrel and said *I Have No Fucks Left to Give.*

She pulled an orange pencil from the pack unable to help thinking that Dax's page didn't fit him as well as hers fit her. Everything going on with her dad *was* horseshit. Dax, on the other hand, did give a fuck. About a lot of things. Lots of fucks. Even when it seemed he didn't.

They colored without talking, surrounded by the sounds of the UNO tournament, for a few minutes.

Then Dax said, "So my dad thinks that all I do is fuck around."

She glanced up but he was still coloring. She returned to the S in HORSE. "Why's he think that?" But she had an inkling.

"Beanbag chairs," Dax said wryly. "The fact that I make a video game for a living. The fact that I'm in business with my best friends and go to Comic-Con and am a hit on YouTube and collect Frank Sinatra memorabilia."

"You collect Frank Sinatra memorabilia?" she asked, momentarily distracted.

"I do. Frank was the man. Suave, sophisticated, successful, but widely admired."

"And sexy," she added.

Dax looked up, at first surprised, then he smiled. "Sexy, huh?"

Jane nodded. "That voice? All the singing about love?" She'd never given Frank Sinatra a lot of thought beyond liking his music, but yeah, he gave off a sophisticated, bad-boy air. A lot like Dax. She shrugged. "I mean, he was just cool, you know? He just had this… attitude. Like life is short so you gotta live it your way." She paused then couldn't help but give Dax a smile. "I think he even sang a song about that."

Dax chuckled. "One of my favorites."

"So, yeah, there's something sexy about a guy who just lives life on his own terms."

Dax eyed her for a moment. Then said, "Sinatra was friends with mob bosses and had a temper. He hated reporters."

Jane thought about that. "Well, they were probably all up in his business. The reporters, I mean. That probably gets old."

Dax nodded. "What about the mob ties?"

"I know he was also a strong advocate for civil rights. Back when that was not popular or common for celebrities. He forced casinos and clubs to hire people of color on their staffs and wouldn't stay at a hotel that didn't let blacks stay there." She wasn't sure how she knew all that, but she definitely remembered learning that about Sinatra and being impressed.

Dax nodded again. "True. So that makes up for being friends with bad guys?"

Jane lifted a shoulder. "We're all complicated and have layers. Who knows why he was friends with those guys? We all have stories that other people only know pieces of."

Dax had put his pencil down. "That's true."

"Which brings us back to the thing about your dad. How can he think you're fucking around when your business is obviously successful, and you're clearly happy, and Sinatra memorabilia is very cool?" She concentrated on filling the S of SHIT in with green, not wanting Dax to see how very interested she suddenly was in any and every story of his.

Yes, every story.

It was true everyone had stories that others only knew bits of, but she wanted to know all Dax's stories. That was crazy.

"He assumes the success is because of the other guys. Though he does give me credit for picking good friends and not pissing them off enough to dump me."

She glanced up. "He actually said that? That way?"

"Oh yeah." Dax grinned. "*He* can't imagine the patience it

must take to be Grant and Aiden, in particular. He knows that Ollie fucks around a lot too."

She thought about that. Then about her first impression of Dax. "Do you have beanbag chairs and gummy bears in your office in Chicago?"

"I do. Of course."

"And Ping-Pong table and cappuccino machine?"

"Yes."

"And has your dad been to your office?"

"Yes. He comes to Chicago about every other month on business and always stops by."

"If your dad *didn't* stop by, would you have those things in your office?"

"I..." He stopped and studied her. "I'm going to tell you something I've never admitted out loud and the guys know only because they've known me a long time."

She smiled, put her pencil down, and leaned in on her elbows. "I'm ready." She really was. This guy was interesting. He was sexy and funny and charming, but he was also surprising. He seemed to be easy to understand on the surface, but there was more there. Somehow, she could just tell. And in spite of her wanting to keep a nice buffer between her and anything that could require more energy and time and work in her life, she was drawn to him.

"I put that stuff in my office when we first started because it was symbolic of something that's been going on with me and my dad since I was fourteen."

"What's that?"

"I've been trying to prove to him that you can have fun *and* be successful."

Jane arched an eyebrow. "And that means gummy bears?"

He grinned. "At first, the gummy bears were symbolic. They're one of the silliest candies. Not just candy. Not just bright colors. But *bears*. Little, cute teddy bears."

She laughed lightly. "Okay. So you symbolically displayed the silliest candy to remind your dad you were having fun making your millions."

He nodded, smiling. "And I found the silliest office furniture and painted my office yellow—like bright sunshine yellow—"

"The silliest color for an office?" Jane guessed.

"Well, one of them. Hot pink might have been worse."

She laughed. "And the Ping-Pong?"

"Silliest way to conduct a meeting."

"You have meetings that way?"

"With my interns and my designers," Dax said.

She shook her head. "Cappuccino isn't really *silly*, is it?"

"To a guy who drinks his coffee straight up black, coffee with foam on it and chocolate or cinnamon sprinkles is silly," Dax told her.

"Ah," she said. "Okay, so you did it all to annoy your dad and make a point."

"I did. And it worked," he said. "But..."

Jane found herself actually leaning in. "His first trip out got canceled. After I had all that stuff in my office. So it was a month before he showed up. And by then, I liked it all. A lot."

She laughed at that. "Really? And you were surprised?"

"The cappuccino was delicious. The beanbag chairs were comfortable, and I got a lot of brainstorming done in them. I loved the yellow office walls and the gummy bears were... well, gummy bears. There's nothing bad about gummy bears."

He gave her a grin, and Jane had the sudden impulse to kiss him. It was just a sudden flash, but he was just so damned attractive right then. Happy, amused, a little cocky, and so genuine. She blinked.

"And, I kid you not, the Ping-Pong was amazing. We had great brainstorming sessions while playing. And I've deduced that when people are doing something a little silly, something that is just fun and totally unrelated to their work, it frees up their brain and lets the creativity flow." He looked around the room grinning. "It just makes people happier and their work gets better."

Jane also glanced around. That was more appropriate than staring at Dax's lips. Her *boss's* lips.

Everyone definitely seemed happier. "So you're brain-washing us all into working better and harder but using silly games to relax us?"

He chuckled. The sound was low and deep. "I'm just making people a little happier. What happens as a result of that is just a nice consequence."

"You'd be encouraging Ping-Pong games and UNO tournaments if it made them work less efficiently and productively?" she asked.

"If it did that, then I'd know those were the wrong activities," he said. "Happy people just naturally work better. If the work suffers, then the activities aren't making them happy. The work is just a measure of the happiness though," he added. "Obviously, there are lots of other ways to tell. Laughing and smiling, opening up, talking, sharing."

She narrowed her eyes. "You're trying to get people opening up and sharing?"

"Sure."

"Why?"

"So I can get to know them." He leaned in. "So I can figure out what they need."

"You want to get to know them?" she asked, her eyes finding it hard to stay off his mouth.

"I do. Some more than others."

She pulled in a breath. "That's a lot of people to play Ping-Pong with."

He gave her a knowing smile. "It is. But I'm up for it."

Jane turned her attention back on her coloring page. She

filled in all the words and started on the flowers. But then she said, "I have a wicked stepmother."

She didn't really see Dax stop coloring so much as sense it. But he didn't say anything. There was something about the fact that he wanted to know more about her that she liked. A few days ago, she would have assumed he'd want to "get to know her" in the sense that he'd want to know how best to get her out of her panties. And that had been appealing for sure. In a way. If he wasn't her boss.

But now, she thought he really did actually want to get to know her. Dax was clearly a people person. He liked people. He liked interacting, knowing how things worked, how people thought.

"So the wicked stepmother makes sense," he said after a moment.

"Yeah?" Cassie very rarely made any sense to Jane.

"I mean, it's no wonder a charming prince came riding into town to sweep you off your feet."

That caused her to look up at him. "Wow."

"I know. Irresistible, right?"

"I just don't know if it's charming to call *yourself* charming." But he was. He really was.

He grinned, clearly unconcerned about her doubting his charm. "Do you get along with your biological mother?"

"She died before I was even two. I don't remember her at all."

His grin fell. "Oh damn. I'm sorry, Jane."

She shook her head. "Don't be. You didn't know. And it's weird... It feels sad I didn't know her, but I'm not really sad from missing her because I didn't know her." She took a breath. "It's just weird."

He nodded. "So your stepmom's been around a long time? Wicked all along?"

"Wicked as long as I've known her," Jane said. Then she

shrugged. "That's not entirely true. She's not really evil or anything. She's superficial and self-centered. She took a vow to love my father in sickness and in health, and now he's in a nursing home because she doesn't want to take care of him. But I know I'm being a little unfair to her. Still, she's mean to my little sister, and she's a bitch to me, and we have nothing in common—except my dad, I guess—and I have a very hard time understanding what he ever saw in her. She's beautiful and about ten years younger than him, and, well, I guess she makes me face the fact that my father really does have horrible taste in women, and it makes me wonder about my mom."

Dax took that in, just watching her, and not saying a word.

"But no, she hasn't been around that long. About seven years. There have been many others though. My dad isn't very good at being alone. But they haven't all been wicked. Like Amanda. That's Kelsey's mom—my little sister. She was pretty cool. She got pregnant, and Dad had her move in with us, and she lived with us for about three years before she decided her dream was to be a flight attendant. She and Kelsey stay in touch, and when she's in town we all go out. But she's a much better once-in-a-while-girls'-night-out person than a mom."

"Wow."

"Yeah." Maybe he'd understand why she had more than enough drama, thank you very much, without adding a Sinatra-loving-gummy-bear addict to the mix.

But dammit, the more they talked, the more she wanted to find out if his kisses were fruit flavored.

She looked down at her coloring page. It was mostly done. It had also been fun. Even though she'd ended up talking about some of the craziness in her life, she didn't feel wound tight like she normally did.

She set her pencils down and closed the book. "I'd better get back to work," she said, pushing back from the table.

"Okay."

She smiled and stood.

"Go out with me Saturday night."

She stopped and stared at him. "I... can't."

"Why?"

"You're..." She should say "more than I can take on right now," but instead she said, "my boss."

"That's a no-no?"

"Probably?" She shrugged. "I've never looked it up because there's never been even the slightest need."

"I'll have Piper look it up. And I'll convene a meeting of the board to rewrite any policies that are a problem."

"The board?" Jane asked. "You mean, your four best friends?"

"Well, sure, if you want to get technical."

She smiled. "There's another I-word that applies to you, that's not irresistible."

"Oh?"

"Incorrigible."

"Not familiar with that one," he said, frowning in pretend confusion.

"Have Piper look that up for you too."

He grinned, and she headed out to work.

It occurred to her about ten minutes later, that she hadn't actually said no to him.

———

H er phone vibrated in her pocket halfway through her third episode of *Schitt's Creek*.

Please God, let it be anyone but Kelsey. She felt immediately guilty for that, of course. She knew her sister was struggling. She was living in a less-than-ideal situation that really sucked. Cassie didn't really mean her *harm*, but she wasn't really doing much to make her happy and well-adjusted either.

Kelsey's biological mom hadn't been back for almost eight months, and when she was in town, it was a day or two layover at the most. They spent the time together shopping and eating and going to movies, like girlfriends. She wasn't someone Kelsey could really confide in. Not that it would matter. Her mom wasn't going to swoop in and save the day.

Nor did Jane want her to. The last thing she wanted was Kelsey being packed up and being moved God knew where. And the last thing she *needed* was someone else in her life doing... anything at all that required a single brain cell or emotion from Jane, including winding Kelsey up, for better or worse.

She pulled her phone out and looked at the screen, holding her breath even as she felt like the worst sister in the world.

It was Max.

With a huge sigh of relief and an actual smile, Jane declined the call and then texted him. *Hey. What's up?*

Max was someone who never needed anything. Not beyond, "What do you think of this shirt?" or "Go with me to see *Frozen II* so I don't feel like a creeper." Those were things she could give.

Come down to Granny's. A bunch of people are out tonight.

Granny Smith's was the local bar. Yes, it was a play on Granny Smith apples, and yes, the last name of the family who owned it was Smith. The interior, like most businesses in Appleby, was decorated with an apple motif, and Granny's specialty was hard ciders served in little wooden barrels.

Don't think so. Sorry. I'm exhausted.

Trust me. You need this.

Maybe next time. She was already in her pajamas.

Her phone rang again. It was Max.

She frowned. If she picked up, he might talk her into stopping by Granny's.

Then again, she was a little hungry, and it wouldn't take

much to slip on some jeans. She supposed she could have one cider while she waited for a pizza to go. Specifically, a small Squealer. All to herself. The Squealer was a pepperoni, sausage, ham, and bacon pizza, and she didn't even pretend to apologize for how much she loved it. It was worth a clogged artery or two.

The call ended and he texted. *Pick up.*

She sighed and called him back.

"Get your ass down here," Max said, far too loudly, when he answered.

"*One* cider, and I'll order a pizza to go," Jane said.

"Oh no, you have to stay tonight, babe. I think you need this."

"Need what?"

"A night out. Some fun," he said.

"I don't think I'm in the mood."

Not that you had to be at Granny's. That was the nice thing. It was laid back and very come as you are.

"How is he?"

She sighed. She knew Max was asking about her dad. "Yesterday was a little rough. I need more *Schitt's Creek* and to go to bed early."

"Well, hey, it's very hard to beat a dose of David and Patrick," Max said of two of the main characters. "But I'm sorry."

She smiled. She had really great taste in friends. "It is what it is."

"It is," Max agreed. "But I might have something for you that's even better than *Schitt's Creek* and a Squealer."

Of course Max would know what pizza she planned to order.

"*Hart of Dixie* and strawberry pie?" she guessed. Because Zoe's strawberry pie was harder to get than a Squealer. Even though the baker was one of her besties. She sold out of that

ERIN NICHOLAS

pie every day, so if Jane didn't get a piece in the morning, she was out of luck until the next day. Pie took longer than pizza. It was science. Or something.

"There is no policy against sleeping with the boss," Max said.

Jane sat up straighter on her couch before she even realized what she was doing. "Excuse me?"

"Looked it up. And also talked to Monica in HR just to be sure. There are no fraternization policies at Hot Cakes. Employees can date whoever they want. Banging for everyone!" he announced. Again, far louder than necessary into the phone.

She winced and pulled the phone away from her ear.

Clearly Max had had a couple of beers already. Or four.

"And you looked this up and talked to Monica in HR about this for what reason exactly?" Oh my God, he'd talked to Monica in HR.

"About you and Dax!" Max laughed. "Of course!"

Well, now she probably had to stop by Granny's. Because she had to kill her best friend and really, tonight, when she could bury the body in darkness, was probably better than waiting until daylight. Though she was really tired tonight. Digging a hole and dragging Max's body to it seemed like a lot of work.

"Max," she said through gritted teeth. "Did you *tell* Monica in HR you were asking about me and Dax in particular?"

"Of course not," Max said, sounding perfectly sober suddenly. "But I did clarify that 'no fraternization policy' applied to bosses too." He laughed. "I'm sure she thinks I have the hots for one of them."

Okay, well, that wasn't so bad.

"She did say that there could be power dynamic issues, blah, blah," Max went on. "But I just wiggled my eyebrows and said, 'I hope so' and then walked out. And," he said, totally

90

serious now, "I *do* mean that. If anyone ever needed someone to just boss her into letting go and having an orgasm, it's you."

Jane felt her mouth drop open. This was Max. She should be used to him being very unfiltered. But this was... beyond. She felt her cheeks heat, and, well, the rest of her heat. Dax Marshall didn't really seem like the bossy type, honestly. But putting him and "orgasm" in the same thought definitely had an effect.

"Max," she said, trying to sound pissed off. "You stepped over the line."

"Maybe," he agreed, obviously not the least bit sorry. "But you needed to be yanked over that line, and if I had to go first and pull you with me, I'd be willing. That's how good a friend I am."

"I don't want to go over this line."

"Yes you do."

"I really don't."

"You totally do."

She sighed and closed her eyes. "Well, hey, thanks for checking into that," she said, changing tactics. "I will file that under 'things I'll never need to know.' Right beside the info you dumped on me about sea urchins and about the best places for biscotti in Rome."

"I already have my 'told you so' GIF ready for when you send me a selfie from Rome, eating biscotti," he told her. "Oh my God!" His voice went up an octave. "Dax would totally take you to Rome! Holy shit, Jane! This could happen! He'd take you diving where you could see sea urchins too, I'm sure of it!"

She pressed a finger against the middle of her forehead. "Max," she said calmly and coolly.

"Yes, baby?"

"I'm not going to Rome with Dax."

"We'll see about that." He sounded way too smug.

And then, suddenly, a bunch of things clicked into place,

like Legos snapping together. "Is Dax there with you tonight?" she asked.

Her stomach flipped and twisted at the same time.

"He sure is. And lookin' *good* too," Max confirmed.

Well... fuck.

"See you in ten minutes," Max said.

"I really shouldn't—"

But Max had already disconnected.

Jane sighed and squeezed her phone. Max knew better than to think this conversation was really over.

She tipped her head back and looked at her ceiling.

So there was no fraternization policy at Hot Cakes, huh? She supposed that shouldn't surprise her. Employees had been dating each other as long as she'd been there. There were three married couples—they worked in different departments—that she could think of, and at least one of them had met at work. It was the major employer in a small town. It stood to reason that people would meet there, and occasionally anyway, get involved. And maybe fifty-some years ago it hadn't occurred to anyone, but maybe now there *should be* a policy.

She should discuss that with someone. Like one of the new bosses.

And she might as well go down to the bar where he was hanging out with a bunch of people she knew and do it now.

That wasn't "going out" with him. That was meeting coworkers for a drink. And talking about how employees shouldn't date the boss.

Big difference.

5

Five minutes later, she slid behind the wheel of her car. She took a deep breath. And hit Josie's number to FaceTime.

"Hey, what are you doing?" she asked when her friend answered.

"Just taking cookies out of the oven." Josie's phone was resting on her phone stand on the countertop, and she bent and pulled a cookie sheet from the oven as she spoke.

Jane smiled. Josie was always baking. At the bakery all day long and then at home. She was the emergency cookie and bar and brownie lady in town. She always had some in her freezer for the moms who had a kid tell them, at eight o'clock at night, that they needed treats for their classroom... tomorrow.

It was a tiny side gig for Josie, and the parents in town with elementary-aged kids kept it a very strict secret. Zoe didn't know and it killed Josie to keep it from her, but it was extra cash and it really helped the parents out.

It had started innocently. A recently divorced dad who had never navigated treat day at school had called her one night, desperate, and she'd happily baked for him.

Then a couple of moms had called two weeks later, begging for help with a last-minute bake sale to raise money for a little boy at school who had been suddenly hospitalized. Josie had, of course, been happy to pitch in.

Then a couple of moms had asked if they could pay her to do their baking for a church potluck because they just did not have time. Another had asked if Josie would do the brownies she needed for the football team's tailgate because she was going to be out of town for work.

Every time, Josie made the treats and the moms put them in pans from home and passed them off as their own. Though every woman with kids between the ages of three and eighteen knew the truth.

It was a secret society of overscheduled moms, and Josie was their baked-goods dealer.

She drew the line at birthday cakes and other things people could get from Buttered Up, but last-minute treats or items for fund-raising were different.

It still bugged her that Zoe didn't know.

"Do they need frosted or decorated or anything?" Jane asked of the cookies.

"Nope, just good old chocolate chip."

"Great, then I need you to come to Granny's with me."

"Oh." Josie paused with a spatula in hand. "Um."

Jane smiled. "I know your hair is up. You have flour on your face. You're in your blue fuzzy pajama pants and have your glasses on, but I need you."

"What's going on?"

"I might, kind of, want to sleep with my boss."

Okay, well, there it was. Out loud. Out in the universe.

"Oh." That was a much more interested "Oh." Josie moved closer and peered into her phone.

"Yeah," Jane said.

Josie smiled and sighed. "That's so great."

Jane caught herself smiling at her romantic friend. Then she frowned. "Wait. What? No, it's not great."

"It's not? He's one of Aiden's friends, right?"

"Yes, Dax."

"Oh, the fun one!" Josie said enthusiastically. "He's so cute too. He's got that smirky smile and that charm." She sighed again. "God, you deserve that, Jane."

Jane shook her head. "You're supposed to talk me *out* of this."

Josie blinked. "Why?"

"He's my *boss*."

"That's hot."

"That's illegal."

Josie laughed. "It is not. You're both consenting adults. Unless he's blackmailing you or something. Is he blackmailing you?"

"Well, no." Jane felt flustered suddenly. "Okay, it's not illegal. It's unethical though. He's my *boss*. There's a definite imbalance of power. He could coerce me or threaten to fire me or something."

Josie nodded. "Okay, that's true. I mean, technically. You're right. That's not cool. But..."

"But what?"

"Well, for one, it's *you*. You don't want to be promoted."

"Oh *God*," Jane said. "I so do not want to be promoted." Promoted might mean more pay, but it also meant more responsibility which meant more headaches.

"Exactly. And if he tried to fire you or whatever, you'd tell everyone about it, and that whole place would walk out. You know that."

Jane thought about that. She didn't think the *whole* place would walk out. But several would. She'd never really given anything like that any thought, of course, but Josie was probably right. Her friends at Hot Cakes would have her back. Just like she had theirs.

Dax and Aiden and the others would have no idea what to do.

Though Aiden would never let that happen. If she told him Dax was doing something like that, Aiden would throw *him* out. She knew that. She trusted Aiden completely.

But... she trusted Dax too. It was weird. She hardly knew him. But Dax would never make her job contingent on anything sexual between them. Or contingent on anything at all, other than her showing up and doing her work, as it should be.

"Or you could sue him for everything he's got," Josie said.

A jar of gummy bears and a beanbag chair? was Jane's first thought, but that was stupid. He was rich. She could sue for part of his gaming company. Hell, she could sue for his part of Hot Cakes. Wouldn't *that* be ironic?

"I so don't want to sue anyone," she said, feeling tired just thinking of it. Or walking out. Picketing. Protesting. Who had the energy for something like that?

"Well, and it's Dax," Josie said, waving that all away. "I don't see him saying that you're fired if you don't sleep with him."

Yeah, okay, that was true.

"It's still the principal of the thing," Jane said. "I can't sleep with the boss."

"All right, I'm with you," Josie said. She started lifting cookies from the cookie sheet to the cooling rack. "I just..." She sighed. "Wouldn't it be great? Just for a little while? To have some fun like that? Some excitement? Not the boss thing, specifically, but to be swept up by a guy you haven't known your whole life? To travel and try some new things? Things we never see or get to do here in Appleby?"

Jane watched her friend through the phone. She smiled. Josie was a romantic at heart, and while she loved their little hometown, she, like everyone they knew, had spent her whole life here. As had her parents. And her grandparents. And all her aunts and uncles and cousins. Her older sister was settled down with her high school sweetheart. Her parents were high school sweethearts. Her grandparents had not only met in high school but had eloped at age sixteen, forging their IDs so they could get married before they were even old enough. They'd kept their parents from breaking it up by getting pregnant.

It had been quite a scandal.

A scandal that had resulted in seventy years of marriage, five children, and twenty-five grandchildren.

Josie loved all that. But she was also very intrigued by the idea of her handsome prince being someone she hadn't met at age five and who could show her more of the world than Dubuque County, Iowa.

Her grandfather and father had wanted to show their wives more. They just hadn't been able to afford to.

"So I should become his short-term mistress because he's rich? Get him to jet me around the world and buy me expensive trinkets? Let him pamper me for a little while?"

Josie sighed, her spatula against her heart. "Yes."

Jane laughed. "Come on."

Josie grinned at her. "Okay, not because he's rich. Just... for fun. A little adventure. A little excitement. Wouldn't it be fun to take a carriage ride in Central Park or go to Griffith Observatory in LA or have a cozy, romantic night in a cabin in the Rocky Mountains, or stay in a bed-and-breakfast in Vermont?"

Jane wanted to hug her friend and would have if they'd been talking in person. Josie wasn't interested in money beyond the idea of travel and having some new experiences. None of those ideas were extravagant nor did they require being a mistress for a millionaire. But they were things that Josie's salt-of-the-earth, blue-collar dad had always wanted to do for her mom and had never been able to afford.

"So just something different," Jane said.

"Different and *fun*," Josie emphasized. "And the pampering sounds pretty good. Massages, foot rubs, long bubble baths, decadent desserts I didn't have to make myself..." She laughed lightly. "Or, you know, whatever turns *you* on."

Jane grinned. "Wipe the flour off your face. Take your apron off. Put on some jeans, and meet me at the bar."

"I'll be there in fifteen minutes," Josie said.

Jane smiled. She really did have good taste in friends. "Thank you."

"But just to be clear," Josie said. "I'm supposed to keep you *from* sleeping with him, right?"

Jane actually paused. "I think so," she finally said.

"Okay." But Josie didn't sound convinced.

Yeah. Jane wasn't so sure she was either.

Dammit.

———

Dax was shocked by the way his heart thumped when Jane Kemper walked through the door of Granny Smith's.

Max had told him Jane spent Thursday nights with her dad, so he'd resigned himself to not seeing her. He'd been enjoying his time with the rest of the Hot Cakes employees that had come out tonight though. He'd bought a few rounds and some pizzas. He'd played a few games of darts. He'd learned at least two new facts about every one of them and met four spouses.

It had been a good night.

Now it was a fantastic night.

Because she was here. They hadn't even spoken yet, but everything in him felt happier.

That was the weirdest thing that had ever happened to him.

Because he was happy 90 percent of the time. He *made* the

happiness happen, for himself and others. To have another person able to make him feel like that, so strongly, just by showing up, was new.

But he fucking liked it. A lot.

"So anytime you feel a little... hungry... just let me know." Dax focused on the woman sitting on the tall stool next to him. He'd taken over one of the small round tables that was situated conveniently between the bar, the front door, the pool tables, and dart boards. That way he could see and greet everyone, no matter what they were doing, and could make sure everyone had plenty of food, drinks, and laughs.

"Hey, thanks, I'll do that," he told Danielle. She was one of his employees. A cute, bubbly blond who had come right over to thank him after he'd bought a round for the place. She'd been hanging at the table for about ten minutes now.

He hadn't missed her invitation. For dinner at her place. For more at her place. He got propositioned all the time. In fact, Danielle was being pretty subtle compared to some of the offers he got.

But he wasn't interested.

And the reason had just walked in. He'd known Jane was the reason even before she'd come through Granny's front door. But now, seeing her here, her long red hair down around her shoulders rather than in the ponytail or French braid she wore at work, in blue jeans and a pale-blue top that fell off one shoulder and did not say Hot Cakes on it, wearing canvas tennis shoes instead of work boots, he realized she was different from his usual type but very much like Danielle.

Danielle was blond and shorter and way more OMG-Dax-you're-amazing than Jane was. But she was a small-town Iowa girl who partied in blue jeans and did actual work with her hands. She probably saw her grandmother regularly and still went to church with the same people she'd known since preschool and probably gave directions by using things like

"Take a left at Bill Reynard's old place. You know, the place where Tom and Mary live now" instead of "Go north for two blocks."

He'd figured out that he and Ollie were probably the only humans in the town who didn't know where Bill Reynard had lived for fifty-two years. But he *hadn't* figured out why they couldn't just say "Take a left at Tom and Mary's place." Though he didn't know Tom and Mary either. And he was amazed there was only one "Tom and Mary" in the town in the first place.

Still, Danielle had everything Jane did as far as just being a new type for him. If that was the draw he felt to Jane.

He was starting to figure out that it definitely wasn't.

"Danielle, I need to talk to Dax. Alone."

Suddenly Jane was there beside the table, standing between his stool and the one Danielle occupied. She didn't look at him or greet him. He considered greeting *her* but decided something more interesting was going on between the women when Danielle arched a brow. She looked surprised but also annoyed.

"Well, I'm not *done* talking to Dax yet," Danielle said.

Dax lifted his glass of cider, hiding his smile. Far be it from him to interrupt two beautiful women who both wanted to talk to him. Alone.

"It's about the employee manual. Specifically, Section 47C," Jane told her, putting a hand on her hip.

Danielle paused with her bottle of beer halfway to her lips. "It is?"

"It can be," Jane said.

"But it's not?" Danielle asked as if clarifying an important point, setting her beer down.

"Not yet," Jane told her.

Danielle narrowed her eyes. Then she looked at Dax, gave him a smile, and said, "I guess I need to go."

"Well, thanks for the invitation," Dax said. "It was nice talking to you."

"Sure. Anytime." Danielle's smile was gone instantly when she looked back at Jane. She spun on the stool and slipped to the floor. "You're kind of a bitch."

Jane shrugged. "Heartbroken as always to see you go."

Danielle flounced off and Jane took her stool.

"So, hi," Dax said, giving her a grin.

"Hi."

"Employee manual, Section 47C?" he asked.

"Danielle knows that section well. It covers theft of company property."

"She steals?" Dax asked.

"Not anymore."

He grinned. "What did she take?"

"Plastic cookie boxes and tape."

His eyebrows rose. "Like a million dollars' worth?"

"I think it came to like a eighty-four dollars."

"And that was a big deal?"

"Not really. I mean, she got her hand slapped for it. She was on probation for a while. But obviously kept her job."

"Good."

Jane tipped her head. "And for the record, I would never turn someone in for that. I do understand stealing from your employer is wrong, and I've disliked Danielle since eighth grade, but I thought the whole thing was ridiculous."

"Okay. And you're making sure I know that because?" he asked, sensing something in her tone.

"Because you should definitely *not* promote someone who would *not* turn someone in for stealing."

"Ah." He nodded. "I'll be sure to put that in your employee file."

She sat up straighter suddenly. "No. I mean, you don't have to do that. Theoretically—"

He chuckled. "Jane."

She stopped. "Yeah?"

"Do you really think I even know where the employee files are kept?"

She thought for two seconds and then nodded. "Good point."

He laughed. "So if you didn't want me to specifically know about Section 47C and Danielle and that you would be the most diligent, rule-abiding person we could promote, what was that about?"

"I was getting rid of her."

"Because *you* wanted to talk to me?" He liked that. He didn't even care what she wanted to talk about. They could talk about asparagus for all he cared. He loved making this woman laugh. He loved that she seemed to know who he was, and that she still wanted to talk to him.

"I did. I just—" She stopped and her eyes went wide. "Oh crap, she wasn't telling you about her grandmother, was she?"

He frowned and shook his head. "No."

Jane sagged a little with relief. "Oh good. God, I just thought of that. That maybe she was telling you how her grandmother is sick. She and Danielle are close."

"Why would she be telling me about that?"

"Well, you..." She frowned at him, almost puzzled. "Well, you make people feel better. You get them talking. And you're very concerned with people being happy. I just thought maybe she was kind of drawn to you and wanted to tell you about it because she knew you'd make her feel better."

Dax honestly didn't know what to say to that for several seconds. He leaned in. "Well." Then he blew out a breath and shook his head. Shit, now he absolutely wanted to make everything better in this woman's life. "I'll be honest with you... people do feel better after they hang out with me, but they don't always come to me intending to spill. They come to play Ping-Pong or grab a beer or to hear one of my stupid stories.

They usually come to me to forget about things. They don't usually fill me in."

He hadn't thought about that in a long time. But he knew it was true and he was okay with it. Ping-Pong, beer, and stupid stories were easy.

"Huh." She was watching him but clearly thinking something through. "So what was she telling you about?"

"How good her pot roast is. And that I should come try it sometime."

Jane frowned and glanced in the direction Danielle had gone. "I knew it."

"You did?"

"I knew she was hitting on you. For a second, I panicked about her grandma, I'll admit, but I was right in the beginning." She narrowed her eyes. "And did you want to hear about her pot roast?"

She was asking about more than actual pot roast. Dax grinned. "Not even a little."

"Good." Then she realized how that sounded. "She's... made pot roast... for a lot of guys."

Dax chuckled and took a drink of the amazingly good hard cider he'd ordered, suddenly feeling really good about, well, a lot of things. "You realize what you've done, don't you?" he asked.

"What?"

"You staked a claim."

"A... claim." But her eyes flickered with realization.

He nodded seriously. "You basically told another woman to back off. From me. In a very social situation. So... guess I'm all yours now." He was so fucking incredibly okay with that, he was a little rocked by it.

"Oh, I..." She glanced toward the bar again, where Danielle was gathered with other women about their age from Hot Cakes. Then she looked back at Dax. And sighed. "Shit."

He laughed. "I assume you know how to make pot roast?" Somehow "pot roast" had turned into a flirty euphemism.

"I am not making you pot roast," Jane said. But the corner of her mouth was twitching.

"Well, you *have* to now," he insisted. "You can't scare another pot roast maker off and then not do it for me yourself."

She lifted a brow. "What if I can do something way better than pot roast? Maybe I saved you from *just* pot roast."

He really did like this girl. "Absolutely wouldn't surprise me," he said honestly. "And knowing you as I do, I'm guessing whatever *you've* got has a lot more sugar."

Yeah, dirty sounding and true. He loved it.

She laughed lightly. "Good guess."

He hoped that was true for any actual food she might make and for well, anything else she was offering.

"So what did you want to talk to me about? If not Section 47C of the employee manual?" he asked. As intrigued as he was with Jane and any sugar she might give him—literal and other-wise—he was equally interested in her wanting to talk to him. He wasn't being self-deprecating when he said people didn't come to him to spill their guts. To have fun, be distracted from their problems, just let loose? For sure. And that was great. But people didn't really seek him out for conversation. Other than his closest friends, of course. That Jane would assume someone would come to him for that was really... pretty damned awesome. Because it meant *she* thought maybe she could do that.

"I was just feeling... kind of... yuck," she said. "And I knew you'd make me..."

She stopped, pressing her lips together.

"What?" he prompted.

"I just realized it might sound a little dirty."

"Love a little dirty," he said. "Love a lot dirty too."

He'd give a million dollars, cash, right now to hear a lot of dirty from this woman, in fact.

She took a deep breath and let it out. "Okay, I knew you'd make me feel good."

Yeah, he would. And he only kind of meant that dirty.

He leaned in, forearms on the table. "Okay, well, I really want to. Make you feel good."

There was a flicker in her expression that said it sounded dirty to her. But that she didn't mind.

"So is this like you're hungry and need food to feel good? Or you had a bad night with your dad and need to feel good?"

She looked surprised by that.

"Max mentioned you spend Thursday evenings with your dad," Dax told her.

"Oh. You asked?"

"Asked where you were? Of course."

She smiled softly at that.

He went on. "Or is this a thing where you need a bunch of liquor to feel good and so also need to know you have a ride home? Or is this horniness and need to feel good in every single way I've been thinking of since I met you?"

Yeah, he'd dropped that last one in there as if it were like everything else on the list. In a way, it was. He'd do whatever she needed, from feeding her to driving her home to stripping her naked and making her forget how to even spell Hot Cakes. But he also really did want her to know, boss or no, inappropriate or gray area, he had been thinking those things. They needed to be very much on the same page there.

She blinked at him. Without saying anything. For a long time.

"You okay?" he asked.

"Just wondering," she said.

"About?"

"If it can be all those things at once."

He felt his grin. Wide and instantaneous. "Oh yeah, it can."

"Then... yes. It's... that."

Thank God. He knew how to fix three of those for sure, and if he was good at those, that fourth one—the one about her dad —might be easier. He had to admit, he was a little intimidated by her actually having real problems to deal with and wanting to talk to him about them. None of his close friends had *problems*. They were all young, vibrant, highly intelligent, good-looking, rich guys. They pretty much had it made. People came to Dax to forget about their problems, not to hash them out.

But he wanted to help Jane. He'd try for her. And if he sucked at it... well, hopefully the liquor would take the edge off that.

And the sex, of course. He knew he was good at that, at least.

"Now I just need the order," he told her.

"Oh, a small Squealer. With extra marinara for dipping," she said. "And a shot of tequila. Just one though, I'll switch to soda after that. But yeah, one shot for sure."

He cocked his head. "I meant the order you wanted those things taken care of, but I guess you answered that."

She laughed. "Oh yeah, sorry. I'm starving."

He chuckled, lifting his hand to signal the waitress to come by to grab Jane's order. "What's a Squealer?"

"Oh my God, their best pizza. Sausage, pepperoni, ham, and bacon." She sighed happily at the thought. "I am unapologetic about how much I love it."

God, there was something about the way this woman ate that he really, really loved. "Sounds amazing."

Her eyes went round. "Are you eating with me? Because if so, we're going to need a bigger pizza."

"How many slices in a small?" he asked as Riley, their waitress, arrived.

"Six," Riley said.

"They're small though," Jane inserted. "Seriously, dude, if we're ordering a small, you can't have any."

He smirked.

"And don't you dare judge me for that."

"Absolutely not." He looked at Riley. "A medium." He glanced at Jane. "Medium?"

She shrugged. "If four is your usual number of pizza slices."

"There are ten in a medium?"

"There are eight. But they're bigger slices than the six in the small," she explained. "I will totally eat four of the medium."

"Huh." He did love a great pizza. "Large, then."

Jane seemed relieved. He laughed. "And two shots of tequila. With salt and lime."

Jane nodded. "And water," she said.

"Got it." Riley moved off to put their order in.

"So, do you need to eat before you tell me about your dad? Or do you want to go into the storeroom while we wait for the food?" he asked.

"The storeroom?"

"The horniness," he reminded her.

"Oh right." She nodded. "So you're offering me a quickie in the storeroom?"

"Absolutely. I'm here for you."

She snorted. "Well, thanks, but if you think I'm going to have sex with a *millionaire* for the first—and probably last—time in my life, in a dingy bar storeroom, you're nuts," she told him.

He grinned. "Tell me more."

"Oh, there better be a huge hotel suite involved, massive king-sized bed, ridiculously high-thread-count sheets, Jacuzzi tub, room service, on-site spa with massage therapist included, one of those fluffy bathrobes to lay around in..." She trailed off. "Tell you what, let me watch *Pretty Woman* again quick, and then I'll let you know if I missed anything."

Dax pulled his phone out and tapped on his Netflix app icon. "Do it now."

She laughed.

Riley set down their shots and two glasses of water.

Jane looked at him. He looked at her. Then they both licked the backs of their hands, she shook salt on both of them, and they clicked their glasses together. Then they licked the salt, shot the tequila, and sucked the lime wedges simultaneously.

Jane didn't even shudder as she swallowed the strong liquor.

"Okay," he said. "Since the hotel suite and all the perks are over in Dubuque and the amazing pizza is here—"

"You really have a hotel suite with all that?" she asked.

"Of course." He leaned in. "And if I didn't, I'd get it."

That made her smile. "So much charm you can't even contain it."

"Something like that." He wanted to kiss her. More than he'd ever wanted anything. "Tell me about your dad," he said instead.

6

He wanted to hear about her dad. Which was strange. He didn't know how to handle that. He wasn't sure he could do a thing to make it better, and he wanted to make things better for Jane in a way he hadn't felt for anyone in a long time. His instinct should be to deflect and distract. Flirt. Maybe talk her into dancing. Maybe one more shot and a game of darts.

Instead, he asked about her dad.

"You really want to hear about that?" she asked. "Even with sex maybe, kind of on the table, you'd want to talk about my dad?"

"If that's one of the things you came to me for, I'll do whatever I can to make it better," he said with more sincerity than he'd felt for something in far too long. The last time was probably when Ollie had come to him and said, "I need you to help me make sure no one leaves this Comic-Con without knowing who we are."

He'd do anything for Ollie.

Or Aiden, Cam, or Grant. Or his mom. Or brother.

And now, apparently, Jane Kemper. A small-town Iowa girl

who worked in a cake factory and had a sick father Dax couldn't do a damned thing about.

She looked a little amazed for a moment. Like she wasn't sure if she should believe him, but then she wet her lips and said, "My dad has this weird disorder. They're not really sure what it is. It's a little like Parkinson's, but they don't think it's that. They think it's caused by exposure to pesticides through his work. But they don't know which one for sure, and he's the only one of the men who got sick from the work."

"What job?" Dax asked, frowning. That was a no-joking, bullshit thing. Someone got sick like that from work they were doing, but no one knew for sure?

"He did crop spraying," she said. "Flying planes to spray the fields with pesticides."

"So he's a pilot? That's cool."

She smiled. "He was. And then he also did farmwork. Various farms and farmers. Different jobs. But obviously exposed repeatedly to fertilizers and chemicals."

Dax nodded. "Weird he'd be the only one affected."

"Yeah. Though they say everyone is different, and how chemicals affect us is still based on our body makeup and genetics and other factors. So it's probably a combination of things."

"Are you investigating? Fighting to find out more? Any litigation?" Dax asked.

She sighed a very heavy sigh. "Honestly? That's all so exhausting. Battling the health insurance company is bad enough. I just... *we* just... go day to day. We try to make today as good as we can. Solve the problems right in front of us, and do the best we can."

He nodded. "I get that. But if these companies are doing something that's harming people, someone should be looking into it."

"They do. They have. But he's just one case."

"There have to be others."

"There probably are. But someone would have to get them all together and prove it." She shrugged. "It's just a lot for people like us to take on."

Dax frowned. "People like you?"

"Regular people, Dax," she said, fatigue obvious in her voice.

He wanted to take that away. He wanted her smiling and laughing and teasing him like she had been a little bit ago. This was why he didn't go into this stuff. This was hard stuff. Real-life stuff. Video game stuff—like lopping heads off trolls—was a lot easier.

"Regular people deserve to have things turn out right for them too," he said. He reached out and covered her hand with his, needing to touch her.

She didn't pull away. Jane studied their hands as she said, "We do deserve it. It's just harder to make happen."

He had some things to look up. Some phone calls to make. He had no idea what he was getting into here, but if he couldn't offer this woman anything else, he could definitely tell her that he wasn't *regular* people. And if he was one of the kinds of non-regular ones that had things turn out right for him more often than the typical person—and he knew he was—then he wanted to help.

"Have you ever had anything you wanted to fix for someone that you couldn't?" Jane asked him.

"Absolutely," he said. "My mother is still in love with my asshole father and hasn't moved on even after he chose his job over her and left us."

Jane's fingers slid between his, and she curled her hand in his. "Really?"

Fuck, he liked touching her. Even this much. "Yeah. She threw him out, but she didn't get over him. They still talk. He still comes over. They even go out sometimes. She definitely never moved on."

"She really loved him."

"Guess so. Hell if I understand why, but it does seem that way." He stroked his thumb over the back of Jane's knuckles. "Do you ever wonder why your dad loves your stepmom?"

Jane shook her head. "No. He doesn't love her."

"No?"

"He decided not to love anyone after my mom. She took his heart with him when she died. That's what he's always said. But he likes Cassie—that's my stepmom's name. She makes him laugh. Or did. I guess. They never fought or anything. They did stuff together. I think they were good... companions? Friends maybe even." Jane shrugged. "He's just not good at being alone. He thought he would be bad at raising daughters on his own. So he always tried to have a woman around for us. If one didn't last, he'd find a new one as soon as he could. I think part of his attraction to Cassie was that she's very 'girlie' with the makeup and the hair and clothes and shoes. She had a daughter about Kelsey's age. He thought we needed her."

Dax was fascinated. With the story, with Jane, with everything about her. "So he did it for you and your sister."

She rolled her eyes. "Some of it was for us, but he also really likes women. He doesn't like being alone. He really doesn't like *sleeping* alone, if you know what I mean."

He chuckled. "I definitely know what you mean."

Her hand was still in his. She squeezed it, seemingly subconsciously. "It's what makes the nursing home so difficult though," she said, her smile fading. "He's alone there a lot. He doesn't have that companionship from a pretty, younger woman like he's always wanted. And he's not at home for Kelsey. Me too, but definitely her to a greater extent. That all makes him a little nuts."

Dax nodded. He doubted his father and Jane's had much in

common—except maybe the penchant for liking a beautiful woman beside them at night—but he couldn't imagine his father dependent on other people for his basic daily functions and not being a fucking asshole about it.

"He's the youngest one in the nursing home and... it just sucks," Jane said with a sigh. "They try. The people there are so great, and they really try to make it as pleasant for him as they can but it's just... what it is. There's only so much any of us can do to make it better. The entire situation really just sucks no matter how much we try to improve it."

"I'm really sorry, Jane," he said sincerely. He was. He felt helpless. He hated that. He wanted this woman to smile, and in that moment, when they were surrounded by liquor and music and all the other things that made bars fun and the perfect places for flirtations, he couldn't come up with a single thing to do or say that would make it better.

"Thanks," she said simply. "I really am too."

They sat looking at each other for a long moment. Then Dax said, "I'm really bad at this."

"At what?"

"Being quiet."

She laughed. "You don't have to be quiet."

"I have no idea what to say."

She looked at him for a long moment. And Dax was pretty sure she understood that him not having something to say was very unusual. And meaningful in some way.

"You always try to say something? In every situation, right?"

"Definitely." He studied her hand in his. Her fingernails were short and neat, unpolished. The least sparkly female fingernails he'd ever looked at up close. "I hated when my mom got quiet. She's very outgoing. Happy. She can talk to anyone. Everywhere we go, she strikes up conversations with total strangers."

Jane smiled, listening.

"But after my dad left, she'd have these periods where she'd just get quiet. She didn't cry. She didn't get mad and throw stuff. She never yelled at him. Even the day she told him to leave, she did it in this very normal tone of voice. But when she got quiet, it was... awful. When it happened, I was always trying to get her to talk and smile and laugh. Even if I could do it for short periods, I'd feel awesome. She would still have her quiet spells, but it was always important to me that I could bring her out of them. Not for good, of course, but at least I could distract her for a little while."

"Kind of like a game of Ping-Pong or a coffee bar in the break room? At least it's a little reprieve?" Jane asked.

He nodded. "A lot like that. She was how I got into gaming. Into designing and creating, I mean. I was into it as a player already, but I realized I wanted to create one because of her."

"Really?" She looked sincerely interested.

"When people game, they... do it on purpose. They turn the game on. They pick up the controller. They're looking for a distraction, to kill time, to get lost for a little while, maybe connect with others online... whatever. But they go *to* the game for whatever it is they need. And I can deliver that. Happily. They know what I've got, and I can give them that reprieve, as you call it. With my mom, I was always guessing. What would work best? A funny story? A movie? A magic trick? A... game of Ping-Pong?"

"You had a Ping-Pong table at your house?"

"We did."

"Did she play with you?"

"Yep. Sometimes."

Jane laughed. And Dax felt tension leave his shoulders. He really liked when she laughed. Especially when it was because of him.

"You want to know something awesome?" he asked.

"Absolutely."

"My mom is a master warrior enchantress in *Warriors of Easton*."

Jane gave him a puzzled frown even as she smiled. "Your mom plays your game?"

"She does," he said. "A lot. I didn't even know until she told me that she'd gotten to Master Warrior level. Then she kept going. She's good."

"So you're still able to give her that reprieve," Jane said, her voice soft.

"Yeah. And now, it's whenever she needs it and it's like she comes to me."

Jane squeezed his hand and shook her head. "God."

"What?"

"Now every time I look at that cappuccino machine I'm going to melt a little and think about how you put that there so people could kind of come to you whenever they need to."

He grinned. "That makes you melt a little, huh?"

She sighed as if annoyed by it but nodded. "It does. And now I'll probably always think Ping-Pong is kind of sexy."

He really, really liked her. "That's awesome."

"No," she said. "It's not. Because Ping-Pong is not sexy."

He laughed and lifted her hand to his mouth without thinking. He brushed his lips over her knuckles, and their gazes clashed and held. The air suddenly got hot.

He had his lips against her skin. The skin on the back of her knuckles, but it was still skin.

"And now I think this might be an even worse idea, then, because you're my boss," she said, her voice soft.

"Why's that?" He put her hand down but didn't let go of her.

"Because I think a lot of my stuff is like your mom's. Ongoing. Not something you can really fix. Something you can maybe give me temporary reprieves from but... I'm not sure that's really enough. For you, I mean. Is it?"

It was a fair question. "First of all, I can *definitely* give you reprieves from it." He gave her a wink. She smiled back. But he decided to be sincere with her. "Yes, it bugs me with my mom that I can't fix things for good," he admitted.

"Yeah. So maybe it's better if you stick with girls who have needs you can fix easily."

As if on cue, Riley set their pizza down on the table, causing them to both shift back and their fingers to slide apart. "Here you go." She set down two plates and two sets of silverware as well.

"Like hunger," Jane said with a wry smile.

Yeah, hunger was a good one. Dax shrugged and gave her a grin. "Hunger and horniness are two of my favorite things to fix." And those were usually more than enough. In fact, those were a relief. They were easy, and yeah, fun for him too.

But this woman. Man, he really wanted to fix it all. Or at least try. Even the not fun parts.

"Well, good thing for you, most girls I know get both of those. On a pretty regular basis," Jane said.

"Good thing for me," he agreed.

She watched him for a moment then turned her attention to the pizza. She served up slices for each of them, and they dug in, chewing and swallowing before saying anything more.

"Damn, this is good," he said.

"Right?" she asked with a smile. She took another bite, watching him now as she chewed. After she'd swallowed a second bite, she said, "With all the stuff in my life I can't really fix, I guess I like the idea that guys have some similar easy-to-meet needs."

He lifted an eyebrow and took another bite, waiting for her to go on.

"Hunger and horniness, I mean," she said.

He nodded. "Yeah, I was following that."

She laughed, and he felt that familiar warmth behind his breastbone.

"Men are very easy," he said. "I'd say if you can take care of the hunger and horniness for them, you've taken care of eighty to eighty-eight percent of their needs."

"Wow, eighty-eight percent. That's very high and very specific."

He shrugged. "The need for sports and, of course, showering, sleep, and bodily functions, taking up the rest."

She grinned. "Well, that explains why my dad's with Cassie. She's a really good... cook."

Dax laughed. "Yeah?"

"She actually is," Jane said. "Surprisingly. She's also gorgeous and ten years younger than him so... well, yeah, it all tracks."

"And I've gotta say, you've got really good taste in pizza and cake pops," Dax told her.

"Oh, so just leading you to food can meet the hunger need?" Jane asked. "No need to actually *make* it for you?"

"For sure. I mean, homemade is great, but when a guy's hungry he's just focused on getting... not hungry, you know?"

She nodded, her grin wide. "I *totally* know all about just needing to get un-hungry sometimes."

"Yeah?" He took another bite. The pizza really was exceptional. "And with your great-food-in-Appleby knowledge, you're pretty good at getting yourself *un-hungry* when you need to?"

No, they were not just talking about being hungry for food.

He loved it. He loved talking with this woman. He loved flirting with this woman. He loved eating with this woman.

He was starting to think he would love doing just about anything with this woman.

Of course, he had very specific ideas about some things he was *positive* he would love doing with her.

"Oh, Dax," Jane said, her tone completely sincere. "I have *never* gone hungry for too long in this town."

He almost choked on his bite of pizza. He gave her an appreciative look. "I have no doubt about that at all."

At least the men here weren't stupid.

They sat, grinning at each other and eating pizza, and Dax thought maybe he hadn't had such a good time in too long to remember. And he played Ping-Pong. At work. And went to Comic-Con. That was definitely saying something. People at Comic-Con thought he was amazing. He had actual fans there.

He'd spent part of *this* evening talking about Jane's sick father and how there was nothing Dax could do to fix that or even help with it. Yet he didn't want this to end.

"So I just want you to know," he said, after he'd polished off his second piece. And watched her and grinned at her like a seventh-grader with his first crush. "If you ever want to talk about your dad more, I'm happy to listen."

She cocked her head. "Really? That doesn't seem like your kind of thing."

He nodded. "It's not."

"But you want to do that with me?"

"I do."

"Huh."

He watched her think about that. Maybe she'd figure out a reason for it other than that he was falling for her. Because that was about the only thing he could come up with.

"I guess I was expecting some more of the thing you *are* really good at doing."

He thought about how to say this delicately. He gave her a half grin. "So the two needs I'm best at meeting both start with H."

"Hunger and horniness," she said.

"And the way I meet those needs both start with F. Feeding and—"

"Got it," she said with a laugh.

He nodded. "And I'm really good at both. Like maybe not

pizza and cake pop good, but I know some pretty great restaurants."

"I'll bet you do."

They weren't talking about the feeding part just then either.

"So you might need to be more specific about which of the things I do that I'm really good at that you thought I'd be doing for you."

"Right. Well, I was referring to the D thing."

His brows rose. "The D thing. That's a little less... polite than I'm used to..."

"Distracting, Dax," she said over a light laugh. "I was talking about how you're really good at *distracting* people from their problems."

"Oh right," he said, nodding. "I am pretty good at that too. Maybe not as good as the F thing."

"You mentioned the great restaurants."

"*Really* great. And my very big... credit limit."

"Right. That was a goes-without-saying thing," she told him.

They did that silly grin-at-each-other-for-several-long-seconds thing. Then he said, "Nearly three percent of the ice in Antarctic glaciers is penguin urine."

She blinked at him.

He took a drink of cider.

"Really?" she finally said.

"Yep. Are you distracted?"

"Completely."

He winked at her.

"That's... interesting."

"There's more where that came from." He knew tons of weird animal facts. For some reason.

"I guess I was expecting more of the flirtatious type of distraction," she finally said. "Less of the animal urine type of distraction."

"Oh." That was good to know. "I can do that." He paused. "I think."

"You *think*? Haven't you been flirting this whole time?"

"Sure. I mean, that's talking-flirting," he agreed. "But if you want sexy-flirting... I'm pretty sure I can pull that off too."

"Why only pretty sure?" She looked genuinely confused.

He decided to be totally honest. They'd shared a lot tonight. He could tell her this. "I'm not sure I've ever sexy-flirted with a woman I really fucking *liked*. I'd rather sit here and talk over pizza than have you dress up in a fairy costume and tell me my staff really is magical."

"Oh my God, please tell me that's a gaming thing," she asked, looking part fascinated and part horrified.

He nodded. "Comic-Con."

"That really happened once?"

"Three times."

"I... um... have no idea what to say."

He grinned. "Exactly. And I bet you've never owned anything from Prada or Louis Vuitton."

"I do know what those are," she said. "But no."

He nodded. "And if you did have an extra two thousand dollars, you'd do something great with it rather than buying a purse."

"*Purses* cost two thousand *dollars*?" she demanded.

"At least."

"That's... that should be... illegal." She shook her head. Then she took a breath. "But you can't judge people because they spend money on purses. To them, two thousand dollars is like twenty bucks to me."

He smiled at her. Not a sexy grin. Not an amused grin. A smile he knew was full of affection and admiration. "I *like* you. I respect the hell out of you. I think you're a better person than any of the women I've ever dated. Not because of how they—

and you—spend money, but just because of who you are. And that's a little intimidating."

She was staring at him as if he'd just told her four more animal urine facts.

"You okay?" he asked after another few seconds.

"*You're* intimidated by *me*?" she asked.

He laughed. "Yes. But not enough to get up, make an excuse, and leave you alone."

She took that in. Then she slowly smiled. "Good. The not leaving me alone part, I mean. Not the intimidated part. You have nothing to be intimidated about."

"I'm a guy who loved video games, accidentally made one that got popular, and now uses his money and success to drive his father crazy."

"You're also a guy who looks around and wants to make things better. A lot of people never even look around. Those who do, don't feel personally responsible for changing things."

"I bought a cappuccino machine."

"Yeah. You *did* something."

"That's not much."

"It's *something*, Dax. It matters."

"You didn't think so at first."

They'd been slowly leaning in closer to one another across the table.

"I was wrong. I was looking at the machine, not the guy behind it."

Yeah, he was falling for her. That was interesting. He wasn't sure that had happened to him since high school. And Bailey Conner didn't really count. He'd liked her mostly because of her game controllers—not a euphemism—and love *for Call of Duty* and *Assassin's Creed.*

"Yeah, well, you deal with a lot of shit, and you're still a wonderful friend and coworker and daughter and sister. You want your workplace to be a great place and your coworkers to be happy and appreciated and have what they deserve when you could be wallowing in all your own crap and not worrying about anyone else."

She looked a little sad for a moment. "I try to do that," she said. "But full confession. I want to go to work, do my job, and then go home. I want it to be simple. I've worked there for so long because it's straightforward. I resented getting pulled into all the drama with you guys coming in and taking over and stirring everything up and scaring everyone."

"But you still got involved," he said with a shrug. "You didn't want to, but you did it. Sorry, but that makes it even more admirable."

"Come on. The fact that I don't want to be involved, even for the great people I work with is admirable?"

"Yes. Because even if you just want to go home at the end of the day and forget about it all, you definitely know something about how important temporary reprieves can be," he said. "Having someone to dog sit, having a simple ride to work... Those little things can make a few moments easier, and that can make an entire situation lighter."

Jane stared at him. But he meant it. The things she did to lighten things up for the people around her were more meaningful than what he did, but they both liked making things easier for others. He loved having that in common with her.

"And you do even more than that," he went on. "You've been pushing for better working conditions and to be sure the new management respects the workers and the things that are already in place."

"I did not want to," she insisted. "I would have loved to have someone else go up to Oliver's office that first day."

"Do you think the great warriors always want to charge into battle? Risk their lives? Face injury and possible death? Of course not. But they do it anyway. That's what bravery is. Not *wanting* to fight. Fighting because it's the right thing to do."

Her eyes widened. He was on a roll. He made a video game full of warriors and battles. This was his shit.

"You're not even really doing battle for your own treasure," he said. "I mean, you don't have kids and dependents. You don't need certain work shifts or jobs. You're healthy and able to do whatever. You have yourself to take care of. But you're in there fighting so everyone else's treasure chests and villages are also protected." The analogies from *Warriors of Easton* were easy. He grinned, pleased. "Fighting to protect someone else's village, when yours is pretty safe, is *very* heroic."

There was a beat of silence. Then she said softly, "Aiden coached me." But she was watching him, taking in every word.

"You went to Aiden for coaching. The warriors often go to mentors. The generals and wizards who have more knowledge and experience. That's just a sign of intelligence and heart. You know what you know, but you want to know what you don't know too so you're as prepared as possible."

She nodded slowly. "Wow. I do sound pretty great when you put it that way."

He laughed. "See? My crush on you is *very* well placed."

Jane lifted an eyebrow, interest sparking in her blue eyes. "Crush?"

"Oh yeah."

"Still really into how I ate that first cake pop?" she asked.

Her voice was more playful now, and Dax felt his gut tighten.

"For sure. And dammit, me being cute and funny and charming isn't good enough for you. All the stuff that's worked on girls and teachers and marketing executives just doesn't work with you."

"You realize that, huh?"

"Yeah. You want me to actually fix something. To actually come to work every day and *try* at something."

"I'm a hard-ass," she agreed. But her voice was soft. And her gaze kept drifting to his mouth.

His body tightened more each time she did it.

"You want to know the best part of it?"

"My sexy work boots?" she asked.

"Well, the fact that you drive a forklift is not something I've forgotten," he told her. He was serious.

She laughed. And her gaze dropped to his mouth again.

"What's the best part?" she asked.

"That when you expect me to *do* something at work, to make a difference, you really believe I can."

Jane's tongue came out and wet her lips. "I do."

"Thank you."

They just looked at each other for several ticks. Then she asked, "No one else does that for you?"

"The guys do," he said. "And Piper."

"I liked her."

"We all love Piper."

"She makes you try?"

"She does."

"So that's good."

"Yeah, but there's something about you that the guys and Piper don't have," he said.

"The forklift?"

He grinned. "Okay, there are two things about you that the guys and Piper don't have."

Jane smiled back. "What's the other thing?"

"I've never wanted to kiss any of them."

Her smile disappeared as she sucked in a little breath. "Not even Piper?" she asked.

"Nope."

He could have sworn she started to lean in again.

"Hi! Oh my God, I'm so sorry I'm late! I went to change, and I burned the cookies that were in the oven, and I had to start over because Lisa really need three dozen, and I've been texting you but you haven't answered, and I called but your ringer is off, and then I called the bar and Dillon said that yes you were here and you were fine and that you seemed like you didn't want to be interrupted."

Jane and Dax both turned to look at the bubbly blond who'd just come up to their table, seemingly rambling and flustered. The appraising, narrow-eyed look she was giving them in return said otherwise.

"Hi, Josie," Dax greeted, fighting a smile.

"Hey, Dax." Josie turned her attention to Jane. "Hi, Jane."

"Hi."

"You forgot you asked me to come, didn't you?" Josie asked.

"No." Jane frowned and shook her head quickly. Too quickly to be convincing. "Of course not."

"Uh-huh."

"She asked you to come?" Dax asked Josie. He looked at Jane. "Why's that?"

Josie leaned in, sort of, on the table between them. The petite woman had to stretch to get her elbows onto the high tabletop and it hardly seemed like leaning when she was on tiptoe, but she pretended nonchalance. "Well, I think it was to keep this"—Josie waggled her finger back and forth between Jane and Dax—"from happening, actually."

"That right?" Dax grinned and looked at Jane again. "What is *this* exactly? Pizza and tequila? Conversation?"

"It's her looking at you the way she looked when Zoe told her she'd made strawberry pie in a jar," Josie said.

"Josie!" Jane protested, her cheeks getting pink.

Dax laughed. "I don't even know what that means exactly, but I like the blush."

The blush got deeper. "It's nothing."

"She *loves* strawberry pie. Strawberry anything, really, but pie especially. And Zoe started making them in jars so they're super portable and easy to keep so you can buy like—what Jane?—ten at a time and stack them in your fridge with no problem."

"*Josie*," Jane said through gritted teeth.

Josie just grinned. "So if she's looking at you like she looked at those jar pies, it means she's never seen anything quite so wonderful, and she's not sure she'll ever get enough."

"Oh my God," Jane groaned and covered her face. "I was not looking at him like that."

"You totally were," Josie said.

"You really were," Dax agreed.

Josie laughed, and Jane shook her head, groaning.

"But in fairness, I was looking at you the same way," Dax said, grinning so big he was sure he looked like an idiot. And he didn't care.

"He definitely was looking at you like... something like that," Josie said.

"Like what?" Dax wanted to know, noticing Josie's pause. "What did you think?"

"Well, along the same lines as Jane and strawberry baked goods." Josie got a sly look on her face and cast a glance at her friend.

Jane peeked between her fingers.

"Like you were thinking about eating it *all* up and then licking the plate clean to be sure you didn't miss anything."

Dax felt his mouth drop open. Then he snorted. "Jocelyn Asher... I really like you."

Josie grinned as if very proud of herself.

Dax focused on Jane. Her cheeks were burning, and she was glaring at her best friend.

"For the record," he said. "She's right about what I was thinking."

"Okay, you two are trouble," Jane said. "I think we're done

here." She leaned over and started to dig in her bag where it hung from the back of her chair.

It took Dax a second to realize she was going for her wallet. "You have to be kidding."

"What?" She looked up, her red hair falling across her cheek.

"One perk of introducing a millionaire to some of the best pizza he's ever had is having him pay, don't you think?"

She sat up straight again. "That is a really excellent point."

"Ooh, thanks." Josie reached for one of the two pieces left.

"Hey," Jane protested.

Josie lifted the slice. "I know better than to go for your pizza without permission, but this is Dax's pizza now."

Jane rolled her eyes and Dax laughed. He signaled to Riley, letting her know to add the pizza and their drinks to his overall tab for the evening. Which was covering pretty much everything being consumed inside the building.

"Well, since I'm clearly too late to keep the two of you from thinking naughty thoughts about each other," Josie said, "I'm going over to talk to Stacey and Kara."

"You show up late, don't do your job, and then leave me alone with him?" Jane asked.

It was clear she was teasing. Dax loved that these women gave each other as much trouble as he and his friends gave one another.

Josie looked back and forth between them. "Well, if I'm sitting here, you'll feel bad about asking him to walk you out to your car, and then how are you going to kiss him good night? You can't do that in front of all these people." She leaned in and said in a lower voice, "He *is* your boss after all."

Jane opened her mouth, shut it, shook her head, then said, "You're the worst."

"Because I've now told Dax you want to kiss him or because

I reminded you that he's your boss?" Josie asked, batting her eyes.

"All of it," Jane told her.

Josie went up on tiptoe again and kissed Jane's cheek. "Love you." Then she started for the far side of the bar.

"Love you too," Jane muttered, watching her friend go.

Dax waited until she finally turned back and looked at him. Almost reluctantly.

"You called for reinforcements?" he asked.

"I *tried* to call for reinforcements. Unfortunately, my reinforcements were elbow deep in cookie dough at the time."

He grinned. "You can just say no to me, Jane."

"Yeah, well, I don't think I can."

He leaned in. "Have I given you the impression that you *can't* say no to me if you don't want to be with me?"

"Not at all."

"Has anyone at Hot Cakes, especially in management, ever given you that impression?" he asked with a frown. A sudden, hot bolt of protectiveness went through his chest. *That* was weird. He didn't get protective.

"No. Never."

"Then what's the problem?"

"I needed someone to remind *me* that this is a bad idea."

Relief washed through him. He gave her a slow smile. "Ah. The irresistible thing again."

"Did you look up incorrigible?" she asked.

He laughed. "I texted Piper about it, but she disagrees, just so you know."

"Does she?"

"She said incorrigible means beyond reform, and she reminded me Grant has been successful in correcting my behavior on more than one occasion."

"How's he do that?" Jane asked, her lips curling up as though she was fighting a smile. And losing.

"Sinatra memorabilia, mostly," Dax said. "He gets some great pieces and then dangles them like carrots."

"Wow, expensive carrots."

"He tried rationing my gummy bears, but I mean, those are really easy to get. It had to be something I couldn't get for myself."

She nodded. "Should have known that correcting your behavior was out of my price range."

"Well…" Dax leaned in. "You do have some things to offer me that I can't get anywhere else."

Both of her eyebrows went up. "Tell me you *don't* mean anything by that that would be inappropriate for a boss to suggest to his employee."

He shook his head, his desire for this woman growing by the minute. "Can't do that. But," he added, "if it's any comfort, Cam is an excellent attorney, and he'd love to sue me for sexual harassment."

She laughed. "You're trouble."

He smiled. "And you're a good girl?"

She tipped her head. "Actually, I think I'm just too busy and tired to be bad."

He chuckled. "There's a lot there for me to think about."

Jane pulled her bottom lip between her teeth, watching him, then said, "Speaking of tired, I really do need to get going."

"Okay." Disappointment jabbed him in the chest, but it wasn't realistic to think he could keep her here talking all night.

The urge was so unusual he thought maybe it was good for them to have a little space too. Maybe it was the tequila. Or something they put in the pizza. How could he be falling for a woman with so much going on in her life that he couldn't even touch? And so quickly?

"But… would you walk me out to my car?"

Fuck yeah. Josie seemed to know Jane well, and she'd

thought Jane would want him to walk her out to her car so she could kiss him good night.

He'd do just about anything to have her kiss him. To have her let him kiss her. To slide his hand into her hair, hold her head, and taste her. Really taste her.

"I don't know if I've ever wanted anything more than to walk you to your car," he told her. "And I *really* wanted that napkin from the Sands with Frank's signature on it."

"That's a big deal?"

"The Sands Casino in Vegas was where the Rat Pack performed together in the sixties," he said, his hand over his heart. "The casino doesn't even exist anymore. So that napkin is... everything."

She laughed. "I'm going to need to read up on Frank Sinatra."

"I can tell you anything you want to know." Dax stretched to his feet. "In fact, we should go back to your place right now and get started. I know a lot."

"Nice try." She slid off her tall chair. "But I have to work at the factory tomorrow. New bosses. Have to impress them."

He stepped close. "Consider that done."

She blew out a breath. "Yeah, see... about that boss thing..."

"Shit," he said. He grabbed her hand and started for the door. "Forget about that. I didn't say a thing. That's nothing."

She tugged her hand free but kept walking with him. He pushed the door open and let her step through.

As she passed him, she said, "It's not nothing."

"It's..." It was going to be nothing. He was going to talk to the guys in the morning. "Jane..."

"How about for right now we just... stop talking completely?" she asked.

He could do that. Probably.

He walked with her to her car. A very basic, blue Nissan sedan.

She opened the driver's side door and tossed her purse onto the passenger seat, then she shut it again, and turned to face him.

"I had a really great time talking with you tonight," he said. "Thank you for telling me about your dad. Thank you for coming out tonight."

"The no-talking thing is pretty tough for you, huh?" she asked.

He nodded. "Really is."

"Maybe this will help." She took the tiny step forward that brought her right in front of him then took the front of his shirt in her hand and tugged him down, putting her lips against his.

7

The first time she'd met him, Jane had wanted to kiss him. She'd told herself she couldn't. It would never happen. It was a bad idea.

But now... now that his lips were against hers, now that he'd made that little groaning sound in the back of his throat, now that his hands were on her hips and he was backing her up against the side of her car and pressing close, angling his head to deepen the kiss, opening his mouth, making her feel like he'd never wanted anything more... well, now she was a goner. Because it was still a bad idea. But, oh man, she didn't care.

He was the new strawberry pie in her life. She'd had one taste of Zoe's strawberry pie and that had been it. Nothing else would ever measure up. She would never not crave it. She would never pass up a chance to have it on her tongue.

Yeah, Dax Marshall was that.

And then some.

He pulled back, breathing hard, staring down at her.

She quickly put her hand over his mouth. "Don't talk. Talking is the *wrong* choice right now."

She was going to have to deal with the boss thing soon

enough. And the millionaire thing. And the he-doesn't-live-here-and-isn't-staying thing. And all the other crap she always had to deal with that made this impossible.

But for another minute—or maybe ten—she didn't want to think about any of that. And if he talked, that would be very difficult.

He pulled in a breath, gave her a short nod that she interpreted as *okay, no talking* and she moved her hand.

Which was the *right* choice, because he leaned in as he slid his hand up the side of her body, skimming over her hip, waist, the side of her breast, up and into her hair. Then he cupped the back of her head and lowered his mouth to hers again.

This time *he* kissed *her*.

And seriously, she'd give up strawberry pie for this.

That was the thought that flickered through her mind as he kissed her, holding her with that hand in her hair, the other slipping under the edge of her shirt just above her hip. His palm met bare skin and just rested there, burning into her like a brand. But he didn't try to move higher, didn't even rub or stroke, just rested it there.

That area of skin, however, whooped it up. Her nerve endings were dancing, and heat streaked from there throughout her body.

She *wanted* him to rub and stroke. Lots of places.

He kissed her hungrily but also slow and deep as if he was savoring. Much the way she ate strawberry pie, come to think of it. She didn't rush through that. She appreciated every bite. She kept it on her tongue as long as possible. She licked the tines of the fork to be sure she didn't miss a bit.

Dax was definitely kissing her like that. Like he didn't want to miss even the slightest bit. Like he wanted to drag it out.

His tongue, his lips, the way he held her, the way he put his whole body against her whole body, the way he felt and tasted and smelled... it was a whole experience.

Jane arched closer, wrapping her arms around his neck, tasting him back. She slid her hands into his hair, running it through her fingers, then down the sides of his face, gliding her palms over his short beard. She let go of the sighs and moans that wanted to escape, letting him know she was all in here, totally and completely.

They made out like that for long, delicious minutes.

When he finally took his mouth from hers, it was to slide it along her jawline, his beard causing goose bumps to trip down her arms and tighten her nipples. In her ear he said gruffly, "I have to talk now."

She laughed lightly. "I didn't think it would last for even this long, really."

"Well, I do love using my mouth this way too." He dragged his lips along the side of her neck.

Her nipples got even tighter, begging for him to drag those lips down there.

"But I can't resist saying—" He lifted his head. "You are the most delicious thing I've ever tasted. And I *really* like gummy bears."

She grinned. "Well... same."

A very sexy kind of surprised but superhot look crossed his face. "What about those jar pies?"

She sighed. "Those are amazing."

"But the kissing..." he prompted.

She knew she shouldn't tell him the truth. The guy's ego didn't quit. Already. But she found herself nodding. "I was *really* hoping you'd be bad at it. Like terrible. Like no-worry-of-dirty-dreams bad," she said.

He arched an eyebrow. "And?"

She sighed. "It was *really* good."

"Dirty-dreams-tonight good?" His voice was rumbly and low.

She nodded. "Unfortunately."

He looked very pleased by her answer. "Better-than-jar-pie good?"

She nibbled on her bottom lip. She was possibly going to regret telling him this. "Yeah, this was better. Don't tell Zoe."

"Do you have dirty dreams about jar pie, Jane?" he asked.

His husky voice caused warmth to twist through her stomach and then slide lower.

"I do," she admitted.

His mouth curled up. "Maybe we should combine the kissing and the pie."

Her eyes widened before she could stop it. That would be... holy crap she would *never* recover. "I can't even imagine that, honestly. I might die."

He laughed, his breath warm against her cheek. He cupped her face, running his thumb along her jaw, looking into her eyes.

"Thank you for letting me kiss you."

"I think *I* kissed *you*."

He nodded. "Thank you for that too."

He was *thanking* her for kissing him? This guy... she honestly didn't know what to think of him. He was so not what she expected nearly every time they talked.

"Do me a favor?" she asked.

"Anything. Except never kiss you again." He shook his head. "Please don't ask me that."

She should. She really, really should. But she couldn't bring herself to say the words. "I was going to say, please don't promote me."

He chuckled. "I don't know. That was definitely promotion-level kissing."

She pushed him back and took a deep breath. She needed some space. She needed to stop thinking about kissing him again—when, where, how long did she have to wait? Could they do it somewhere that would be conducive to taking off clothes? "It really was. I was *really* good just now," she said. "I can understand you wanting to reward me. You have to resist."

He let her go, tucking his hands into his back pockets, but he was grinning the grin that, honestly, was a huge part of what had led to this kissing thing in the first place.

"But no promotions," she said. "I'm serious. I *will* stop kissing you if you promote me."

"I hear you," he said. He reached past her and opened her car door, holding it for her to get in.

Jane resisted the urge to kiss him again. She was not going to keep doing that. He'd told her not to ask him to never kiss her again. Okay, she hadn't asked him that. But that didn't mean she couldn't just *not* do it again.

"So just expensive gifts, then?" he asked. "Jewelry and stuff. As a 'reward.' Since you won't take a promotion."

"Absolutely not. I will pawn it all and pocket the money *and* stop kissing you." She slid into the driver's seat then looked up at him. "I had a nice time tonight."

"Ditto," he said.

"Thanks for the... pizza."

"I'll... eat pizza... with you any time," he said, pausing the way she had, making it into a funny, hot euphemism. "And," he added, "I'll also eat pizza with you any time."

She smiled. So he'd enjoyed just the pizza and conversation too. Yeah, that had been nice. And also a reason she'd kissed him.

She rolled down her window then pulled the car door closed. "I'll see you tomorrow at work."

"You will." He grinned. "I'll have the paperwork for your raise all ready to go. Since you won't let me promote you or buy you things."

Jane shook her head. "Don't even think about it."

"Go out with me Saturday night."

Damn. He was so freaking tempting, and now that she'd

kissed him she was really going to have to shore up her defenses. She could *not* have a fling with the boss. She barely had time to do all the crap she had to do on a regular basis. When would she fit fling-time in anyway? And Dax would be... a lot. He was just a big personality and would be very hard to pigeonhole into a booty-call box.

"Can't," she said. But she paused. She bit her bottom lip. She tried not to say it. But in the end she said, "But you could go out with me Saturday morning."

"Yes."

He didn't ask what they'd be doing, what time, anything. Just yes. Jane's heart tripped a little at that.

"And I'll let you buy my coffee and muffin at Zoe's."

She'd be at Zoe's anyway, and if he met her there for coffee it was only kind of a date. For all anyone knew, they'd just both happened to be there at the same time. If she drank coffee and ate pastries with him in the morning, she would not be tempted to spend the night with him. Something she was *sure* would cross her mind if they went out to dinner or to the bar again. She wouldn't be even able to spend the day with him. She always went from the bakery to see her dad. Kelsey usually met them there unless she had dance practice or a school trip or something. So Saturday morning coffee and muffins was the safest way to see Dax. It would be in public. It would have a time limit on it, and it would be a less-typical time of day for banging.

Though the idea of being in bed with Dax at 10 a.m. on a Saturday morning was not the craziest thing she could imagine.

"Breakfast, and I'm not even waking up with you?" he teased.

"Yeah," she said, nodding. She ignored the jab of jealousy over the thought that he'd probably awakened with and gone to breakfast with plenty of women.

He nodded. "I'll be there at ten."

"Well, I'll be there at eight," she said. Her internal clock was too well set to sleep much past seven. She wished she could sleep in and be leisurely in the morning, linger over her coffee, lie in bed and watch Netflix or read before getting up and at 'em. But she'd been getting up early for too long, and once she was awake her brain wouldn't stop thinking about all the things she could be getting done if she wasn't lying in bed.

"Eight?" He sighed. "You're a morning person."

"Have to be." And he wasn't. Big surprise. They were total opposites.

Except for the fact that they both tried to take care of one of their parents while having issues with the other. And that they both liked and cared about the people who worked at Hot Cakes—she really did believe that Dax cared about them as people after working with them for the past several days. And they both liked pizza. And each other.

She really did like him. Even though anything long term, other than friendship, would be impossible. So friendship. Yeah, they could do that. They could joke and tease and even kiss... Okay, maybe they shouldn't kiss.

"I'll be there at eight," he finally said. Then he added, "Maybe eight fifteen."

She laughed. "I'll wait until eight twenty, but I've got places to be."

"Fine. But I'm going to expect some *very* good... muffins."

Yeah, he absolutely said that with an-inappropriate-for-a-boss-to-use-with-his-employee tone.

A warm shiver went through her.

"You show up by eight oh five, and your chances of getting those are much better," she said. With that same inappropriate tone.

Though it was true. You had to get to Buttered Up early. There was always a morning crowd even on Saturdays.

"Duly noted," he said.

She could have sworn that along with that amused grin, there was a little bit of affection in his expression.

Like *friends* would have looking at one another.

Friends could be affectionate. And eat pizza together. And spend a Saturday morning together.

And make out against her car again at the end of the night...

That would be *very* friendly.

She was in a lot of trouble here.

———

"You're a real pain in my ass, Marshall," Grant said as he came through Dax's office door the next morning.

"Missed you too," Dax said with a grin at the guy who liked to seem perpetually annoyed with them all but who loved Fluke Inc., and the energy and dynamic between the five men who made it up, as much as any of them did.

Grant Lorre was the oldest of the five partners, a year older than Aiden and Cam and two older than Dax and Ollie. He'd been a business management and econ major at the university when they'd all met. He and Aiden had met at some dorky seminar for business majors and had struck up a conversation that had extended past drinks after the seminar and well into pancakes and coffee the following morning. They'd been fast friends, and when Aiden and Cam had "discovered"—their word, not his—Dax and Ollie down the hall in the dorm working on their idea for a video game, Grant had gotten looped in.

Dax annoyed Grant. On purpose. The guy was so fucking serious about everything. Grant thought he was looking out for Dax and Ollie when they went on their crazy trips to conferences and fan meet and greets, but the truth was, Dax and Ollie felt it was their duty to get the guy out of the office, out of his suits, and out of his routine.

It was thanks to Dax and Ollie that Grant had *any* interesting stories to tell. They reminded him of that and told him he was welcome, on a regular basis.

Grant kept a bottle of Tums and one of ibuprofen in his desk drawer. He wrote DAX on the side of the antacids and OLLIE on the side of the painkillers.

That was fucking funny, and Dax loved Grant's dry, subtle sense of humor.

He also loved doing things that made Grant reach for those bottles. Because that meant he'd done something to spice things up for his I-live-by-spreadsheets-and-planners friend.

Grant didn't like messes. Literal or figurative. His fucking apartment in Chicago was all sleek lines and polished surfaces. He was a neat freak, a bit of a germaphobe, and took everything seriously.

Dax loved shaking things up. From surreptitiously rearranging Grant's tie rack in his closet to calling him at 3 a.m. to come pick him and Ollie up somewhere.

The fact Grant stuck around and had even considered investing in yet another business with them, told Dax everything he needed to know.

Grant liked him. In spite of their differences.

"Grant." Aiden was clearly surprised to see their partner in Appleby.

Dax was a little surprised too. He'd called Grant last night —well, this morning, since it had been 2 a.m.—but he'd really thought Grant could handle what he'd proposed via phone and email.

"'Morning," Grant greeted Aiden. "You're on my list too," he said to Ollie, who was lounging in the blue beanbag.

"Me?" Ollie sat up a little straighter. Or as straight as you could get in a beanbag. "What I do?"

"You didn't talk Dax out of this craziness," Grant said. "And you let him dial my number at two a.m. We talked about the rules for that."

Ollie nodded. "Hospital personnel, law enforcement personnel, or criminals and duct tape have to be involved before we call after midnight." He looked at Dax. "What did you do?"

"You weren't with him?" Grant asked before Dax could respond.

"No. Are we talking last night?" Ollie narrowed his eyes, studying Dax. "He was out at the bar last night and spent most of his time with a certain sassy, gorgeous redhead." Ollie leaned forward in the beanbag. "Did you marry her or something?"

"How did you know I was with Jane last night?" Dax asked, ignoring everything else.

Ollie shrugged. "Someone told Piper, who told me."

"Who told Piper?"

"I don't know. But the entire factory was there last night, right? I mean, it's not like you were sneaking around. But seriously, did you go to Vegas or something?"

"Why would I be *here* right now with you if I'd whisked her off to Vegas and convinced her to marry me?" Dax asked.

Not that he *wouldn't* do that. And they all knew it. It just didn't make sense that he'd be here now with *them* if he had.

"The private plane could have gotten you there and back," Ollie said.

"Technically," Dax agreed. "But that doesn't take into account the twelve hours straight I would have her naked in a suite at the Waldorf Astoria."

"Ah." Ollie nodded. "That's true."

"So you had nothing to do with the call?" Grant asked Ollie.

"Nope. I don't know what you're talking about."

"Well, he..." Grant looked around. "For fuck's sake, Dax, is there a regular chair *anywhere*?"

Dax grinned and crossed to the office door. He ducked

around the corner to Aiden's office, grabbed one of his chairs, and brought it back in for Grant. "Here you go, old man. I forget about your aging back and knees."

"Fuck off." Grant took the chair and pushed it up to join the beanbags.

"Cappuccino?" Dax asked. "Gummy bears?"

Grant hated everything about Dax's office in Chicago, and this one was very much like it. To Grant, coffee, dry erase markers, and leather chairs should all be black.

"I'm good," Grant said with an eye roll. "Piper is going to get me a muffin and coffee at the bakery."

Ollie perked up. "I want a muffin from Buttered Up." He shot to his feet and started for the door. "Piper!"

Piper appeared in the doorway before he was even halfway there. "For God's sake," she told him. "I'm not your child or your dog. Stop yelling for me."

Dax wished he had a dollar for every time their executive assistant scolded Oliver. Ollie didn't actually mean anything with the yelling or even the "Get me a muffin" type demands he made. He just didn't *think*. He got excited, and as thoughts and ideas were crashing around in his head, they just kind of fell out of his mouth sometimes.

Ollie was the dreamer and the visionary. If you could pull his head out of the clouds and get him focused, amazing things happened. But the focus was generally short lived, and the ideas were usually a little crazy. At least until Dax formed them into something other people could see and understand. Then Grant would crunch numbers, tell Dax to tone it down or pull back on a few things. Which he would do. Usually. And once that all happened, Aiden could sell it to anyone. Cam would make sure the contract was very lucrative for Fluke. And they all lived happily ever after.

Honestly, the hard parts of the process were getting Ollie's ideas from his head to paper and giving up on things on Dax's wish list like life-sized troll dolls in their merchandise line. Everything else seemed to fall into place, and all five of them ended up being happy.

"Sorry." Ollie did manage to look slightly contrite. "Just wanted to catch you before you left for the bakery."

"I'm already back from the bakery," Piper told him, stepping into the room with a cardboard tray of coffee cups and four bakery bags.

"Oh, I just was hoping for some lemon poppyseed muffins in my life," Ollie said with a dramatic sigh.

"I got you lemon poppyseed and an orange muffin," she said, handing him the bag.

"Do I like orange?" he asked, taking it and peering inside.

"You will," she said confidently.

"You're the best, Piper." Ollie looped an arm around her waist and pulled her close, planting a smacking kiss on her cheek.

And in a very, *very* rare moment within the offices—in Chicago or Appleby—Piper Barry looked flustered.

Only Ollie could do that to her.

Dax grinned. *He* could have kissed her right on the mouth, with tongue, and she wouldn't have done anything but laugh, push him back, and tell him to knock it off.

Ollie was the only one who made her blush and not be able to find her words right away.

He was also the only one who made her grind her teeth.

She had a bottle of ibuprofen in her desk too and Grant wrote OLLIE on it for her as well.

The only problem with any of that, was Oliver was completely clueless about his effect on their pretty, capable, amazing assistant.

Grant, Aiden, Cam, and Dax knew, though, and Grant jumped in to cover Piper's blushing before Dax could.

"Dax wants to sell his part of Hot Cakes."

Oliver let Piper go and swung to face them. "What?"

Aiden sat forward in his beanbag with a frown. "What's going on?"

Dax sighed. "I'm not leaving Fluke. I just don't want my share in Hot Cakes."

"Why not?" Aiden looked not only confused, but a little offended.

Hot Cakes meant a lot to him. Appleby was his hometown, and the people working here were friends and neighbors. He felt strongly about saving the factory and the jobs as well as making it all even better than it had been before.

"Because he's in love," Grant said.

Dax shot him a look.

Grant sat back in Aiden's office chair and opened his Buttered Up bag. He looked smug.

Every once in a while, Grant succeeded in one-upping Dax and making *him* the eye-rolling one who had to deal with a bunch of chaos and questions. It was rare, but Grant enjoyed it immensely.

"You're in *love*?" Aiden asked.

"With someone other than yourself?" Ollie quipped, reclaiming his seat in the beanbag and digging into his bakery bag as well.

"I didn't say love," Dax told them. Though he wasn't really protesting the term.

Jane was amazing. He wasn't sure he was in love with her yet, but he wasn't a dumbass. *Not* falling in love with her would be pretty stupid.

Especially after that kiss. That kiss was why he'd still been awake at 2 a.m. and had decided to fix the "you're my boss" protest Jane kept offering up. There was an easy solution, and he was more than willing to do it to have her.

"You said you had met someone and that you'd never felt

like this before and that the only way to be with her was to give up your portion of Hot Cakes," Grant said.

Dax nodded. "Love doesn't appear in that sentence anywhere."

"Well, let's see," Ollie said, licking an orange muffin crumb from his finger. "You've felt lust and curiosity and affection for women before. You've also felt frustration and annoyance and fear."

"Fear was *one* time, one girl, and that was all her, not me," Dax protested. "She was a nutjob."

He'd actually had a stalker for a while. She was *very* into *Warriors of Easton* and had been obsessed with its creators. Once she'd met Dax and Ollie at a few cons, she'd latched on to Dax. She showed up *everywhere*, sent him emails and letters and packages, posted on fan forums. It had been over the top, and the packages with her panties in them had been *a lot*, but it hadn't been until she'd broken into his hotel room and he'd come in to find her in a full *Warriors of Easton* princess costume —complete with a sword—that he'd really gotten concerned.

He'd called Grant at 3 a.m. about that one. Grant had been just a few doors down and had been there, with the cops, in minutes.

"I'm just saying," Ollie replied. "That you've felt a lot of things for a lot of women, so to say you've never felt *this* way before only leaves a few emotions. And," he added, "this orange muffin is freaking amazing."

Okay, Ollie had a point. Dax hadn't really been trying to label what he felt for Jane, but it was very different, new, unique. And he loved *that* at least. He wanted to be with her all the time. He wanted to know all about her. He wanted to make everything better for her. Around her. For the people she cared about. If anything was even touching her life and wasn't exactly what she wanted it to be, he wanted to fix it. He knew he couldn't. He did acknowledge that. But he wanted to and that was new. The only people he felt that way about were his mother, the men in this room, Cam, and Piper.

"All I know is I want to be with her, and Hot Cakes is in the way, so I want to get rid of it."

"Is it Jane?" Aiden asked, watching Dax with an expression that was part surprise and part concern.

"Yes," Dax told him, meeting his gaze directly.

Aiden nodded. Jane was a friend of his. They'd gone to high school together. Zoe, Aiden's girlfriend, was one of Jane's best friends. It was important Aiden know Dax wasn't just fucking around here.

That was also new. Usually Dax didn't care if people thought he wasn't taking things seriously. *He* knew what he was serious about and gave those things his all. What other people thought didn't matter. Unless it was Grant, Aiden, Ollie, or Cam.

And there was also a niggle at the back of his mind that said he wanted *everyone* to know he was serious about Jane.

Which was interesting, because until that very moment, he hadn't even told himself he was *serious* about her. He just didn't get serious very often, about anything.

"You don't have to give up your part of the business," Ollie said. "That's ridiculous."

"She won't date me because I'm her boss."

Ollie snorted. "You're not really her boss."

"I own the company she works for," Dax said. "At least a percentage of it. That does make me her boss."

Grant lifted a brow. He was clearly surprised Dax would argue with Ollie but probably more so that Dax would consider himself a boss.

"And you want to date her that much?" Grant asked.

Dax shrugged. "I need to see what can happen with her more than I need to own twenty percent of a snack cake company."

"You need to see what will happen with her?" Aiden echoed. "What could happen? You go out, have some fun, have some sex, and then you leave, right? Is that really worth giving up an investment like this?" His tone wasn't confrontational though. He sounded more curious.

"I think there's a chance there's more there," Dax admitted. For the first time out loud but probably for the first time to himself too. "She's... amazing. Different than most women I know."

"Worth giving up millions for?" Ollie asked.

Dax nodded. "Yeah." He could admit it helped that he'd still have millions in the bank. He didn't want to blow this "sacrifice" out of proportion. He wasn't giving up fame and fortune here.

"And you want to make this grand gesture, right?" Grant asked. "That's pretty typical. Do something big and crazy to make a point."

It was totally typical. "Well, the thing is," Dax said, "and I'm sure you'll find this amusing," he told Grant specifically, "I'm not sure she'll go out with me anyway."

"No?" Grant asked. "When you take the one thing she's worried about out of the equation?"

Dax shook his head. "I think the boss thing is a convenient excuse. There's more reasons why she doesn't want to let me too close. But I'm definitely up for showing her I'm serious here."

Aiden was watching him carefully. "Jane is special," he said. "She's not at all like your usual girls."

Dax nodded. "I promise you I realize that. I won't hurt her."

Aiden gave him a small smile. "I think I'm more afraid that she'll hurt you, man."

Dax frowned. "What do you mean?"

"Jane doesn't have time for anything extra, anything silly or outrageous."

Dax gave him a nod. Aiden's words jabbed him in the chest. "Got it. I'm silly and outrageous."

"You are," Aiden agreed. "Intentionally."

"Maybe Jane needs a little silliness in her life."

"Maybe," Aiden said. "But that's going to be short term. The seriousness in her life isn't going to go away. You're not going to be able to just help her through a tough time and make it go away. That tough time is her reality."

And Aiden didn't think Dax had what it took to help someone through a tough time on any kind of ongoing basis.

That hurt.

But the worst part? Dax thought maybe Aiden was right. He'd helped his mom through her lowest periods, but he certainly hadn't been able to get her to a happy place on any kind of permanent basis.

"And this is going to hurt *me* how?" Dax asked Aiden.

"You're going to have to eventually just let it be what it is. And that's hard for you. You keep trying to reform your dad, for God's sake, and everyone knows he's the man he's going to be."

Dax really hated this whole fucking conversation suddenly.

"Just buy my shares out, and then when this all goes to shit, you can buy me a five-pound bag of gummy bears and get me black-out drunk," Dax said.

"Is that how you deal with broken hearts?" Ollie asked.

Dax could honestly say he'd never had a broken heart. Not over a woman anyway. He looked at his best friends and shrugged. "Fuck if I know."

8

The next day sucked.

Not because of the tequila shot or the later-than-usual night out at the bar or the fact that she'd had a hard time falling asleep because of all the thoughts of Dax and that kiss running through her head.

But because her stepmother really was wicked at times. And her sister was a drama queen.

"Kelsey," Jane broke into her sister's ranting. "I am on my way over. Do *not* throw any more dishes."

Cassie had basically grounded Kelsey because she'd gotten a C on her chemistry test. That meant Kelsey couldn't go to the school dance that weekend. *That* meant Kelsey was going to be insufferable to live with, which meant Cassie was going to be even meaner and... Jane was going to be getting a lot of calls from both of them.

"It's not fair! She's not my mom! I don't understand why she gets a say in this at all!" Kelsey said. Her voice was wobbly with tears, but they weren't sad tears. They were teenager-pissed-at-the-world tears.

"Because you got a C. That's not her decision. That was

something dad and I put in place, and you know it," Jane said, heading out the door of the factory toward the parking lot. Thankfully, her work shift was already over, and she hadn't had to duck out early.

She *really* sympathized with Kelsey. Her sister was in a very tough situation in general. Her own mother was flitting around the world while her father sat in a nursing home, and she lived with the stepmother who punished Kelsey for anything she had—friends, great hair, a natural talent for dance and a place in the front row of the dance team at school—that Aspen didn't.

But Kelsey also used her my-mom-was-never-there-for-me and my-father-is-sick stuff as an excuse to be a brat.

Jane had been there for her. Jane was still there for her. She didn't do Kelsey's laundry or cook for her or sleep under the same roof, but she went to parent-teacher conferences, showed up to every dance team performance, and went to bat for her when Cassie leaned too hard.

But Kelsey had to get good grades. She was capable of it. She just didn't try because she hated chemistry.

Well, I have to do a lot of things I hate every day, Jane thought. Kelsey needed to grow up a little. Throwing dishes against the wall in the kitchen was not grown-up.

"I got a C!" Kelsey said. "Big deal! That's passing! And she only grounded me because of the dance. If I didn't have anything fun going on she wouldn't have even bothered. And you wouldn't even know about the C!"

"Well, to be fair, I know about the C because there are two plates lying in pieces on the kitchen floor." Cassie had called Jane immediately. She'd even sent a video of Kelsey heaving the second plate across the kitchen.

"She would have told you anyway," Kelsey said.

"Probably," Jane agreed. "But that would have surely been after *you* told me because you know how much I hate hearing that kind of stuff from her."

"It's just one stupid test," Kelsey muttered.

"And the rule is 'no C's,' so it doesn't really matter."

"You *have* to get me ungrounded." Kelsey's tone turned pleading.

"*You* have to get *yourself* ungrounded," Jane told her. "Talk to your teacher about some extra credit. Do more chores. Beg. But this is on you."

"You could take me out Saturday," Kelsey said, ignoring everything Jane said. "And then I could go to the dance from your place."

Sister time with Jane never counted as "going out," so the grounding rules wouldn't apply. Jane could take Kelsey anywhere and anytime, for the most part. There had definitely been times that Jane had let Kelsey spend a weekend or even three or four days with her just to give them all a break. She suspected Cassie liked that as much as Kelsey did. But this wasn't going to be one of those times.

"You can hang out with me this weekend if you want," Jane said, compromising. It was Friday night. Kelsey could spend her grounded weekend on Jane's couch with ice cream. That was better than her shutting herself in her room to avoid Cassie, Jane supposed. "But you're not going to the dance."

"Come *on!*"

"No. I'll be there in ten minutes, and I'll help you with the chores, but you're not going to the dance, and I'm not sweeping up broken plates. Pull yourself together. Clean the kitchen up, and I'll see you soon."

Jane took a deep breath and blew it out. Maybe she should start doing yoga. Josie's younger sister, Paige, ran Cores and Catnip, a yoga studio and cat café. Jane could head over there right now, in fact. Cores offered yoga classes of all kinds along with a juice bar and cat adoption center. The sign even had a cat playing with an apple core on it. Paige really liked the cats best, but the yoga and juice bar actually made money while collecting cats did not.

Cores was the opposite of Buttered Up in almost every way. The bakery was decorated in bright yellows and had display cases brimming with multicolored treats full of fat and sugar. People came in to get a shot of sugar and caffeine so they could face their workday. On the other hand, the yoga studio was all soft creams and tans and was a quiet place. People came in and did yoga while cats lay around on the mats and purred. People stretched, breathed deep, drank smoothies, and petted cats. They even adopted them sometimes. If Paige could part with one.

Yoga sounded good. Relaxing. All that. Hell, maybe Jane needed a cat.

But truly, she probably needed to take up kickboxing. Pent-up frustration seemed to need something more like beat-the-hell-out-of-a-punching-bag than stretching and breathing. Or purring.

Jane tucked her phone away and mentally went over the cleaning supplies that were at the house, wondering if she needed to stop to get anything on her way over.

So she was about thirty feet from her car before she realized there was a man leaning against it.

Her heart thumped and she felt her lips curving. It wasn't just any man.

It was her very hot, very charming, hell-of-a-kisser boss.

And yes, she'd had dirty dreams about him and pie last night. Together. At the same time. Combined.

"I can't wait until Saturday to go out with you," he said with a shrug.

The stupid warm, twisty, aww-I-really-like-him sensation bloomed in her stomach at that.

"Saturday is tomorrow," she pointed out, coming to a stop in front of him.

God, he looked good. He was in jeans, a black Hot Cakes t-shirt stretched over his chest and shoulders, and black work boots on his feet. They were pretty clean and a little shiny compared to most of the boots around here, but otherwise, he didn't look awkward in them. He wore them with the same easy attitude he seemed to do everything.

Except kissing. The kissing had been pretty intense.

"Yeah, *tomorrow*," he said. "And you didn't come into the break room today."

He'd been looking for her. *Awww*.

"I got a call from my stepmother I had to return over lunch," she said.

He frowned slightly. "Everything okay?"

"Everything is... typical."

"So not okay."

She nodded. "Right. But it could be worse. So typical."

"Well, I can't stop thinking about you," he said, pushing off the car and straightening. "And eight o'clock on Saturday is fourteen hours and thirteen minutes from now." He stepped forward, nearly on top of her. "That's too long."

Again, *awww*.

Guys didn't make her go *awww*.

"Well, I've been thinking a lot about you too," she admitted. "But I've already got plans tonight, and you're still my boss so... we'll have to wait until tomorrow."

Her plan for tomorrow included bright sunlight and public places and other people and activities that would be appropriate for a woman who was showing a new guy around town in a casual, platonic way. Even her boss.

"Take me with you to do whatever you're doing tonight. Oh, and no, I'm not."

"You want to come with me?" she asked, imagining introducing Dax to Kelsey, Aspen, and Cassie. *Wow, that would be... interesting.*

"Of course."

"You don't even know what I'm going to be doing."

"It doesn't matter. Just want to be with you."

She put a hand on her hip and tried to pretend that didn't make her heart thump a little harder. "There probably won't be any opportunity for more kissing."

He grinned. He wasn't touching her, but he was absolutely in her personal space. And she wasn't doing a thing to change that.

"I really do just want to hang with you."

Oh. "So you won't even *try* to kiss me? Or talk me into kissing you?"

"I didn't say that."

That was better. She smiled. "Well, I guess..." She frowned as something occurred to her. "Wait a second, did you say 'No, I'm not' when I said you're my boss?"

"I did."

"But you are," she said. "I mean, I guess if you're not directly my manager or whatever and *say* that you're not going to promote me or give me a raise or special treatment, I understand, but you still are. I can't kiss or date or sleep with the owner of the company I work for, Dax. In spite of there being no fraternization policy. Which we should maybe talk about at some point, by the way."

"I understand," he said.

Okay, *that* little stab of disappointment was stupid and unexpected. She wanted him to understand this. It made sense. It was *very* understandable. But she wanted him to insist it would be okay, *a little* more.

"Good," she said with a nod.

"Which is why I gave up my shares this morning."

Jane stared at him. She repeated his words in her head. She frowned. She tipped her head. Finally she said, *"What?"*

He reached up and brushed the pad of his thumb over her

cheek. He lifted it to his nose and sniffed. "Powdered sugar?" he asked.

Jane's hand flew to her face, wiping the rest of the sugar away. "We dropped a huge bag in the warehouse, and it was *everywhere*. I was in the process of cleaning up in the locker room when my sister called and I just headed out. I didn't remember I hadn't gotten it all."

He put his thumb to his mouth and licked the sugar off.

Her belly, and lower, clenched.

"So, um..." Her thoughts were spinning. In part because this guy just did that to her. He was very distracting. But also because she was still trying to fully understand what he'd said a minute ago. "What do you mean you gave up your shares?"

"Oh," he said, his hand back at his side. He shrugged. "Grant, Aiden, Cam, and Ollie now each own twenty-five percent instead of twenty."

"They divided up your shares?"

"Right. Or they will. They're in the process. We just met about it this morning."

"And that leaves you with what? Zero? Nothing? You just don't own any of Hot Cakes now?"

"Exactly." He smiled. "That doesn't mean I won't be in there playing Ping-Pong every day though. In fact, it means I can play *more* Ping-Pong. I'm just consulting now. I don't really have to do anything but sit around and drink cappuccino and watch the Game Show Network."

She had no idea what do say. Who did that? Who just gave up twenty percent of a multimillion-dollar company? "You're... crazy."

He grinned again—this was slower and sexier. He lifted his hand to her face, this time cupping her cheek, and leaned in. "Oh, and I also now get to fully pursue a woman I'm becoming completely enamored with. I can ask her out. I can kiss her. I can sweet-talk her into coming back to my hotel room with me —and not leaving for about a week."

Jane felt hot bubbles fizzing through her bloodstream. "Why doesn't that sound creepy and like you're going to stalk me and hold me captive?"

"Because you *want* me to ask you out and kiss you and sweet-talk you and take you to my hotel room," he said.

Well, that was a very good point.

"The problem is," she said, realizing she sounded very breathless suddenly. "You're not the boss now, so you can't really get me out of work for a week to lie around naked in a hotel room with you."

His eyes flared with heat, and he leaned in, putting his mouth against her ear. "If they fire you, I'll just be able to keep you in my hotel room even longer. I promise you won't even remember where you used to work, and you certainly won't care."

She laughed, though she sounded completely seduced. Which she was. She imagined that laugh was the soft, breathy, oh-my-God-you're-Dax-Marshall laugh that he heard a lot from girls at Comic-Con. She got it. She really did. And she didn't even know that much about his video game.

"You didn't *really* give Hot Cakes up so I'd say yes to going out with you."

He pulled back and looked into her eyes. "I did. I absolutely did."

"But..." That just wasn't sinking in. Who did stuff like that? "That's nuts. You don't even know that you really want to date me. We haven't even gone out."

"Well," he said. "I hate to tell you, but last night was kind of a date."

"It wasn't. We both just happened to be at the same bar at the same time surrounded by coworkers and friends." Yeah, that wasn't true and she knew it.

"And we talked and got to know one another and realized we want to know each better, and I got a little crazier about you, and then you laid a kiss on me I couldn't forget even if I wanted to. Which I absolutely do not."

Jane pulled in a deep breath. "I'm assuming your friends will let you buy *back* into Hot Cakes if you suddenly decide this is all a huge mistake."

He frowned slightly but said, "I'm sure they would. But I'm not planning on calling *that* meeting anytime soon."

"Well, maybe we should actually try this out and see. That way you're only out a few million by the time you realize you messed up."

He smiled. "Excellent idea. I'll let them know you will be very late getting to work tomorrow."

She gave a soft laugh. "I wasn't actually talking about *that* part. I think you should see what hanging out with me really entails."

He narrowed one eye. "You're going to try to scare me off?"

"No. I'm not going to try. But I'm going to show you my real life, and, well, if you get a little scared, I won't blame you."

"I'm not worried."

"Of course you're not." Jane wondered if Dax ever actually got scared about anything.

"Can I kiss you at the end of the night?" he asked.

She didn't have to think about that for long. "If you still want to at the end of this night, then yes."

"Then I can brave just about anything."

If she was the swooning type of girl, that might have done it.

"We'll see," she said flippantly, instead of throwing her arms around his neck and kissing him right now.

Though maybe she should. Just in case he was no longer inclined to kiss her at the end of the night...

"So let's go," he said, stepping back and moving to open her car door. "Let's get this night started."

Yeah, that's what they should do. She should show him what being in her real life actually meant. He'd probably be in Aiden's office with his checkbook out, trying to buy his shares back tomorrow morning.

"The deal for the guys to buy your shares is just in process?" she asked as she slid into the driver's seat.

"Yeah. Paperwork and shit," he said.

"Okay." That was good. They could just tear the paperwork up tomorrow. "Get in."

He loped around the front of the car with a huge grin and got in.

"This is going to be fun," he told her.

"Sure." Though she had to admit the idea of millionaire, playboy, computer genius Dax Marshall witnessing a Kelsey-Cassie-Aspen showdown could be entertaining.

They drove the few blocks to her childhood home, her pointing out a few things in town—like the ice cream parlor and the arcade. Those seemed like places Dax might like.

She pulled into the driveway behind Aspen's shiny red sports car. Her dad had given it to her for her birthday four months ago. She'd already had to fix a dented fender and pay a speeding ticket. Kelsey didn't have a car and relied on friends or Jane to get her to and from school because she refused to ask Cassie or Aspen for rides. Or for anything really.

Jane turned off the ignition and took a deep breath as she focused on the front door. Everything seemed really normal looking at that front door. The house was a typical two-story with white siding and dark gray trim and shingles. The lawn was well cared for, thanks to Kelsey and Jane, and the flower beds looked great. Also a Jane thing.

She would admit keeping the house up and doing chores kept Cassie off Kelsey's back and gave her less to complain to Jack about, but Jane did it for more than just that.

This was where she'd grown up. Everything here was dear

and familiar. The new fixtures were Cassie and Aspen. And, of course, the furniture Cassie had insisted on buying. But the house and yard, the structure, the big, solid, unchanging parts were still Jane's home, and she took pride in keeping it looking nice.

Not that she thought Cassie would let it go. She'd never live in a dump, that was for sure. But she would have hired someone to do things like the yard work and tree trimming and landscaping. Probably even housekeeping. That would mean dipping into her joint account with Jack. The account that paid for his nursing home stay and his medications and the things he needed. Jane wasn't about to let Cassie get them to the point where her carpets were being steam cleaned before Jack's prescriptions were being filled.

"This is it," she finally said to Dax. "You ready for this?"

"I have no idea," he said. "I'm not sure what I'm preparing for exactly, so I don't know *how* to prepare."

She smiled. "Fair enough." She opened her door.

"So still no hint?" he asked, also pushing his door open.

"Nope. I walked into the break room one day to find a wall knocked down, a cappuccino machine, and a Ping-Pong table moved in, and an UNO tournament going on. This is payback."

That was *not* fair. What he was about to walk into was nothing like a break room with a Ping-Pong table. Because a break room with a Ping-Pong table could be *fun*.

There was nothing fun about walking into that house with two dramatic teenage girls who had no real adult supervision and were intent on making each other miserable.

"I do love surprises," he said. He rounded the bumper and came to stand by her, studying the front of the house. "I think this is going to be fun."

Jane snorted. "Dax, I think we're about to walk into the one place even Ping-Pong can't make better."

He got a thoughtful look on his face.

"Challenge accepted."

Oh boy. There was something about this guy saying those two words that made a tickle of trepidation go down her spine.

He grinned down at her. "Grant gets that same look on his face when I say that."

———

Dax followed Jane up the front steps to her dad's house. It was quaint. That was a good word for it, he decided. It was the kind of house you saw in movies. It was two stories, had big front windows that probably glowed with a soft yellow light at night, warm and welcoming. It also had a big front yard where he would fully expect to see a dad and son playing catch after dinner, a guy pushing a lawn mower over the grass on a Saturday afternoon, and a big old snowman in the winter. It was a family home. He would be sorely disappointed if there weren't a thousand Christmas lights dangling from the eaves in December, and he almost didn't want to look at the huge oak tree for fear there would *not* be a tire swing hanging from a branch.

Jane knocked on the front door and Dax asked, "Did you ever have a lemonade stand out on the curb?"

She glanced over her shoulder and nodded. "Yeah. A couple of times."

Dax put a hand over his heart and breathed out. "Thank God."

"What are you talking about?" she asked, looking bemused.

"This house was made for having a lemonade stand out in front of it," he told her. "How about a dog. Did you have a dog?"

"We did when I was little."

"Perfect." He grinned and looked around. "Did you pile leaves up in the fall and jump in them?"

She still looked puzzled. "We did."

"And you hung a wreath on this door at Christmastime, right?"

The door was perfect for a wreath.

She nodded slowly. "Yes."

"Awesome."

"What is going on?"

"This is a picture-perfect family home." He pointed to the flower beds. "Those are perfect. And..." He took the chance and glanced at the tree. "There's a damned tire swing." He grinned. "Perfect."

Jane looked around too. "It's pretty... typical."

"It is. And I love that. I've never jumped in a leaf pile or had a lemonade stand," he said.

She looked up at him. "Huh."

"It's kind of tragic, don't you think?"

"I never really thought about the fact that some kids don't do those things. But it makes sense. Kids who grow up in apartments in the city wouldn't, I guess. Those are just things I took for granted."

He nodded. "Those things just always seemed like the epitome of childhood."

"Because of movies and TV," she said.

"A lot of it, yeah."

"Well, a house that has a pile of leaves or a lemonade stand out front isn't automatically perfect," she said. "Remember, that's just the front. The stuff you can see."

Dax sobered immediately. He looked down at her, feeling a tightness in his chest that was unexpected. The intensity of it and the timing. This woman had a way of changing his perspective with the snap of her fingers.

He liked that. He needed new perspective. Everyone did. Getting outside the box you were used to, whether you liked the box or not, was important.

"You're right," he said.

She gave him a little smile. "But thank you for saying the flower bed is perfect. That's my flower bed."

"You planted this?" he asked, looking at it again.

"I did. Every year I do it and take care of it."

"Well, I love it."

"Thanks."

They were smiling at one another when the door whipped open. "Finally!"

A beautiful teenage girl with long, dark hair greeted them. She was wearing cut-off jean shorts and a blue tank top. Her hair was pulled back into a ponytail that hung to the middle of her back. She was slender and about two inches shorter than Jane.

They didn't look much alike until she met his gaze.

Those eyes were Jane's blue eyes.

"Sorry, it took a little longer to get away from work," Jane said, stepping through the doorway.

Dax felt a flicker of what might have been guilt. He was the reason she'd been hung up in the parking lot rather than coming straight over here.

"Kelsey, this is Dax. He's..." Jane glanced at him.

He lifted a brow. What was he? He wasn't her boss anymore. Were they friends? Yeah, that felt right. But she'd definitely not kissed him like a friend last night. He just grinned, waiting for her to finish her thought.

"He's new at Hot Cakes," she finally said.

That sounded weak and he smirked. Kelsey must have thought so too because she gave Jane skeptical look. But before she could say anything more there was a scream from upstairs.

Not a there's-a-guy-with-a-chainsaw-in-my-closet scream but a I'm-going-to-use-a-chainsaw-on-someone scream.

Kelsey blew out a frustrated breath. "Well, it's a shitshow here."

"What's new?" Jane muttered. She looked at Dax. "Remember, you wanted to do this."

"I'm totally in." He had *no* idea what he was in for, but this had to be more interesting than his hotel room. Unless Jane came back to his room with him, of course.

Another teenage girl came pounding down the stairs off to their left just then. She was also beautiful. She had long blond hair and was wearing a sundress. He didn't know what color her eyes were, but even from ten feet away he could see they were shooting sparks.

"You *have* to be kidding me!" she said, holding up what looked like a lipstick tube. "You're such a bitch."

Kelsey crossed her arms, facing the blond. "Well, at least I know you can spell *that* word."

"This was brand new and cost more than *all* your stuff put together!"

"Aspen," Jane said to Dax. "Stepsister."

"Got it."

"What is going on?" Jane asked, raising her voice.

"She—" Aspen said, thrusting a finger at Kelsey, "wrote all over my side of the mirror with *my* lipstick! She totally ruined it!"

Jane sighed and looked at Kelsey. "What's up with that?"

"She wrote LOSER on my side of the mirror with my shaving cream. Used it all up. And she didn't even spell it right. She wrote LOOSER."

Dax did *not* grin at that. That would be inappropriate. But if it was his group of friends, there would definitely be a conversation about if the author had actually meant LOOSER.

"What did you write?" Jane asked, looking concerned.

"It's called a dictionary," Kelsey said.

Jane frowned.

"That's what I wrote on her side of the mirror."

Dax deduced that the girls shared a bathroom with, he was

guessing, two sinks and one big mirror. Clearly that didn't go so well.

"I only wrote *one* word! She wrote a bunch!" Aspen protested. "It's a way bigger mess to clean lipstick off than shaving cream too!"

"That doesn't make it okay that you wrote on *her* mirror," Jane said.

"And it's not like *you're* cleaning it up!" Kelsey shot back. "Why do you care if I make a bigger mess? I'm the one who has to do *all* the work!"

"You know what?" Aspen said. "That is a great point."

She pivoted on her heel and started back up the steps.

"Oh no." Jane stepped forward and caught the back of Aspen's dress. "You're not going back up to make it worse."

"Oh yes I am." Aspen narrowed her eyes at Jane. "You always take her side."

"I don't. You know that," Jane said. "But why did you write on her mirror to start with?"

"Because she poured out my favorite hair gel," Aspen said, glowering at Kelsey. "She knew I wanted to wear my hair curled today, and she knows that hair gel is the best for curls."

"Oh, for God's sake!" Kelsey said. "I don't give a flying frig about how you wear your hair, Aspen! I never touched your hair gel. You used it up and didn't replace it and are blaming me!"

"Your hair looks a lot better than usual," Aspen said, eyeing Kelsey from four steps up. "You're telling me you didn't use *my* products?"

Kelsey gritted her teeth and pulled in a breath. "I didn't use your products. Your products smell like rotting avocados."

Aspen gasped. "They do not!"

"They do. And Wade wasn't talking to me after school because of my hair." Kelsey propped a hand on her hip.

Ah, this was actually about a guy. Dax was catching on.

"Then why was he talking to you?" Aspen said, looking down her nose at Kelsey.

"Because I'm *nice* and because *I* can *spell*," Kelsey told her.

Aspen's eyes narrowed. "You are such a—"

"I think jojoba oil is better than avocado for hair actually."

All three females in the entryway turned to look at him. Dax shrugged. This was dangerous, he knew. He was with the one woman who had broken his I-can-charm-anyone-into-anything streak and now her little sister and stepsister. There was no guarantee he was going to do anything but make this worse.

But he still couldn't shut up. "I do," he said. "But the best is coconut oil. Love the way coconut oil smells on a woman's hair."

Jane raised both eyebrows. Both teenagers just stared at him.

"Who are *you*?" Aspen finally asked.

"I'm a friend of Jane's. We work together."

"Oh." Aspen frowned, but she studied Dax, almost as if she hadn't noticed him at all before. "Coconut oil, huh?"

"Yep. And easy to get at most grocery stores." Of course, he was in Tiny Town, Iowa. "Or you can order it online."

"We have coconut oil," Aspen said, wrinkling her nose. "My mom uses it to cook sometimes."

He nodded. "Well, there you go. Same stuff. Some of the most versatile oil in the world. And you don't have to worry about replacing your hair gel, then."

Aspen flounced down the stairs. "Fine. I'll do that, then." She glared at Kelsey. "You're lucky."

"Yep," Kelsey said, nodding. "I tell myself how lucky I am every single day."

Aspen rolled her eyes and continued to flounce, right past them and down the hallway Dax assumed led to the kitchen.

"Do *you* use coconut oil on your hair?" Kelsey asked, her gaze going over his head.

He grinned. "Nope. I'm just blessed with amazing hair genes."

"So you know about the coconut oil from women you know?" Kelsey asked. Her gaze flitted to Jane and the corner of her mouth curled up. "Just... friends?"

Dax liked Kelsey. "Yes. Some of my friends have used coconut oil on their hair." He'd actually been told about it by one of the cosplayers who was a regular at the cons Dax and Ollie attended. She had great hair. She was also happily married and one of the few women who thought Dax was amazing, loved *Warriors of Easton*, and who *didn't* want to sleep with him.

"Right," Kelsey said. "And you make a habit of smelling women's hair?"

"Whenever possible," he said with a nod. "Assuming we have *that* kind of... relationship."

"Of course," Kelsey said, fighting a smile. "What does Jane's hair smell like?"

"Cake," he answered immediately. Then realized he'd just more or less confirmed they had a hair-smelling-is-appropriate relationship. *Well done, Kelsey.* He grinned at her.

Kelsey laughed. "That's true. Of course, *all* of Jane smells like cake because of the factory."

Dax glanced at Jane. She was watching him and Kelsey interacting as if fascinated and confused.

"Well, I'll have to take your word for that," he told Kelsey, his eyes still on Jane. "For now anyway."

Kelsey snorted, and Jane's eyes widened as she snapped her head to look up at him.

"Okay, enough of that," Jane said. "It sounds like we have a lot of cleaning up to do in the bathroom."

"*She* made as much mess as I did," Kelsey immediately

protested. "And Wade is *not* her boyfriend. She has no right to be mad he was talking to me."

"Kels," Jane said, sounding tired. "If we don't clean it up, Aspen will tell Cassie, and Cassie will tell Dad. Then he'll be upset you're fighting and be concerned about Wade and...." She sighed. "I'll help you clean it up. Let's just... get through it. Just another couple of years."

Kelsey looked like she was going to cry for a minute, but she finally sniffed and lifted her chin. "Fine. Whatever. I'm not sorry though. I'm not apologizing."

"Okay," Jane said. "Except about the smashed plates. You need to apologize for that and buy new ones out of your allowance."

Kelsey shrugged. "I already gave Cassie money. She's out buying new ones now."

Jane shook her head with a sigh. "She's out getting away from the two of you fighting."

"That too," Kelsey agreed.

"Mother of the Year," Jane muttered. Then she looked at Kelsey. "I did *not* say that and you will *not* repeat it."

"I know."

Dax watched the exchange with interest. So Cassie just bailed when the girls started fighting? And Kelsey was a plate thrower? Wow. And it seemed that perhaps Jane said a lot of things about Cassie that Kelsey shouldn't repeat judging by Kelsey's answer.

He was not having a terrible time. This was infinitely more interesting than anything he'd be doing at the hotel.

Unless Jane was with him.

He couldn't resist adding that little afterthought every time he thought about how boring his hotel room was.

"So go grab the supplies," Jane said. "I'll meet you in the bathroom." She looked at him. "You can watch TV or some-thing, if you want. Living room is in there." She pointed. "I'm sure Aspen will shut herself in her bedroom and will be reading up on how to use coconut oil in her hair, and Cassie will stall coming back here for as long as possible. Especially because she knows I'll be here."

"She knew you were coming over?" Dax asked.

"She'll assume Kelsey called me, and I always come over when the girls are fighting. Partly because Cassie always bails," Jane said.

"Got it. But I'll help," he said. He wasn't going to sit in the living room and watch TV when he could be hanging out with Jane. And Kelsey.

"You'll help?" Jane asked. "You'll help clean the bathroom?"

"Why not?"

She looked at up him, hand on her hip. "Have you ever, in your life, cleaned a bathroom?"

"Sure. There was this time in Vegas..." He shrugged. "It just didn't seem fair to make the housekeeping staff clean *that* up."

Jane and Kelsey's eyes were both wide. He looked back and forth between them. "See, one of my friends was—"

"Nope." Jane held up a hand. "Don't want to know."

"I do," Kelsey said.

"No, you don't," Jane told her.

"I do." She looked at Dax. "Is it super gross?"

He studied her. "Well, that depends. Are you the squeamish type?"

"No—"

"Stop it," Jane said. She pointed down the hall. "Get the cleaning supplies," she told her sister. Then she looked up at him. "If you're going to help, you have to be good."

He gave her a slow grin. He couldn't let the moment pass without commenting. "I'm always good."

"Yeah? And why do I think you're *just* the guy to ask about how to get lipstick off of a mirror?"

He laughed. "Rubbing alcohol."

Jane nodded. "Figured. And I don't want to know that story either."

"There's more than one story involving lipstick and mirrors," he said. It was true, but he also loved teasing her. "And windows."

"Nope." She shook her head. "No stories about Vegas, lipstick, bathtubs, showers, or... maybe no stories at all. How about that?"

He chuckled. He wanted to kiss her. Badly. He wasn't sure he'd ever wanted to kiss a woman more.

"I don't know if we have rubbing alcohol," Kelsey said.

"Hair spray will work too," Dax said. "Guessing you all have plenty of that."

"It will?" Kelsey asked.

"Yep, it's the alcohol in it. Just like the rubbing alcohol. And hair spray is easier when you're covering a large area. If it's just like a single lip print or a heart or something, you can just use a cotton ball and the rubbing alcohol, but if it's a big area like with words and stuff, then the spray is easier."

Kelsey grinned. "Yeah, we have hair spray. I'll raid Cassie's bathroom for the *big* bottle."

"You wrote in big letters?" Dax asked, really liking Jane's little sister.

She nodded. "Very big."

She headed down the hallway, presumably to gather supplies. Dax watched her go then turned to Jane.

"Lip prints, huh?" she asked.

He nodded.

"Guessing you're pretty used to having lip prints in *lots* of places."

Okay, he really liked the little flash of jealousy he saw her in her eyes. Was he going to tease her? Oh yes. "I have a little experience," he said nonchalantly, tucking a hand in his front pocket.

"But soap and water will probably get most of them off?" she asked.

Insinuating that most of the lip prints had been on skin.

God he liked her. "Well, you gotta use rubbing alcohol or hair spray to get lipstick out of clothes."

"Maybe you should hang out with people who can wait until the clothes are out of the way to start applying their lips," Jane said.

Yep, she was definitely a little jealous.

"Or maybe I should hang out with people who don't wear lipstick." He lifted a hand and ran his thumb over her bottom lip.

Her eyes heated a little, and her tongue darted out to trace the same path his thumb had taken.

"Yeah, maybe you should," she agreed.

He grinned. "It's definitely a good idea. It took me half an hour and two trips to the store to clean the last lip print up."

She frowned. "What?"

"Lipstick is a bitch to get out of carpet."

Jane closed her eyes and took a breath. "Do *not* want that story."

He laughed.

Kelsey rejoined them just then with a plastic bucket full of cleaning supplies in one hand and a large can of hair spray in the other. "Okay, let's do this." She was actually smiling.

Dax felt a stupid rush of satisfaction at that. He didn't think Kelsey smiled about cleaning the bathroom very often.

He followed the girls up the stairs to the bathroom on the second floor. It was actually pretty good sized. As he'd guessed, there were two sinks in the long vanity with a huge mirror. One side of the mirror had white streaks that looked like dried shaving cream. The other was covered in words written in bright pink lipstick.

Dax had to laugh. Girls were brutal.

"Okay, you've got mirror duty," Jane said to Kelsey. She plucked a bottle and a sponge from the bucket. "I'll do the tub."

"What do I get to do?" Dax asked.

"You can pick between the sinks, toilet, or floor," Jane told him. "And just so you know, this is only room one. We have the kitchen to clean and the living room to dust and vacuum."

"Awesome."

She snorted. "Well, it's definitely not Ping-Pong."

But it could be. Not Ping-Pong exactly, but it could be fun. He chose a bottle from the bucket as well and looked at the label. "Toilet, it is." Then he lifted the bottle and spoke into it like it was a microphone. "And my first selection will be, of course, 'Chicago' by Frank Sinatra."

"We're going to listen to Sinatra while we clean?" Jane asked.

"No, that's my song for the lip-sync battle."

Jane blinked at him. Kelsey asked, "There's a lip-sync battle tonight? That's so cool. Where?"

"Right here," Dax said. "What's your song going to be?"

"Huh?"

"We're going to clean for fifteen minutes. Then one of us is going to do their lip sync. Then we'll clean for fifteen minutes more. Then the other will go. If I were you, I'd grab my earbuds and listen to my song and practice while I'm cleaning. I'm *really* good."

Kelsey grinned at him. "Seriously? We're going to do a song every fifteen minutes?"

"Yep. And I know you're younger than me and the sister of the girl I'm really trying to impress, but I will *not* go easy. Lip-sync battles are serious shit. And did I mention I'm really good?"

Kelsey was laughing. "You did mention that."

"So, yeah, I'd find my headphones or whatever if I were you and pull that first song up."

"Okay." She started for the door. "I'm going to do 'Sweet but Psycho.'"

Dax laughed. "Awesome."

Kelsey ducked out of the room, and Dax turned to find Jane grinning at him. "'Sweet but Psycho.' You sure *you* shouldn't do that one?"

He moved in close, taking the chance to pull her in and put his mouth against her neck. "Aw, you think I'm sweet."

She sighed and tipped her head back, letting him kiss down her neck and along her collarbone. "I do," she admitted.

He kissed back up her neck to her mouth. "And all it took was coconut oil and a toilet brush."

She kissed him, going soft in his arms, letting him tease her lips open and meeting his tongue with hers. She arched into him, sliding her hand into his hair.

But after a few seconds, she pulled back. "That's not all it took," she told him.

"No? Then what was it?"

"The realization that you jumping in with coconut oil and a toilet brush is completely in character for you. You're not even really trying to win me over here." She smiled. "You're trying to make my sister smile. And you'd be doing it even if I weren't here."

Dax had to swallow hard. He should be flippant and charming and flirtatious here, but damn. He couldn't do it. That meant a lot to him. "I would."

"Thank you."

"I—"

"Oh, see, that's not fair," Kelsey protested as she came back into the room. "If Jane's the lip-sync-battle judge, you can't be kissing her and stuff. That will bias her vote."

Dax and Jane both laughed and moved apart. "She can be the judge if you want," Dax said to Kelsey. "But I'm telling you, it's going to be very obvious who's winning this thing."

Kelsey propped a hand on her hip. "Bring it on."

"Gladly." He pulled his earbuds from his pocket and tucked them into his ears. "See you in fifteen."

Kelsey grinned and stuck her earphones in as well, tapping the screen on her phone then tucking the device into her pocket.

"What if I want to lip sync?" Jane asked.

He turned to her. "What song would you choose?"

"That's easy."

"Oh?"

"'I've Got You Under My Skin.'"

Dax's eyebrows shot up. "A Frank classic."

She nodded with a sly little smile. "I might have looked up his greatest hits."

Dax pointed a finger at her nose. "If I hadn't already given up my shares in Hot Cakes, that would have done it."

She laughed and turned away. Dax watched her squirt cleaning solution into the tub and kneel to begin scrubbing. Kelsey had already sprayed the mirror with hair spray and was working on the lipstick.

This was the weirdest date he'd ever been on.

He loved every second of it.

9

Dax hit the play button on his music app, and as Frank filled his ears, he studied the toilet. This couldn't be that hard, could it? He lifted the bottle of toilet cleaner, turning it to read the back label.

The directions for use were pretty straightforward, but he looked around and didn't see a toilet brush. Was he supposed to use a sponge like Jane was using? That sounded disgusting.

He turned, intending to ask her, but found she'd moved in behind him, and he bumped into her, stepping on her foot.

"Ow!"

He pulled the earbud from one ear. "Oh shit, sorry."

"You don't know how to scrub a toilet?" she asked. Clearly she'd seen him checking out the label.

"I do. I just read the instructions," he said. "But I need to know—if I *don't* put my hands in the toilet and scrub with a sponge, does that completely knock out the chance of a kiss tonight, or would you still consider it?"

She shook her head, grinning. "Your chances of getting kissed are *far* better if you *don't* stick your hands in the toilet."

"Awesome."

"So you need to use the scrub brush." She pointed to the cupboard under the sink nearest him.

"Got it."

He opened the cupboard and pulled the brush out and then, well, he scrubbed a toilet. For the first time in his life.

When the timer went off at fifteen minutes, everyone stopped and turned to look at one another.

Dax pointed at Kelsey. "You ready, or do you want me to go first?"

"Oh, you have to go first," Kelsey said. "I need to see how this works."

He nodded. "I'm on it."

And he proceeded to reduce both of the Kemper girls to giggles and twinkling eyes, serenading them with Frank Sinatra, via toilet brush.

He had to admit Kelsey absolutely brought her A game when it was her turn. But in the end, he and Kelsey both agreed Jane was the winner. The way she lip-synced to Frank showed she'd listened to that song a number of times too, and that pleased Dax more than he ever would have imagined.

An hour later, the house was clean. Everyone had performed, and Dax was officially falling in love with Jane.

"Ice cream time," he announced after all the supplies were put away.

"*Yes*," Kelsey said enthusiastically.

"I don't know..." Jane laughed and put her hands up as they both turned to her at once. "What am I saying? Yes, ice cream, of course."

Kelsey ran upstairs to grab her shoes, and Dax took the opportunity to put his hands on Jane's hips, back her up against the front door, and kiss her.

She didn't resist. In fact, she wrapped her arms around his neck and pressed close.

They kissed for long moments, then Dax lifted his head.

"Wow, what was that for?" she asked.

"Frank Sinatra, being an amazing older sister, being sexy as hell, letting me come along."

She smiled. "Oh. Okay, then."

He chuckled. "You're awesome."

Her expression softened. "I don't know about that. I'm kind of wishing I could *not* take my little sister out for ice cream right now. That's not very awesome."

"You don't want to take Kelsey for ice cream?" Dax asked.

"Well, it means it will be longer I have to wait to have you alone."

Oh, he liked that a lot. He leaned in. "You want me alone?"

"I really do," she admitted.

"We can cancel ice cream," he said quickly.

She laughed and pushed him back. "You *really* don't know how teenage girls work."

On cue, Kelsey came bounding down the stairs.

Dax let Jane step around him and took a second before turning, making sure Jane was in front of him. He didn't know if Kelsey would notice how happy Dax had been to be up against her sister, but it was safer to block the view.

"I'm ready!" Kelsey said, her smile bright.

"Where are you guys going?"

They all looked up to find Aspen on the staircase.

"Ice cream," Dax said. He glanced at Kelsey and Jane and then took a risk. "Want to come?"

He wasn't sure who looked more surprised, Aspen or Kelsey.

"Um... really?" Aspen asked. Her gaze also skittered to Kelsey.

"Yeah, really. If you want to," Dax said.

He couldn't see Jane's face, but she didn't say anything. He heard Kelsey sigh, but she didn't protest.

Aspen seemed very torn. She chewed on the inside of her

cheek. He wouldn't have blamed her for saying no. After all, things were tense with Kelsey. Going out and eating ice cream together might be awkward.

But she finally nodded. "Yeah, that would be nice."

"Grab your stuff," he said. "We're on our way out."

"Okay." Aspen turned and ran up the stairs.

Dax braced himself for Kelsey and Jane's reactions.

"Ugh," Kelsey said. She sounded more resigned than angry though.

"Sorry," he said. "Just thought maybe extending an olive branch would be good."

Kelsey rolled her eyes. "I guess."

"You don't actually hate her, do you?" he asked.

Kelsey frowned. "I don't *hate* her. I hate sharing a bathroom with her, and she can be super obnoxious and petty and unreasonable. But..." She shrugged. "Aspen doesn't have a lot of friends, and she hasn't figured out that it's entirely her own fault. But I think she will eventually. I feel sorry for her sometimes. Her mom isn't helping make her a better person *at all,* and she's got a weird, broken-up family just like we do." Kelsey looked at Jane. "And she doesn't have a cool sister to help her through it." Kelsey focused on the floor. "I feel bad that I'm not a better sister to her. She's just so difficult, and I lose my temper and fight with her instead of trying to be her friend."

Jane reached out and pulled Kelsey into a hug. "It's not on you to make Aspen better. But you'll never be wrong being the bigger person."

Kelsey wrapped her arms around Jane's waist. "Is that your way of saying I shouldn't touch her makeup anymore?"

"It is," Jane said. Then she kissed the top of Kelsey's head. "And I think you're a very cool sister too."

Dax felt an ache in his chest. He'd never seen a woman he wanted to do very dirty things to, interact with her family. He'd met one mother of a girl he was dating one time, and he hadn't

ERIN NICHOLAS

really seen them just being together. So maybe he would feel this warm, soft, urge to hug them both very tightly if he'd seen other women with their families. But he doubted it.

"I'm ready." Aspen joined them at the bottom of the steps. She actually looked shy.

"Okay, let's go," Dax said, clapping his hands. "I had no idea cleaning toilets could make me so hungry."

"I guess I wouldn't really know," Aspen said, her smile small and tentative.

Kelsey snorted loudly. "That's for sure." But she actually gave Aspen a grin.

"Your lip sync was really good," Aspen told her.

Kelsey's eyes rounded. "You saw it?"

"I love that song. I looked out to see what you were doing." She shrugged. "But I guess I'm not surprised. You're really good at dance."

Kelsey had added choreography to her lip sync and Dax would agree it had been impressive.

Kelsey looked stunned at Aspen's compliment. "Uh... thanks."

"Maybe next time I can help in the bathroom," Aspen added, "if you'll teach me some of that choreography."

"Holy crap. I will *happily* exchange dance lessons for help with chores," Kelsey said enthusiastically.

"Do you think you could help me get good enough to get on the dance team?" Aspen asked.

"Yes," Kelsey said without hesitation. "But you have to quit being a bitch to me."

"Kels!" Jane protested.

But, her cheeks pink, Aspen nodded. "Okay."

"Okay," Kelsey said as if that decided it. She turned to Dax. "We're ready."

They all headed for Jane's car, but Jane grabbed Dax's hand, pulling him up short and letting the girls get to the car while they were still on the front steps.

"You know that 'you're awesome' thing you said to me a little bit ago?"

He nodded.

"Well... ditto." Then she lifted up on tiptoe and kissed him. "And eat your ice cream fast," she said against his lips.

He reached down and squeezed her ass. "I have a feeling I'm in for some major brain freeze."

She settled back on her feet and gave him a naughty little smile he was instantly crazy about.

"I'll warm you back up," she said. Then she headed for the car.

Dax took a breath. It was no surprise Sinatra and ice cream were solid ingredients for a seduction. But a toilet brush? He never would have guessed. But he knew without that particular tool, he would not be anywhere near as close to getting Jane Kemper naked.

He would happily scrub toilets every day.

———

J ane loved her little sister.

She really did.

She also loved ice cream. A lot. Not as much as pie. Or cake. Or cookies. But it was very, very good.

Yet here she was, eating fast, impatient with her sister's chatter—even though happy chatter from Kelsey was lovely and not common after a run-in with Aspen. Then again, Kelsey and Aspen eating ice cream together after one of their blowups had *never* happened, so this was an unusual night all around.

About as unusual as the idea of a playboy millionaire turning her on with a toilet brush.

Of course, that wasn't really what turned her on about Dax Marshall.

It was... pretty much everything.

Jane scooped up another spoonful of strawberry ice cream, listening to Kelsey telling Dax about the upcoming dance competition in Des Moines as her chocolate ice cream with marshmallow and graham-cracker-crumb topping melted in her bowl. Jane cast a glance at Aspen. Her stepsister was just sitting there quietly eating her vanilla with caramel sauce. Jane tried to remember the last time she'd been around Aspen that hadn't included Cassie. She couldn't come up with anything.

Was it possible Aspen fed off her mother more than her actually disliking Kelsey and Jane? The girls did butt heads, and Aspen did seem jealous, but they were two teenagers living in the same space, wanting the same things. And Cassie did pit them against one another, now that Jane thought about it.

Huh. Maybe she needed to give Aspen more of a chance. Maybe the girl needed some positive female role models and just some freaking attention that wasn't about the things Kelsey had that Aspen didn't.

Jane felt herself frowning. *Dammit, Cassie.*

"Hi, Kelsey."

Jane was pulled out of her thoughts by the young, male voice. There were four guys about Kelsey's age standing around the table now. They looked like they could be athletes, based on their builds, and they were pretty cute. For guys *way* too young for her to really notice.

Kelsey was trying to look cool, but Jane could tell she was surprised by the guys' presence. "Hi, Matt."

"We were wondering if you wanted to come sit with us," Matt said. He glanced at Aspen, who was studying her ice cream intently. "Both of you."

Aspen looked up quickly, clearly shocked.

"Uh." Kelsey looked at Jane. "I think we're almost done, actually."

"Oh okay." Matt shrugged. "Just thought we'd say hi."

"Okay." Kelsey nodded, clearly puzzled.

"Um, you're Dax Marshall, right?" Matt asked, lingering behind Kelsey's chair.

Dax nodded. "I am."

"We are *huge* fans, man," Matt told him. "*Warriors of Easton* has been our favorite forever, but this newest edition is *kick ass*."

Dax smiled. "Thanks. I really appreciate hearing that."

"Yeah, I heard you were one of the new owners at Hot Cakes," another of the boys said. "That's really cool too. We had no idea you might come to town though."

Dax gave Jane a look. She knew she was staring, but this was... weird. She'd known about the video game, of course. She knew Dax made appearances at Comic-Con and other gaming cons. She knew he had a huge social media following. But even after looking everything up and seeing some video footage, it hadn't really sunk in that he was famous. At least in his corner of the world.

"I'm going to be spending a lot of time here," Dax told the boys. But he was looking at Jane.

"That is *amazing*," another of the guys said. "This town is so small and boring, but we've got the *Warriors of Easton* inventors here. That's just wild."

"Is there any chance you guys would do like a gaming event here or anything?" Matt asked. "It would be super cool if you did."

Dax shook his head. "I don't know. Something to think about though. We're really focused on Hot Cakes right now, but I'll keep that in mind. You guys would be up for helping out?"

"For *sure*," Matt said, and the other three nodded adamantly.

"Great. Why don't you give Kelsey and Aspen your

numbers, and I'll get ahold of you if we put anything together. They'll be our go-between. I assume you talk to them a lot at school and stuff?" Dax asked.

"Uh... yeah," Matt said.

Dax looked at Kelsey. She rolled her eyes.

"I mean... we can. We want to," Matt said. "Very happy to be in touch with Kelsey and Aspen."

"Great. Girls, why don't you give the guys your phones, so they can put their contact info in?" Dax said.

Both girls reached for their phones, handing them over as if waiting for someone to yell "Psych!"

In the end, all four guys put their numbers into both phones and headed toward a back booth after gushing again over Dax and how much they'd love to have a tournament or a con in Appleby.

When they were out of earshot, Kelsey leaned in, her eyes on Aspen. "Oh my *God*."

Aspen leaned in too. "I know!"

"I have Matt Porter *and* Landon Summers's phone numbers in my phone!" Kelsey said in an excited whisper.

"And Tanner asked if we were going to be back in here next Saturday. A bunch of people are getting together after the baseball game!" Aspen said.

"They looked like athletes," Jane said, scraping the bottom of her bowl with her spoon and taking the last bite of her Strawberry Supreme.

"They are *the* athletes," Kelsey said. "Those four are good at everything and captains of like every team. They are the *hottest* guys in school." She turned round eyes on Dax. "I had no idea they were gamers though. Oh my God." She grabbed Dax's arm. "They think we are so cool just because we know you!"

Dax smiled, clearly used to this kind of reaction. "Well, you'll have to let me know if they say anything interesting about *Warriors*."

"I can't believe you set up a way for them to talk to us," Aspen said. "I didn't even know Matt knew my name."

"Well, I don't want them calling me directly all the time," Dax said with a laugh. "Plus I did *them* a huge favor."

"Yeah, you're going to set up a huge gaming con in Appleby for them," Kelsey said with a laugh.

"I don't know about that," Dax said, chuckling. "But I do know I gave them all very good excuses to talk to two beautiful, fun, smart girls. They don't have to come up with their own lame lines now."

Aspen blushed and Kelsey laughed. "Yeah, they were just *dying* to talk to us."

"Well, if they weren't, they will be after a few conversations," Dax said.

"I know nothing about *Warriors of Easton*," Kelsey said. "Sorry," she added.

"Me neither," Aspen said.

"I can teach you anything you need to know," Dax told them. "But I'm thinking they'll find new topics to talk to you about after a bit."

Kelsey smiled as if pleased and Aspen sighed. "That would be nice."

"Is everyone done?" Jane asked. She was ready to get out of here. Really ready. Dax was...too clothed. And not close enough to kiss.

"Yeah, I guess," Aspen said.

"Not quite," Kelsey replied.

"Hurry up," Jane told her.

"Hey. What's your problem?"

"I've got..." She looked at Dax. "Stuff to do."

He smirked at her and her inner muscles clenched. Wow. That was new. And not unpleasant.

She reached for her sister's ice cream dish and headed for the garbage.

"Hey! There's some left."

"Then you can eat it in the car." Jane turned toward the door, still carrying Kelsey's ice cream.

"Oh my God!" But Kelsey scrambled after her.

By the time she was behind the steering wheel, Kelsey was in the back seat with her dish, and Aspen and Dax were climbing in as well.

She glanced at Dax. He looked smug.

Well, that was fine. He could be as smug as he wanted to be. As long as he kissed the hell out of her the second they were alone.

No, the second they were back at the Hot Cakes parking lot where no one would interrupt them.

She tried to focus on the girls in the back seat, talking happily about the guys that had called goodbye to them as they left the ice cream parlor. That did make her happy. Of course.

But maybe not as happy as kissing Dax would.

She pulled into the driveway. "Okay, ladies, good night. Love you."

Aspen hesitated getting out. "Hey, Jane?"

"Yeah?"

"Thank you for letting me come along."

That caught Jane off guard. She smiled. "You're welcome."

Aspen nodded then looked at Dax. "And thanks. This was all really fun."

"You bet," he told her.

"Hey, Aspen," Jane said as the girl got out of the car.

"Yeah?"

"Let's make things better tomorrow too. You can help with that, right?"

It was clear Aspen knew exactly what Jane was talking about. "Yeah, I can."

"Great."

"'Night." Kelsey leaned over the seat and kissed Jane's

cheek. Then she leaned over and kissed Dax's cheek. "Nice to meet you."

He chuckled. "Ditto. Work on your lip sync. We'll enter the lip-sync competition in Chicago as a duo."

Kelsey gasped. "Really?"

"Sure."

"Okay!"

A minute later, both girls were finally out of the car and heading up the path to the front door. Once they were safely inside, Jane shifted into reverse. But before she moved the car, she looked over at Dax. "Have you ever had sex in a car that cost less than eight thousand dollars?"

His eyes were hot when he met her gaze, but he smiled. "I don't think I've ever even *been* in a car that cost less than eight thousand dollars."

She grinned. "You don't think?"

"I'm pretty sure. *Maybe* a guy in college or something."

"Right."

"In case you're wondering," he added, "I'm *very* okay with doing anything you want in this car. Or any other car. Or any other place for that matter."

"That's good," she told him. "That's very good."

Then she backed out of the driveway and pointed the car toward Hot Cakes.

They didn't talk on the short drive back to where Dax's car was parked. The lot was much less full, but there was a third shift, so there were still cars in the lot.

She pulled in next to his roadster and shut off the ignition.

"Jane, I—"

She unhooked her seat belt and turned to face him. "Yes?"

He shook his head. There were tall lights around the lot that kept the interior of the car from being completely dark, but they weren't directly under or next to one. In the dim light she saw him smile. "I don't know."

"You don't remember what you were about to say?" she asked.

"I don't know what I thought I was going to say," he admitted. "I'm usually pretty good in these situations, but with you it's different."

He amused her. He was so confident, so used to charming everyone, that she knew he didn't even have to try. It was natural that he'd never be at a loss for words and never actually nervous about anything. But his honesty and moments of self-deprecation always made her smile. He always seemed surprised to find himself less than completely in control.

"These situations?" she repeated. "What situations would those be?"

"Alone with a gorgeous woman."

"Ah. I'm guessing you're pretty good even when you and the gorgeous women aren't alone. And with less-than-gorgeous women." She knew that was true. Dax was used to fame and incredible privilege, but he honestly treated every person the same, no matter who he or she was, how they dressed, or what their job was.

"I'm very rarely off my game," he admitted.

"But you are right now?"

"I don't know that I've really been *on* my game with you for even one minute," he said.

She liked that. "I don't want this to be a game. I don't want you to be playing around," she said. Lip-syncing while cleaning the house, Ping-Pong in the break room, coloring books all seemed like playing around, but she could honestly say that as she got to know him, she realized more and more that those weren't games either.

"Maybe that's it," he said after a moment, holding her gaze. "This isn't a game. And I'm not used to that."

She wet her lips. "Well, if it's any consolation, I'm not used to any of this either."

"Good." He didn't even hesitate with that answer. He unhooked his seat belt and leaned over the center console. He cupped the back of her head, sliding his fingers into her hair. "Thank you for tonight."

"Thank *me*?" she asked. "You're the one who saved the day."

"You let me. I'm guessing you don't let people swoop in and take the reins very often."

They were leaning in, almost nose to nose. His hand was hot against her head, and all she could think about were all the other places she would love to feel that heat. "Most people aren't even half as good as you are with those reins," she said.

"A lot of people think all I do is fuck around."

"A lot of people aren't paying very close attention, then."

Even in the near darkness she could see his slow smile. "Are you paying attention to me, Jane?"

"I can't stop thinking about you," she confessed softly.

"Thank God." He met her lips with his, kissing her sweetly.

But she didn't want sweet. She opened her mouth, sliding her tongue along his lower lip, then in along his tongue when he groaned and opened. Her hands went to his hair, holding him still so she could pour everything she was feeling into the kiss.

She admired him. She was grateful to him. She wanted him. But more than anything, she *liked* him. A lot. She would have never believed it a few weeks ago, but Dax Marshall was someone she could seriously fall for.

And that was all kinds of complicated. They were very different. He lived in Chicago. He might find her lifestyle interesting because it was new for now, but nothing about her regular life resembled his at all. And he had been her boss twelve hours ago.

But apparently that was one thing she didn't have to worry about anymore.

She was breathing fast when she pulled back and looked at

him. He was amazing, and he was making her look at everything differently.

"Temporary reprieves can be very, very nice," she said softly.

"I will reprieve you any time," he said with a wicked smile.

"I mean it," she said, running her hand along his jaw. "I see how it can be important and can lead to more, even lasting, things."

His smile died and he swallowed hard. "I'm glad."

"There's a lever on the side of your seat," she said. "I would really like it if you would move your seat back as far as it will go."

He did without question or pause.

Jane climbed over and into his lap, straddling his thighs.

His hands settled on her hips and she cupped his face. "I'm not going to ask again, but know this," she said. "If you did *not* give up your shares in the company and you *are* still my boss after this, I *will* do terrible things to your gummy bears."

10

D ax huffed out a laugh. "Noted. Headless gummy bears if
you end up having sex with the boss."

"I was thinking more like poisoned gummy bears," she said.
"But let's say headless, poisoned gummy bears to cover it."

"Got it."

Then she kissed him. Deep and wet and hot. He tasted like
hot fudge with a hint of salt from the peanuts in his sundae. A
man shouldn't taste that good.

She wiggled on his lap, loving the way his fingers curled
into her hips as if wanting to hold her closer. He was hot and
hard behind his zipper and she pressed close, grinding, not
caring that she hadn't made out in a car since high school. A
guy also shouldn't feel this good.

Dax's answering groan, and the way his hands spread out
on her ass pulling her down against him even more firmly fired
her blood. She wanted him. She'd never wanted a guy like this.
She'd been holding back for a number of reasons, but none of
them mattered when he reached down to the side of the seat
and hit the lever that tipped the seat back nearly flat.

She went with him, not wanting to stop kissing him. Ever.

His hands slid up and down her back, rubbing, teasing her skin through the cotton.

It was nice. He wasn't in a huge hurry to strip her. He seemed content just to kiss and touch.

But she wasn't. Jane sat up suddenly, whipping her shirt up and over her head, tossing it into the driver's seat.

She was wearing a basic bra. It was a nude color. There was nothing special or skimpy about it. It didn't even have lace. But the way Dax looked at her in the faint light coming in through the window made her feel like she was the hottest thing he'd ever seen.

He ran a hand up and down her side, gliding over bare skin, but not touching her breasts. He just looked at her.

"Now you," she said, her voice husky. She started to push up the bottom of his shirt and he quickly obliged her, grabbing the shirt and stripping it off.

She'd been thinking about his chest and abs since that first day when he'd exchanged his button-down shirt for a Hot Cakes tee.

Jane ran a hand over his chest, the soft hair tickling her palms, making her nipples tingle with the thought of rubbing back and forth over that hot skin. She slid her palm over his abs, loving the way they jumped under her touch.

She really wanted him to do the same. To touch and stroke and tease. She reached back to undo her bra and Dax reached to help, hooking a finger in the front of the bra and drawing it down her arms. She tossed it... somewhere. She wasn't even sure where it landed because Dax did touch her then, cupping a breast and rubbing his thumb over her nipple.

She felt her pelvic muscles clench tight and heat wash through her. Just that simple touch and she was ready, a few perfectly placed strokes away from an orgasm already. She shifted restlessly on his lap, rubbing against his very obvious erection. The pressure good but definitely not perfect.

"God you're gorgeous," he said gruffly. "You look like a goddess sitting up there. You know exactly what you want, don't you?"

She nodded, reaching to pull her hair from the ponytail. She felt like a goddess suddenly, and it seemed that goddesses would wear their hair down. She shook her head, her hair falling around her shoulders. "I know exactly what I want."

"You want it here? Like this? Because I will gladly take you back to my hotel and pamper the hell out of you."

He plucked at her nipple and she gasped.

"I don't need pampering," she said breathlessly.

"What do you need, Jane?"

"You. With your pants down."

He grinned, an almost wicked grin. "Same."

She laughed and reached for the button and zipper on her jeans. She shifted and wiggled to get one shoe off and one leg out of the jeans.

He just watched her.

"Sorry. Cramped quarters," she said. "But I don't want to get off of you."

"I have no problem with that. Grinding against me like that is almost killing me, but I like what the wiggling does to your tits."

She huffed out a surprised breath. For some reason, laid-back, good-time-guy Dax didn't seem like a dirty talker. And maybe "tits" was not exactly dirty talk. But it worked for her. She was hot and ready to go. She settled back on his thighs, one leg in her jeans and one leg out. But that was all they needed.

His gaze dropped to the front of her panties. Also nude in color and very basic. In fact, she had to think hard to even come up with a pair of underwear she owned that wasn't black, white, or nude. She thought she might still have a pair of red ones somewhere. And there was a pair that was white but had lipstick prints all over them. A lot like that tie Dax had worn to their first meeting, come to think of it. She had no idea where, or why, she'd gotten either pair. The guys she slept with were a lot more interested in getting the panties off than they were in how those panties looked, and she was hardly the striptease kind of girl.

She figured Dax had experienced plenty of fancy, colored, skimpy panties in his time though. This was real-life, regular-girl, small-town, front-seat-of-a-car sex. It was good to expand his horizons.

She reached for his zipper at the same time he reached for her panties. He got there first. And she forgot what she'd been about to do. He ran his finger up and down her center, brushing over her clit and, no doubt, feeling just how hot and wet she was.

Jane closed her eyes and took a deep breath. It had been a while since someone other than her had touched that particular area. That area was very grateful for the attention.

"Really need your pants out of the way," she said, her voice tight.

"I'm busy," he told her, rubbing up and down again.

"Dax," she ground out. She was trying very hard not to just start begging him to slide his finger in...

His finger slipped under the edge of her panties and he stroked over her with no barrier. Jane couldn't breathe, and her thighs tightened on either side of him, squeezing.

"I..."

"Yes, Jane?" he asked, circling her clit leisurely. "Were you going to say something?"

"I... don't know." It was just his finger. Something better and bigger was just a few inches away, but his finger was *right there* doing very nice things, and she couldn't think about anything else suddenly except that digit teasing and filling her. She tipped her head back and gripped his wrist. She lifted slightly, guiding his hand down to right where she needed him, and then sank down, his thick middle finger sliding into her.

"Oh yes," she said, almost panting.

"Fuck," Dax answered. "That's so hot, Jane. Show me exactly what you need."

Her eyes flew open and she met his gaze. His finger was pumping in and out of her and his thumb was circling her clit. It was awesome. But he'd said she could show him *exactly* what she wanted, right? She leaned in, bracing her hand on the seat above his shoulder. It put her breast right at mouth level for him.

"Make me come, Dax," she said huskily.

"My fucking pleasure." He added a second finger as he took her nipple in his mouth, sucking hard.

She cried out at the sensations ripping through her. God, she needed this. This was the culmination of all the feelings and fantasies about this guy she'd been trying to fight.

She wasn't fighting anymore.

He licked and sucked, thrust and circled. He told her how much he wanted her and how she really did smell, and taste, like cake everywhere, and how perfect her curves were, and how hot her bossiness was. She shifted, putting her mouth against his and moving her hips wantonly against his hand.

And then lightning struck and a swift, hard orgasm shot through her.

"Dax!" she cried out, letting it all go. "Oh yes!"

"God, Jane," he rasped. "Yes. Hell yes."

She took his face in her hands and kissed him again. Pleasure was still coasting over her, and the orgasm had been intense and so very needed, but she still wanted more.

"Pants," she said against his mouth. "Please get your pants out of the way."

He chuckled, the sound rumbling through her too. She sat back and was shocked, and turned on, when he slid his hand from her panties and lifted it to his mouth. He sucked his fingers clean, his eyes on hers. "Better than cake."

That was so hot. She shook her head. She'd expected him to be playful with sex but not necessarily dirty. She didn't know why. "I'll take your word for it."

"Seriously." He lifted one of those magical fingers to her mouth. "Want to see?"

"Uh, no."

"Forget chocolate," he said, sliding his finger over her bottom lip. "This is what I want to dip strawberries in."

Instinctively her tongue darted out to follow the path. She didn't taste anything unusual—he'd sucked that finger pretty clean—but it felt dirty anyway.

And she really wanted to take a big old bowl of strawberries to bed with Dax.

"Strawberries in bed would get very messy," she told him.

"Yes," he agreed. "It would take a lot of licking and sucking to clean up."

Her muscles, which had just been treated to a very nice orgasm, clenched at that.

"Not to mention a nice long shower after," she said. A fully naked Dax, wet and slippery, backing her up against the shower wall? Yes. Yes, yes, yes.

"Exactly." He reached between them and unbuttoned his fly. "Now, what were you saying about my pants?"

"They are very much in the way."

"I agree." He reached into his back pocket and pulled out his wallet. "You want to do zipper duty or condom duty?"

"Both." She quickly reached for his zipper, pulling it down and then wiggling the denim and boxers over his hips, freeing his erection.

His cock was amazing. Long and thick and hard, and a shiver of pleasure went through her as she wrapped a hand around it and stroked.

"Jane," Dax said.

It sounded like he was talking through gritted teeth and she looked up. Still stroking. "You okay?"

"About thirty seconds away from embarrassing myself and ruining the chance to thrust up into that sweeter-than-cake pussy," he told her bluntly. "Move your hand."

She didn't want to. She hesitated.

Dax wrapped his fingers around her wrist and pulled her way. "Girl, you're going to kill me."

He put the condom packet to his mouth, ripping it open with his teeth, apparently not trusting that he could let go of her wrist.

He was right. She wanted to touch him. She wanted to take him into her mouth. She wanted to explore every inch of him and make him crazy.

Dax reached between them, rolling the condom on one-handed. Then he let her go. She stroked her hand up and down his cock, smoothing over the condom. He just let her, but his abs were tight, and he was barely breathing.

Emotions washed over her just then. It was so dumb, the timing so strange, but suddenly she was overcome with affection and happiness. This man was something else. They were going to have sex in the front seat of her car and he wasn't batting an eye. Sure, he would have whisked her off to his hotel suite and put her down on eighteen-hundred-thread-count Egyptian cotton sheets, ordered strawberries from room service, and made a mess that someone else would have to clean up. Though he was probably a really great tipper. He absolutely seemed like a great tipper. Also a huge point in his favor.

He also would have gone back to her place with her and wouldn't have cared that she hadn't made her bed in a week or that she had laundry sitting in a basket on her kitchen table. Or that she would have wanted to *not* make a big mess with strawberries because *she* was the one who would be cleaning that up.

Turned out, Dax Marshall wasn't as high maintenance as she'd initially thought. In fact, he was helpful and supportive and... really, really wonderful.

"You're..." She started. But her throat got tight, and she didn't know what she'd been about to say for sure anyway.

He paused, studying her, waiting for her to go on. But after a moment, he seemed to sense she couldn't.

"Fucking crazy about you," he told her, reaching out and clasping her waist. "And in desperate need of feeling you wrapped tight around my cock and moving that gorgeous body on me." He moved her forward.

She gratefully let sex take over for the words. Or the lack of words. She lifted up and then sank down on his length.

They moaned together as he filled her, sliding deep.

Jane stayed still for a second, just absorbing the feel of him. Then he squeezed her waist and started moving her. She quickly joined in, lifting and lowering, taking him deep, feeling the stretch and friction send sparks of heat and desire through her body.

They moved with an easy pace for a few minutes, their ragged breathing the only sound in the car. But quickly the heat and need grew, and Jane picked up the pace as she felt another orgasm hovering there, wanting to wash over her. She wanted that orgasm.

"Yes, Jane, fuck, yes," Dax panted.

"You feel so good," she told him, her voice breathy. "This is so good."

He thrust up into her as their tempo built, and Jane felt her climax winding tight, ready to let go.

"Yes, fucking grip me like that," Dax ground out.

She tightened her muscles around him and he groaned. Then he reached between them and found her clit.

It only took a few strokes to send her flying.

"Dax! Oh yes!" She came apart, clamping down on him.

He groaned, and then he was coming too, surging into her, holding her tightly against him.

For several long moments, they just panted and gasped. Jane slumped forward on top of him. His arms went around her. Their chests moving up and down together.

Slowly, her skin started to cool, and her breathing returned to near normal.

Though she wasn't sure the rest of her would ever return to a pre-Dax state. She'd never had sex like that. It wasn't the front seat or the darkness or the fumbling with the clothes. That had all happened before. It just had never felt so... right.

Everything about this night had felt like it clicked. Like it was exactly the way it should be.

Like *they* were exactly the way they should be.

Laughing, teasing, dancing, and singing, dealing with teenage-girl drama together, and then fucking in the front seat of her car because they couldn't wait to get anywhere else.

There was something that told her that even if they were really *together*, had a relationship, had been doing this for months, or even years, even if they owned a bed together only a few minutes away, they would still get frisky in the car from time to time.

She liked that thought.

Too much.

Jane pushed herself up and looked down at him, taking a deep breath. "So that was definitely better than cake."

He chuckled and reached to brush her hair back from her face. "How about strawberry pie?"

Yeah, he knew that was her weakness. "Well... we might have to do it again sometime, just to be sure, but it was *really* close."

"I'm happy to keep working until I'm right on top of your list of favorite things," he said with a grin.

Jane's heart tripped in her chest.

She was pretty sure he was headed straight to the top of that list. If he wasn't already there.

Uh-oh.

Jane shifted off of him, rolling into her seat and reaching into the compartment on the side of her door where she stuffed all the napkins she got when she went to the gas station for sandwiches or carried food out from the diner. She handed them over, assuming Dax could deal with the condom somehow. He was the more experienced one after all. She worked on getting her jeans back on, then lifted her hips, pulling her bra and shirt from under her butt and slipping into them as well.

By the time she was sort of put back together, Dax was too, and his seat was upright again.

Jane took a deep breath, tucked her hair behind her ear, and finally looked over at him again.

He was watching her as if waiting to see where she'd lead the conversation next.

"Are we still on for tomorrow?" she asked. She wanted to see him. She wanted to spend time with him. She wanted to kiss him. A lot. And she kind of wanted to take him to her house, and she was pretty sure she'd be okay with a strawberries-in-bed mess.

"We are absolutely on for tomorrow," he said. "And any other time you'll give me."

She wanted to take him home with her right now.

But she also wanted to have a little time and space. Just to think about it all. Just to be sure she wasn't on some ice cream high or that the cleaning solutions hadn't gotten to her or something.

Could she actually be falling for Dax?

She needed to figure that out before she saw him again.

And then she needed to decide how she felt about that if it turned out she didn't want to lick him from head to toe just because he'd been nice to her sister.

And stepsister.

Yeah, yeah. He'd been nice to Aspen too. Something Jane was ashamed to admit she hadn't been able to pull off in the past few months very well.

Her feelings for Dax really might just be because he was a nice guy with a great body. That she absolutely wanted to lick from head to toe. That would make things easier if that was true. For sure.

"Meet me at the bakery at eight," she reminded him.

"Right. And I'm promised amazing *muffins* if I'm no later than eight oh five," he said.

She grinned. "Honestly? I'll save you the good muffins even if you're not there 'til eight thirty."

He lifted a brow. "Eight thirty. Wow, I must have done well tonight."

She laughed. "You did very well."

He leaned over and kissed her. She was surprised for just a second, then she started to melt into him.

He pulled back. "I'll be there well before eight thirty."

"Yeah? Well, *I* must have done very well tonight too. To be worth getting up early for."

He nodded, but instead of teasing, he brushed his thumb over her cheek. "Very worth it."

Something in his tone made her throat tighten and her heart flip again.

Thankfully, before she could cry or beg him to come home with her, he opened his door and got out. She watched him slide into his roadster, aware that even their cars showed how very different they were.

But he waited for her to pull out of the parking lot in front of him and gave her a little wave when they went in opposite directions at the stop sign at the entrance.

They were different. But, man, she *really* liked him.

Maybe even enough to be convinced to stay in bed with him on a Saturday morning and miss the strawberry-cream-cheese muffins Zoe only made on the weekends.

Maybe.

———

"Good morning!" Jane entered the bakery through the back door the next morning, a definite friends-with-the-owner privilege.

Both of her best friends were in the kitchen, busily preparing for the big dessert tasting in Dubuque later that morning. The dessert tasting was a part of a huge bridal fair, and the focus was on unique and fun options for wedding receptions outside of the typical wedding cakes.

Josie and Zoe did amazing wedding cakes, of course, but they'd embraced the idea of bringing new ideas to the tasting as well, including cake pops, brownie bites, and pies in a jar, the newer specialties in the bakery. Those items now outsold the usual bars and cupcakes, and Zoe, a longtime stickler for tradition and the tried and true, had finally admitted trying new things could be good.

Jane gave them both huge grins as she grabbed plastic gloves and prepared to help out however they needed her.

Jane hadn't lied to Dax. The bakery was open and was doing its usual Saturday morning business, but this morning she was here to help Zoe and Josie get their sweets ready for the event while Zoe's mom and dad handled the front of the bakery.

He'd still be able to get muffins, and she was happy to get a table with him once he arrived, but she had been called in as more than a patron today. She was happy to help. Not just because she loved the idea of Zoe and Josie showing off their talents to a wider audience and offering some limited shipping options for those outside of Appleby for the first time, but because now Jane had them both to herself for a little bit, and she could tell them about Dax.

And ask for their advice.

"Good morning." Josie gave her a grin from where she was boxing up cake pops. "Hey, you're wearing a dress."

Jane looked down at the navy-blue sundress with the white flowers. "I am."

"You almost never wear dresses," Josie said.

"I know."

"So you're in a dress kind of mood," Josie mused.

"Yes, I am."

"Okay, what is going on around here with you two today?" Zoe asked, looking from Josie to Jane.

"I have a date later on," Jane said. "With Dax."

"Ah." Zoe nodded. "So that's why you're so chipper. Do you have a date too?" she asked Josie.

"Too?" Jane asked.

Zoe tipped her head toward Josie. "She's been humming all morning."

Jane looked at Josie. "Oh really?"

Josie laughed and waved her hand. "I'm just in a good mood. Maybe I'm excited about this event. We've never done something like this before."

Zoe and Jane shared a look.

"Sure," Zoe said.

"Right," Jane agreed.

Josie giggled, and Jane was certain she saw a little blush on her friend's cheeks.

"Well, I am excited about my date," Jane said, going to the table set up with the apple, cherry, blueberry, and strawberry—

her favorite—jar pies. "But I'm also in a really good mood because of the sex."

Jane started putting the little mason jars into the box that was padded with Styrofoam peanuts and tissue.

Both of her friends immediately stopped what they were doing and turned toward her.

"The sex?" Zoe asked.

"Yeah," Jane said, her grin huge and, she was sure, goofy. "The sex last night."

"Who did you have sex with?" Zoe asked.

Jane laughed. "I'm going on a date later with Dax."

"So you said."

"And I had sex last night."

"You also said that," Zoe agreed.

"You think I had sex with someone last night and am going out with someone else today?" Jane asked.

"So you *did* have sex last night with Dax?" Josie asked.

"Yes." Jane grinned and kept packing jars.

"Oh my God, Jane!" Josie said. "That's awesome!"

She laughed. "It is?"

"He's so good looking and funny and charming." Josie sighed.

Zoe shook her head. "I thought you were adamantly against that," she said to Jane. "Since he's your boss and everything." She held up a hand. "Not that I don't love Dax. He really is awesome and I know you've been flirting. But why did you change your mind?"

Jane paused with a jar in each hand. "Well, for one, he went over to the house with me and helped me and Kelsey clean last night."

Josie gasped. "He did? Wow. That's pretty sweet."

"And he totally mediated this whole situation with the girls, and then he took us all out for ice cream and made the girls hugely popular with the hottest guys in their class." She told them the whole story.

Through it all, Zoe's smile continued to grow, and Jane thought Josie might actually swoon at some point.

"Wow." Josie had her hands on her chest, her eyes wide, as Jane finished. "Just wow. That's so sweet. He's just so... heroic," she decided. "He must really *like* you to go in there and fix things like that."

"That's the thing," Jane said. "I don't think he was even trying to fix anything." She sighed. "That's just who he is."

Josie sighed too with a dreamy smile.

"So he was awesome yesterday," Zoe agreed. "And you decided that was more important than him being your boss?"

Zoe didn't actually think Dax being Jane's boss was a problem. She knew Dax and Jane. She knew Dax wouldn't reward Jane at work for sexual favors, and she knew Jane would never expect or want that. But she agreed it didn't *look* good to other employees, potentially.

"Actually," Jane said, shooting a glance at Josie, sure *this* would make her friend swoon. "He gave up his shares in the company."

Zoe's eyes got round, and Josie made a little squeak-gasp-choking sound.

"What?" Zoe asked.

Jane nodded. "Yep."

"To date you," Josie clarified. "He gave up his part of the business... that could have made him millions... so he could date you?"

Jane lifted a shoulder. "Evidently."

"Oh my God. I need to sit down." Josie reached for a tall stool nearby and slid onto it.

Jane laughed. "He can get it back. Of course. The guys would sell it back to him. In fact, the paperwork isn't even finished yet." She looked at Zoe. "Aiden didn't say anything?"

"No, but Grant's in town, which is unusual, so they took advantage of all being in the same place, in person, at the same time and had a big meeting." She grinned as she put air quotes around *meeting*. "Which I think means they went out and ate and bullshitted and drank a lot. He came in really late and crashed in the other bedroom so he wouldn't wake me up. There was a sticky note on the bathroom mirror, but I haven't seen him yet this morning." She shook her head. "It's a little hard on them all being apart, not being in the same office together every day. It's pretty cute that they miss each other."

Jane agreed. She knew the guys had all been friends for a very long time, and the things they'd accomplished together were definitely impressive. Which made it even nicer Dax had chosen to spend the evening with her. Sure, he might not be a Hot Cakes partner right now, but the guys getting together had been about more than business. It was longtime friends hanging out. But he'd chosen Jane. She felt a little warm at that realization.

"So," she said, starting to pack jar pies again. "I was thinking that, before it's all official and he's *really* given everything up, I need to let him truly see my life. Really see what being with me would be like."

"You mean with your family?" Zoe asked.

Jane nodded. "With everything. But he's already seen the factory and knows what my job is like and how I feel about it. He's met Kelsey and Aspen, and he's heard about and gotten a look at what Cassie is like. So now he needs to meet my dad." She looked up. "Right?"

"That's big for you," Zoe said, studying Jane.

"It is."

Jane was very protective of her dad. He hated people seeing him in the nursing home. He didn't want visitors other than Jane and Kelsey and Cassie.

"You don't think Dax will change his mind just because

your dad is sick, do you?" Zoe asked, frowning.

"No. I don't, actually," Jane said. "But he's making this *huge* gesture in giving up the business. I just feel it's only fair for him to really see what my life is like. And I want Dad to meet him."

"Will your dad be up for that?" Josie asked. She often said how much she wished Jack would let her come and visit. Zoe and Josie and Jane were close, and they knew one another's parents well.

"I don't know. I think if I tell him Dax is important to me, he'll make an exception."

"You're not using this as a way to scare Dax off, or test him, hoping he reacts badly and gives you a reason to not see him anymore?" Zoe asked.

"I'm not," Jane said truthfully. "I don't think this will scare him off anyway. I think he'll pass with flying colors."

"You're falling for him," Zoe said, still watching Jane closely.

Jane's instinct was to deny it, but she couldn't. She didn't introduce guys to her dad. She didn't introduce guys to Kelsey, for that matter. Guys were just a once-in-a while diversion. Until now.

She nodded. "Yeah, I think I am."

Josie smiled and gave another big, happy sigh. "That's so awesome, Jane. I'm so happy for you."

"Thanks." Jane took a deep breath. "So introducing him to Dad is a good idea, right? I want him to know all these parts of my life."

"I think it's awesome," Zoe said. "Dax seems like exactly the type of guy you need. Fun, confident, generous, laid back."

Jane agreed. With all of that.

"Me too," Josie agreed. "I hope Dax understands what a big deal it is, but *we* know. I'm so happy you're falling in love."

Jane was too. It was a strange feeling, one she hadn't felt in a very long time, if ever, but she liked it.

"So what about you?" she asked Josie. "Did you get lucky too?

Josie blushed and shook her head. "Not the way you did."

"No sex?"

"Nope."

"Then why the humming and blushing?" Zoe asked.

"I had a... romantic encounter with someone," Josie said. Then she frowned slightly. "Well, I thought it was romantic. But he seemed annoyed."

Jane laughed. "What happened?"

"Last night after Zoe left, I was just finishing things up and wanted to refill the flour canister. So I was up on the step stool reaching for a bag on the top shelf. My shoulder's been bugging me, and I got a major twinge of pain when I grabbed the bag, and I almost dropped it. I jerked, and I almost slipped off the stool. Suddenly there was this guy there, catching me." She sighed and lifted a shoulder. "I thought it was very gallant and said something about him being a knight in shining armor. He just set me down on the floor and said, 'For fuck's sake, you need to be more careful.'"

Jane snorted, but Zoe's eyes were wide.

"Well, he's right," Zoe said. "What if you'd fallen and gotten hurt? You were here alone. You can't do stuff like that when no one's around."

"I didn't even think about it," Josie protested. "I needed the bag of flour so I climbed up to get it."

Zoe shook her head. "Well, thank God he was there. And he just caught you? You just fell into his arms?"

"It wasn't *graceful*," Josie said. "I fell, and he kind of just kept me from smacking the floor. But he *did* save me. And..." She sighed. "He was very good looking. Big. Smelled amazing."

"Who was it?" Jane asked. "Oh my God." Big, good-looking, amazing-smelling guys were definitely not as common around Appleby as the female population would have liked.

"I… can't tell you," Josie said, focusing her gaze on the cake pops she was now wrapping again.

"You can't tell us?" Zoe asked. "Excuse me? Why not?"

"Because I don't know."

Josie's cheeks were bright red now.

"You don't know?" Zoe repeated. "He was a stranger?"

"Yep. Never seen him before."

"He didn't tell you his name when you introduced yourself?" Jane prompted.

"Nope. He stared at me for a few seconds then asked if I was Zoe. When I said, "No, I'm Josie," he turned on his heel and walked out the door." She finally looked up. "And that all sounds pretty stupid when I tell the story out loud."

"He didn't even tell you his name?" Jane asked. This was a crazy story, but for some reason she was grinning. Maybe because Josie actually looked a little starry eyed about the whole thing.

"He didn't. When I said I wasn't Zoe, he walked out. Not another word." Josie sighed. "He had a great, low voice too."

Jane shook her head. "Wow, you're half in love with a guy who said like a dozen words to you and walked out? That's pretty rude, isn't it?"

"Yeah. It was weird," Josie agreed. "But there was something about the way he looked at me."

Jane arched her brows.

"But… you were *humming*," Zoe said, looking puzzled. "Why were you humming?"

"Because whenever I think of it, I smile," Josie said. "And because of the tingles."

The last two words were almost too quiet to hear.

"The tingles?" Jane pressed. "He gave you tingles."

"Major tingles," Josie confirmed. "And I swear he must have felt something too. He let go of me super quick, like he'd gotten shocked or something."

"Why are you so enamored with this guy?" Zoe asked.

Josie shrugged. "It was the most romantic thing to happen to me in a *very* long time."

"That was romantic?" Zoe demanded. "He kept you from breaking your neck and then asked for me and walked out?"

"I can't explain it," Josie said. "It was just a *moment*."

Jane caught Zoe's eyes and gave her a little head shake. Josie was a sweetheart and a romantic. There was nothing wrong with that. The guy was a stranger, probably stopping by to try to sell Zoe some new cake pans or something. Josie would never see him again, so it didn't really matter if they'd had a moment.

"Hey, Jane, there's someone here to see you," Maggie, Zoe's mom, said, popping her head into the kitchen.

Jane felt her heart flip. Dax was here. She had to admit, she kind of understood where Josie was coming from. Sometimes there were just moments. Simple chemistry. Even before they'd had sex in her car, there were definitely moments where Dax made her hum. Or would have if she were the humming type.

"Thanks, I'll be right up."

"Oh, I have to see this," Zoe said, setting the full-sized pie she was wrapping on the worktable and wiping her hands.

"See what?" Jane asked, starting for the door.

"You in love," Josie said, sliding off the stool. "We've never seen that before."

Well, she had a point.

11

He'd dreamed of Jane last night.

That didn't surprise him. He'd absolutely gone to bed with her on his mind.

What did surprise him was that the dreams didn't include her naked and bent over the sofa in the living room of his suite, or her naked and on her knees in front of him in the shower, or her naked and tangled up in the sheets on his king-sized bed.

She wasn't naked in his dreams at all.

She was sitting at a big table, somewhere outside—the place didn't look familiar—with people from Hot Cakes and her sister and stepsister and Zoe and Aiden and Josie and Piper and Ollie and Grant and Cam. And Dax's father.

They had all been there, sitting around a big table laden with food and drinks. They'd all been just talking and laughing.

Then he'd come to the table, carrying a tray of strawberry pies and had passed them out before bending and kissing Jane and then taking his seat next to her.

They'd basically been hosting a dinner party for all the people in their life. As a couple.

It was the most normal, almost boring, dream he'd ever had. And he'd awakened from it feeling happy and in the best mood he'd been in for a while. Which was saying something. He was generally in a good mood.

Then when he'd looked at the clock beside his bed and saw it was only 7 a.m.—thirty minutes before his alarm was set to go off—he was even further convinced Jane was magical.

So he'd been whistling when he stepped into Buttered Up at ten to eight.

"Oh my God, are you sick or something?" Jane asked, coming through the door from the kitchen.

He moved to the end of the bakery case. Jane came around in front of the case, and Zoe and Josie stopped just behind it. An older woman and man were serving the customers at the register.

"I feel amazing." Dax slipped an arm around Jane's waist and kissed her temple.

She gave him a big, wide-eyed stare that clearly said, "What the hell?"

"Good morning," he said with a grin, unconcerned about her reaction.

She put her elbow against his side, trying to push him away. He laughed and dropped his arm.

"'Morning, Dax," Josie said, looking back and forth between them curiously.

He liked that having a man kiss Jane publicly seemed unusual. "Good morning, Josie," he said. "How are you?"

"I'm great. And you?"

"I've never been better." He looked down at Jane. "Serious-ly." He wanted her to see his sincerity too. He was a well-known goofball, but he was crazy about her, and he wanted her to know he meant that with everything in him.

"I heard a rumor about you," Josie said, putting three

lemon-poppyseed muffins into a carryout box and passing them to the man who was helping the customers.

"Oh?"

"I heard you're no longer an owner at Hot Cakes," she said.

"Oh, that's true. Feel free to spread it around," he confirmed.

"Really?" Josie cast a glance at Jane. "So it's not a secret either?"

"Of course not," Dax said.

"Are we also allowed to talk about the reason for it?" Josie asked.

"No."

"Sure."

Jane and Dax spoke at the same time, then looked at each other.

"You're not going to tell everyone why you are thinking about giving up your shares," Jane said. She narrowed her eyes. "Unless there's a reason other than the one you told me about last night."

"You," Dax said. "You are the reason. The only one. And I'm not thinking about it. I did it."

She swallowed hard, and when Dax glanced at her two best friends, they were both watching with huge smiles.

"You can't tell everyone that," Jane said, lowering her voice. "You shouldn't really tell people you're giving up your shares at all."

"Why not?" Dax and Josie were the ones speaking simultaneously this time.

"Because when it doesn't work out and you buy those shares back, everyone will know, and that will require even more explanation," Jane said.

Dax turned to face her more fully. "I have no reason to believe it's not going to work out."

"You live in Chicago."

"For now," he agreed.

"We're very different."

"In wonderful ways," he said.

"You don't want to be a part of my crazy life long term, Dax."

"I think I do, actually."

"One night with the girls and you're so confident."

Dax laughed. "Admit it. The way I handled them was at least thirty percent of why you got naked with me in your car last night."

Jane gave a squeak-cough and looked at her friends again.

"Your car?" Zoe said. "You left that detail out."

Dax grinned down at Jane. "You told them the naked part though?"

Jane rolled her eyes as Josie confirmed, "Oh yes."

Jane shook her head and looked at him again. "Maybe you saving me from Kelsey and Aspen's dramatics was the *whole* reason the car happened."

"Nah," he said with a shake of his head. "You've been wanting to get into my pants since we first met."

Zoe laughed and Josie said, "Yeah, I saw you two at Granny's together, remember? The naked-in-your-car thing was just waiting to happen."

Dax gave Jane a smug grin. "And don't try to tell me I got you all softened up with the ice cream, because you were giving me that look when you saw me leaning against your car at Hot Cakes."

"I was not." Jane's cheeks were a little pink.

And she didn't ask *what look?* She totally knew. Dax grinned. "You totally were."

She shook her head. "So we'll just move into my tiny apartment together, and you'll do your video game stuff from my kitchen table?"

He shrugged. "Or we can buy a house. Or build one. Or I could rent some office space."

Honestly, if her entire protest was the size of her kitchen, he was so in.

"You're really going to have to throw me harder challenges than that," he said.

"How about I don't like gummy bears or beanbag chairs and refuse to paint even a single wall in my home yellow?" she asked, crossing her arms.

"All the more reason for me to rent office space," he agreed.

"Like I might *never* let you have gummy bears in my house."

He shrugged. "I can make you like gummy bears."

"No, you can't."

He gave *her* a look. A look that was full of all the dirty thoughts he was having about her and his favorite candy. "Dare me."

She cleared her throat.

"But an office somewhere downtown will be better anyway," he said, letting her off the hook. Kind of. They were going to come back to this conversation at some point.

"Because you can't be left alone all day?" Jane asked. "You'll be bored or get into trouble?"

"Or both," he agreed. "I'd rather have an office where people might come in and where I can pop out for lunch." Even as he spoke, he could imagine an office with a huge front window where he could watch the traffic and wave to people walking by. "I could put a cappuccino machine in and have a candy bar there," he said. "I'd encourage all the local business-people to stop by to chat and grab some candy or coffee."

"Ahem," Zoe said. "I *sell* coffee. You can't have free cappuccino in your office just because you might get lonely."

He grinned at her. "I guess I can just pop in here whenever I get bored."

Zoe smiled even as she arched a brow. "And that would be, what, three or four times a day?"

"Oh, way more than that."

She laughed. "Maybe you could rent an office at Hot Cakes. Then you could have Aiden and whoever else around to talk to."

"Maybe," he said. "Or maybe they could move down here. That would make Hot Cakes more a part of the local business scene, right? We'd mingle with the other people who make this town work. And that will help out some local business owner who has space they need to fill."

"You don't think management should be on scene at the factory?" Jane asked. Then she shook her head. "You know what? Never mind. Having management off-site might be great."

He laughed. "And if I'm based here, we can actually put together that gaming conference here those friends of Kelsey and Aspen's were interested in. That would be a big boon to the town and local economy." He started to nod as the idea took shape. "Yeah, great idea. I'll have to hand a lot of it off to Ollie. These big plans are his thing." That would also keep his friend in town longer. Dax would miss Ollie the most if he were back in Chicago. "We'll leave our headquarters in Chicago, but this can be a second location for Fluke Inc." He grinned at her. "Thanks for the great idea, Jane. That's awesome. When should I bring my stuff over to your place? That will really cut down on my drive time too."

She was just staring at him. Then she looked at her friends.

Zoe held up a hand and shook her head. "Don't look at me. Aiden walked back in here day one saying we were going to get married, and I thought he was nuts, but look at me now."

Yeah, now she was madly in love, happy, and engaged to be married.

"Can you put a few strawberry muffins in a bag and on my

tab?" Jane asked, completely changing the subject from moving in together. "We need to go."

"Of course." Josie wiggled her eyebrows at Jane and Dax laughed.

"Not like that," Jane said quickly.

Josie nodded. "Okay."

"We have somewhere to be."

"I believe you." Josie grabbed four muffins and slid them into a bag.

"Seriously," Jane said.

Josie handed the bag over. "Enjoy *whatever* you'll be doing."

Jane just took a deep breath and then blew it out. "See you later."

"You will," Josie promised.

"Wine night Monday night," Zoe said.

Jane glanced at Dax then back to her friends. "Yeah, I think I'll need that."

Dax didn't know why exactly, but that made him feel proud. Like he was achieving something here that he didn't even fully understand. But being something Jane wanted to discuss at wine night with her friends—which was obviously what they all meant—seemed like an accomplishment.

Jane started for the door, but as he went to follow her he heard Josie whisper, "Dax."

He turned back. "Yeah?"

"She's not used to having a lot of positive attention focused on her. She's the one always focusing on everyone else and what they need and how she can help them."

"Okay." That definitely seemed to be exactly who Jane was.

"So just keep it up," Josie said. "She's going to feel a little discombobulated at first. She's pretty used to taking charge and knowing what needs to happen next. Just keep coming at her with this you're-amazing-and-I'm-completely-into-you stuff. She really deserves that."

"It's all real," he felt compelled enough to say.

Josie nodded with a smile that was almost affectionate. "I know."

"That's why we're not leaning over this bakery case and threatening to make your life a living hell," Zoe added.

He gave her a wide-eyed nod. "Duly noted."

Zoe smiled. "Just remember, to melt unsweetened chocolate takes low heat and time and patience. You add the sugar in slowly. You just keep stirring. Eventually, it will melt. And once it does, it's smooth and sweet."

Dax nodded. "Got it." He started after Jane then turned back. "Oh, except the low-heat part." Then he gave Jane's best friends a wink and went after her.

———

D ax joined Jane on the sidewalk outside the bakery. "I have a surprise for you," he said.

"Oh?"

"I've come up with the perfect date. The surefire way to your heart. The only thing I could do once I heard about it."

She tilted her head with a curious smile. "What is it?"

"The bridal fair."

Jane's eyes went wide and she gave a little laugh. "Five minutes ago, we were just moving in together. Now you want to do wedding planning?"

Dax grinned and moved in closer to her. "Don't tease me, Ms. Kemper."

"You're a little crazy." She said it softly, looking into his eyes.

He nodded. "Crazy about you. And the perfect way to make you a little crazy about *me* is to take you somewhere we can eat all the desserts we could possibly want... for free."

He could see the humor in her eyes.

"I have to admit you pretty much nailed it as far the perfect date to take me on."

He nodded. "Movies schmovies. Candlelight dinner? Please. Surprise flight to Paris? No way. But all-you-can-eat sweets... bingo."

But instead of laughing, she took a deep breath. "I actually can't go."

"To the bridal fair?" he asked. "I was kidding about wedding planning. We're just going there to make sure none of the bakeries have to take leftovers home." He paused. "We can always do the wedding planning next weekend."

She did smile then. "As much as I would love to eat pie and cake all day with you, and you know I really would, I spend Saturdays with my sister and dad."

Okay, that wasn't an absolute no. "Well, that's fine. We'll take them with us."

Jane shook her head. "That's sweet but I don't think so."

"They don't like cake?"

"They both love cake."

"Then what's the problem?"

"My dad," she said. "He's not very social lately. Well, for the last several months. His condition has made him depressed, and he really just wants to stay in his room all the time."

"Okay, well, we should at least ask," Dax decided. "He can say no, and we'll just hang out there with him. But maybe we can convince him. Some sunshine and fresh air and sugar could be good for him." Then he frowned. "Wait, is sugar okay for him?"

Jane smiled. "Yes. He can eat whatever he wants for the most part." Then she sighed. "It's not a lack of sunshine and fresh air. It's true depression."

"I know something about that," he said. "My mom's was too."

Jane nodded. "It helps that you understand that. A psychologist sees him every other week and is helping him with his depression and anger, but it still isn't unusual for him to ask even me and Kelsey not to come see him. If he's having a bad day because he's feeling weaker than usual or if it's just a particularly emotional day, he doesn't want us to see him like that."

"I totally get that," Dax said. "Parents want to be the ones taking care of their kids, not the other way around."

She nodded.

"I know being told no over and over is hard." He reached out and grasped her upper arm, rubbing up and down. "It sucks to try, to want to help, and to have them reject it. Especially if it's time with you they're rejecting."

Jane looked into his eyes, her bottom lips between her teeth again. He could tell she saw his sincerity.

"But," he went on. "If you stop asking, stop trying, then they never have the chance to say yes. And even if the yeses are lot less common than the nos, they are so sweet when they come."

She gave him a little smile. "But... he's also in a wheelchair."

"You mentioned that," Dax said. "The other night at the bar when you told me some people had just showed up to build a ramp at the house." He frowned, thinking about the house last night. "Hey, the ramp wasn't at the house. Is it in back?"

Jane swallowed hard. "Cassie had it taken out. She didn't like how it looked and once Dad moved to the nursing home, she said there was no reason to have it."

Dax scowled. Wow, he really disliked Jane's stepmother. "What about when he wants to come home and visit? Holidays and stuff?"

Jane shook her head. "Nope. He doesn't do that. We went out to a restaurant at Thanksgiving, and that was such an ordeal he refused to do anything but have us come to the nursing home for Christmas."

"Why was it an ordeal?"

"The wheelchair is heavy and takes up a lot of trunk space,

and then we have to help him in and out of it, which can be hard when he gets tired, and then we have to make room at the table for the wheelchair, and he was really embarrassed by that."

Dax didn't know Jane's dad. But he had an idea, knowing Jane and having met Kelsey, that he was a good guy. "No offense, but your stepmom is kind of a bitch."

Jane snorted at that. "She's a piece of work."

"So we can make this happen," Dax said. "I can help lift him and the chair and whatever. And the fair is being held in a bunch of buildings in a park outside of Dubuque, right?"

Jane nodded. "The park has a 'old town' area with buildings that look like buildings from the time the city was founded. They have fairs and events there a lot."

"So big buildings with good paths. We won't have to worry about tables crowded together in a restaurant," Dax reasoned. "And if it sucks or makes him uncomfortable, we'll leave."

Jane took a breath. "I don't know."

Dax watched her face. He knew her dad's situation broke her heart. He knew she did her damnedest to make things work for her family. He knew she often felt helpless to really make anything better. He could definitely relate to that. He'd been there with his mom more times than he liked to remember. His brother to an extent as well.

He wanted to help Jane. He wanted to show her she didn't have to do it alone. He wanted to make things easier, on her and her family.

In fact, it was becoming a *need* more than a desire.

"Let's just go see him," Dax said. "We'll talk to him, and see what he thinks. We don't have to do it, but it *is* an option. I'm certain I can help with the wheelchair and everything."

"Your car's trunk can barely fit the spare tire," she said, her tone lighter.

"Then we'll take your car. Or I can rent one. How about a

van with a wheelchair lift on it? Maybe we should just buy one?"

She laughed and put her hand on his face. "And I know you're not kidding."

"I'm totally not," he assured her. "If you're trying to shut me down, you're going to have to come up with something that I can't throw money at."

Her expression was one of wonder and affection. "I'm not trying to shut you down."

He pulled her hand from his cheek to his lips. He pressed a kiss on the back of it and then put her hand over his heart. "Good."

"Okay, let's go talk to my dad."

"Can't wait."

They walked, hand in hand, to her car. "I'll just text Kelsey and tell her to meet us over there," Jane said, digging in her bag once she was behind the wheel.

"I can text her while you drive," Dax said, pulling his phone out of his pocket. Their house wasn't far from the nursing home. Kelsey could easily walk the few blocks.

"You have Kelsey's number?"

"Yeah."

"I—" Jane broke off. "Great."

He grinned. "Told her she can call me any time. Especially if she needs something during your work hours."

Jane frowned slightly. "I don't mind her calling me."

"I know."

"Did you say that as my boss, because you don't want me to take personal calls while I'm at work or as my..." She bit her lower lip.

"As your..." He trailed off the same way she had. "And Kelsey's friend." He paused. "And I'm not your boss."

She nodded.

"I know you work your ass off, and that place would fall

apart without you," he added. "I don't care if you sit in that break room and color and drink cappuccino all day."

She smiled. "Too bad you're not my boss anymore, then."

He leaned over and cupped the back of her head, pulling her in for a kiss. A long, slow, wet kiss. When he let her go, she blinked at him several times.

"What was that for?"

"Reminding you that you're very happy I'm *not* your boss."

A smile teased her lips. "Right. I almost forgot."

He growled and said, "Take me to meet your dad before I forget I'm too good of a guy to haul you back to your place and keep you naked all day."

She gave a little shiver. "Right. But... later. We can be naked all night."

"Deal."

She was coming around. He knew he'd blown in and turned her life upside down and that she didn't want to feel all the things he was making her feel. But she was feeling them anyway. And maybe even starting to like them.

Jane started the car and pulled out onto the street. He sent Kelsey a quick text: *Going to see your dad. Meet us there?*

He got an almost instantaneous reply: *There better be a muffin for me.*

Of course. He also added a strawberry.

See you there.

They pulled up in front of Sunny Orchard Living and Care Center a few minutes later. Jane took a deep breath.

Dax just waited for her to speak.

"Let me go in ahead. At least into his room," she said. "He's funny about guests."

"I can do that." Dax really didn't want to make this harder, but he was eager to meet Jane and Kelsey's father.

"Okay, thanks."

They had just reached the front doors when Kelsey called

to them from the sidewalk. They waited for her to catch up with them.

"Hi!" She seemed in a good mood.

"Hey." Jane gave her a quick hug.

"I'm so glad you're coming to meet Dad," Kelsey said, reaching for the door.

"Yeah?" Dax asked, glancing at Jane.

"Definitely. He doesn't usually let people come visit him but us. I'm glad he said you could come."

They followed her through the door.

"Well, I haven't told him yet," Jane told her sister. "Dax is going to wait out here for me to kind of ease Dad into it.

Kelsey frowned. "Oh. Well, he'll be okay, right? I mean, he'd want to meet your boyfriend."

Dax saw how that made Jane freeze for just a second. He lifted a brow, just waiting to see how she might handle that.

But she surprised him by turning to Kelsey. "Do you think so?"

Kelsey nodded. "Of course. I mean, he doesn't want his old boss coming just out of guilt, and Aunt Amy will totally make a huge deal out of everything and insist on doting on him and make him crazy. And he doesn't want his friends to see him like this." She looked a little sad but she shrugged. "But Dax is different. He's the guy you're in love with. Dad will totally want to know him."

Dax's grin grew as Jane's mouth dropped open. But she didn't deny anything Kelsey had just said.

His chest got warm and a little tight. He wanted to grab her. But if he did, he'd back her up against the nearest wall, and it would become very inappropriate very quickly. Especially for the lobby of a nursing home. Though, the way he was feeling, it would probably be inappropriate for even the lobby of a sex club at the moment.

"Okay," Jane finally said slowly. She glanced at Dax, and he just gave her a big, cocky grin.

She rolled her eyes. But the corner of her mouth curled.

"Let's go see him first though," she told Kelsey. "Just to warm him up."

"Fine," Kelsey said. She looked at Dax. "I will talk you up big time."

"Thanks, Kels," Dax said sincerely. "I'll just hang out." He looked around. The lobby had two leather-covered couches and a few armchairs gathered around a fireplace. There was a coffee and water station in one corner and a huge fish tank in the other. The reception desk was to his left.

"Hopefully, it won't take long," Jane said.

"No problem."

She hesitated as if she wanted to say something more, but finally she just nodded, and she and Kelsey started down the long hallway.

Dax tucked his hands in his pockets and sauntered toward the coffee station. But he wasn't really in the mood for a cup of coffee. He watched the fish for a little bit. He looked at the artwork on the walls—nice, kind of typical scenes of farms and rolling fields and a sunset over a river he imagined was the Mississippi. He checked out the magazines on a couple of the side tables. He put three pieces into the jigsaw puzzle that was laid out on the big, round table near the windows.

Finally, he took a seat in one of the armchairs and opened a browser on his phone. He had never in his life been in a nursing home. He had a vague idea what he would find here, but he was curious.

Nursing home layouts was his first search. Then he searched *typical day in a nursing home*. Then *depression in nursing home residents*. Then *innovative nursing home programs*. Innovative was one of his favorite words in all situations.

He read four articles then sent off a message to Piper and

another to Grant. They each said the same thing. *What do you know about nursing homes? Do we know anyone in the business?* They were the two most connected and knowledgeable about their business network.

A glance at the clock told him things down the hall with Jane's dad were not going as smoothly as Kelsey had anticipated. Dax was surprised to find himself disappointed about that. He'd like to meet the man, and he'd like to assure him that Dax had only the best intentions and that he'd be there for Jack's daughters however he could be. Surely that would be reassuring for the man. Wouldn't it? Or maybe it would just be a reminder that Jack couldn't do all the things for them he wanted to. That would suck. Dax was going to have to be careful here.

He approached the reception desk. "Hi."

The young girl—weekend help, he assumed—was busy looking at her phone. She looked up as if surprised to find someone standing there. So security guard she was not.

"Uh, hi."

"I'm Dax."

"Taylor."

"Have you worked here for a long time?"

She shrugged. "About a year, but I only work after school two days a week and weekends."

"Do you like it?"

"Sure."

"Tell me your favorite part."

Just then his phone rang. He looked down to see Grant was calling.

"Damn, hang on. I have to answer this."

"Okay." Taylor seemed very unconcerned about having their conversation interrupted.

"Hey," he answered, starting toward the fish tank.

"What are you up to?" Grant asked.

"What do you mean?"

"Why are you asking about nursing homes?"

"Because I'm in one right now."

That made Grant pause for a moment. "Why?"

"Jane's dad lives here," Dax said.

"Ah."

Dax could picture Grant nodding as if he'd just figured everything out.

"So that makes sense?" Dax asked.

"Of course. You're the most curious guy I know and you just walked into something new. Of course you're going to try to figure everything out about it." Grant said it with a very familiar slightly exasperated, slightly amused, slightly proud tone. He used that tone with Dax and Ollie a lot.

Dax knew he gave his friend heart palpitations, but he also knew Grant could have left Fluke a long time ago and been just fine. He could have made money and had much more important friends who didn't give him migraines. But he'd stayed. Because, whether he would admit it or not, he liked them.

"Well, nursing homes are definitely new to me," he said. "Never gave them much thought, you know? Pretty different than anything else I've ever done."

"True," Grant said. "But that isn't the new thing you just walked into that I was referring to."

"What were you referring to?"

"Being in love."

Dax grinned. "Well, yeah, there's that too."

"So you realize you're in love?" Grant said.

"Yeah. I was pretty sure I was falling from almost day one. But yeah, I'm there."

"And the woman that you gave Hot Cakes up for has a father living in a nursing home, so naturally you're interested in how those work."

Dax nodded. "Exactly. It's a part of her life, so I want to know more."

"Do not buy that nursing home, Dax," Grant said.

Dax didn't answer right away. His mind was spinning too fast.

Grant interpreted his silence correctly. "Shit. You *weren't* thinking about buying it?"

"I hadn't gotten quite that far," Dax said. "But I probably would have at some point."

Grant sighed. "Dammit. And now I gave you the idea."

Dax laughed. "Don't beat yourself up. I almost always get to *hey, I should buy one of these* with most things eventually."

Grant groaned. "Dax, you know nothing about nursing homes."

"Which is exactly why I texted you and Piper." He rolled his eyes. "I'm not an idiot."

"You're impulsive."

"I'll give you that." Then Dax laughed. "But don't run out for more antacids just yet, G," he said. "I was actually just thinking I could maybe make a donation so they can implement some new programs for depression. Sounds like most nursing homes need extra funding, and depression is very common among residents."

There was a beat of silence on Grant's end. Then he said, "Jane's dad's depressed?"

"Yeah."

"And it's hurting her?"

Dax took a breath. "Yeah."

"Okay," Grant said. "Then you should totally make a donation. I can get some resources together to see what kinds of programs are available and reach out to see what kind of funding would help most."

Dax smiled. Grant Lorre was a good guy. He wanted to protect his business interests from Dax and Ollie's reckless and sometimes ridiculous ideas. He wanted to protect his friends too, for that matter, from scams and people out to defraud them because of their fame and money. But the bottom line was Grant cared about them and believed in them. When they had a good idea or a true passion project—and not something that just occurred to them on a whim or when they were on an endorphin high—he was behind them 100 percent.

"Thanks," Dax said. "I'd appreciate the help researching. I'm going to do more of my own too."

"Oh right, you have more free time now," Grant said. "What with not being a part of Hot Cakes anymore."

Dax grinned. "Tell you what, I'll do my research in the Hot Cakes break room. I hear they have great cappuccino. Then if you guys need me, you'll know where to find me."

Grant gave a grunt that was supposed to be laughter. "Great. When I need a quick game of Ping-Pong, I'll be down."

Which meant Dax would never see him in the break room. Grant didn't play Ping-Pong.

Just then, Jane stepped into the lobby. She found him immediately and motioned with her hand in a *come on* gesture.

Yes. He was in. "Gotta go. Talk to you later."

"Don't spend any money before we talk again," Grant cautioned.

"Only on cake and pie today," Dax agreed.

"Cake and pie?"

"Big dessert-tasting thing. Buttered Up is going to be there, so Jane and I are going to take her dad and sister out there."

"Buttered Up?" Grant asked sharply. "Zoe's bakery?"

"Yeah."

"Zoe will be there?"

Dax frowned. "Yeah."

"Anyone else?"

"Her assistant, Josie," Dax replied.

There was no sound on Grant's end.

"Hello?" Dax asked.

"Yeah. Okay. Nothing. Talk to you later." Grant disconnected before Dax could reply.

Well, that was weird.

"Everything okay?" Jane asked as he joined her.

"Yeah. Probably. That was just Grant."

"Okay. So—" She took a deep breath. "You ready for this?"

"You sure he's good with it?"

"He's... willing."

"Took a while."

"Yeah. We eased into it. And had to discuss Kelsey's chemistry grades and her grounding and..." She sighed. "Anyway that's all done, and he knows Kelsey thinks you're amazing and that you were nice to Aspen and that you have the coolest car. Which he agrees with."

"How's she know about my car?" he asked with a grin as they started down the hallway.

"Oh, it's not plastered all over your social media?" Jane gave him a look.

"Right. Yes, it is."

"Yeah." She shook her head. "I'm still getting used to the idea that you're kind of famous."

He laughed. "You're probably not the target demographic for my message."

"I don't know," she said without looking at him. "I think I've received your message about living in the moment and making it as great as you can, pretty clearly."

He stopped her, turning her to face him. "That means a lot to me."

She met his gaze. "I'm glad."

He thought about kissing her, but she turned and started walking again.

The hallway was wide, stark white, with a white tile floor. It was brightly lit by fluorescent lights overhead.

The first room on the right seemed to be some kind of community room. There were several round tables with chairs and wheelchairs pulled up to them. There were about eight people in the room along with a woman who looked like a staff member, judging by her lavender scrubs and the name tag he could see but not read. It looked like they were working on some kind of craft project.

The next room was empty but was clearly a small chapel. On the left was a much larger room filled with exercise equipment of various types. Two staff people were working with two residents going through a set of leg exercises. He gave them a smile as they continued on.

They passed the office of the nursing home's director, empty at the moment, and finally got to rooms that seemed like resident rooms.

There was a lot of noise—a lot from televisions in the rooms, but also some conversation—and a variety of smells. There was a medicinal disinfectant smell underneath the smell of food being prepared.

Finally, they reached the end of the hallway, where two more hallways led off in either direction. In the middle of that intersection of hallways was a round desk where staff, who were clearly nurses, typed on computers or leaned over writing on papers.

They took the hallway to the left and went four doors down. Jane hesitated just outside. "Oh, also, you should know my dad thinks you're my boyfriend."

"I'm totally good with that. In fact, I think we should just make that official."

She rolled her eyes but was smiling. "Okay. That would help so I don't feel like I'm lying to him."

"Great." Dax felt that warm feeling that had settled in his chest earlier, spread. "And does he think we're going to this bridal fair because we're talking about getting hitched?" he asked. He could totally play along with that too.

"Oh no, he knows it's all about the cake and pie for me."

Dax laughed. "Right. He probably knows you pretty well."

She nodded. "But he and Kelsey think it will be fun to pretend we are getting married and we're there to make plans."

Dax liked Jack already. "So at the event we'll have to act like we're in love and like I'm ready to throw an elaborate, over-the-top party to declare you off the market and totally monogamous to only me."

She lifted a brow. "Well, *you* will also be off the market and totally monogamous only to *me*."

He liked that little flicker of possessiveness. He leaned in and stole a kiss. "Damn right," he said against her lips.

She gave a little sigh and then pulled back. "So you can pull this off?"

"Acting crazy about you and that I love an extravagant party?" he asked. "Absolutely." He let a beat pass and then said, "No acting required. For any of it."

For a second she looked like she was going to confess something, but she just nodded and said, "You are so the extravagant party type."

"I'm the extravagant everything type."

12

"Now this is my kind of forking around," Jane said, dragging the tines of her fork over her tongue slowly and thoroughly because of the way it made Dax's eyes darken.

"We're taking some of this pie home with us."

"Please," she said, letting her voice get husky.

They'd been eating dessert and teasing with frosting and sprinkles and whipped toppings for two hours, and she wasn't sure she'd ever had more fun.

Kelsey and Jack seemed to be having a great time as well. They'd not only sampled desserts but had also done a couple of passes by the hors d'oeuvres tables and had checked out all the other booths, including the ones showing off honeymoon packages and tuxedo rentals and we-can-build-it-in-a-day gazebos.

"I want to suck this whipped cream off your nipples and lick this strawberry glaze off your clit."

Jane's eyes flew to Dax as she made a little gasping-choking sound. "Dax!"

He grinned. "No one can hear me."

"But..." She felt a flush go through her. "Yeah, you should definitely do both of those things."

She'd never been with a guy who was dirty and sexy and sweet and playful all at the same time.

She was completely addicted and almost giddy. Giddy. That was a word she'd never used to describe herself before. Of course, that was probably because she'd never *felt* giddy before. She wasn't the giddy type.

She watched Dax lick whipped cream off of his index finger —slowly—catching her eye and giving her a wink.

She was definitely the giddy type now.

"And finally, we're thrilled to announce our grand prize winners!"

There was a woman on the makeshift stage at the front of the largest building set up for the bridal fair. She was going through the winners of several door prizes, including a basketful of goodies from Buttered Up.

Jane had been past Zoe and Josie's table a couple of times, and they always had a cluster of people in front of them, tasting their desserts and asking questions and placing orders.

Josie was thrilled. Zoe looked overwhelmed.

But she'd be okay. Aiden would talk her down, and they'd all pitch in to fill orders if needed. Jane was so happy for her friends and grateful to Aiden for coaxing Zoe out of her box to try new things.

"The couple's weekend at Pine Grove Bed and Breakfast includes the Diamond Suite, a couple's massage, tickets to the local production of *Wicked*, and gift baskets from The Sweet Spa, Rutherford Winery, and a shopping spree at Naughty and Nice Lingerie and Gifts," the woman said excitedly.

"I think we should take some of the cupcakes from that place over by the other door too," Dax said.

Jane nodded. "Yes. But we can*not* tell Zoe."

"Never," he agreed. "We can take all the contraband back to my hotel room. Then there's no risk of her even seeing a wrapper."

Jane grinned up at him. "That's pretty smooth."

"What?" he asked innocently.

"Making going back to your hotel room *practical*."

"I'm just presenting facts," he said with a shrug. "I'd hate to hurt Zoe's feelings."

"But you'd also hate to leave this pie and those cupcakes behind."

"I would hate that so much," he said with a nod. And a wicked grin.

"You know, this could seem kind of like a guy trying to lure kids into his unmarked white van with candy," Jane teased. "You know if you dangle strawberry pie, I'll do almost anything."

"No," he said. "I know if I dangle strawberry pie, you *will do* anything. No *almost* about it."

She laughed. "You're using my weakness against me?"

He took a big bite of the pie in question and grinned, unapologetic.

The truth was, *he* was her new weakness.

"Fine," she said as if put upon. "I'll go back to your hotel with you tonight."

He swallowed. "We're going to give a new meaning to *orgasmic* strawberry pie."

"Do people refer to strawberry pie as *orgasmic*?" she asked.

"They should."

"Dax Marshall and Jane Kemper!"

They both jerked at the sound of their names coming over the loudspeaker. They looked at one another then toward the stage.

"Oh my God!" Suddenly Kelsey came jogging toward them pushing Jack's wheelchair. They were both grinning widely.

"What's going on?" Jane asked.

They were toward the back of the crowd, away from the stage, and people were starting to turn.

"You won!" Kelsey laughed and then high-fived Jack. "You're the grand prize winners!"

"We are?" Jane looked at Dax. "We didn't do anything."

"We s-signed you u-up," Jack said,

Jane was frozen for a moment, just looking at her father. She hadn't seen him smiling that big in far too long. He looked younger and healthier. Her heart tripped.

"We signed you guys up for a ton of stuff," Kelsey said. "We went around to all the booths and got samples and entered all their draws with your names. Since you're the bride and groom." She winked at them.

"You condone this?" Jane asked Jack.

He just grinned.

"And hot damn, the grand prize!" Dax said. "That's awesome. What did we win?"

"You didn't hear any of it?" Kelsey asked. "It's like this huge package with wine and massages and a free stay in a B and B." She looked immensely proud of herself. "You're welcome."

"Wow, they just drew our names?" Jane asked. "That's amazing. But... we're not even really engaged. Are they going to throw us out when they find out?"

Jack shook his head. "D-don't t-t-tell."

Jane gave him a look. "Lie?"

"F-f-for fun. It's free st-stuff." Jack also looked proud of himself.

"Oh yeah, you can't give it back," Kelsey said quickly. "Dad had to write an essay to win that!"

Jane felt her eyes widen. "An essay?"

"Yeah," Kelsey said. "I wrote it but they were his words. And it's awesome." She grinned at her father. "*Very* mushy. All about how happy he is that his daughter found true love and how he couldn't have picked a better guy and how he knows Dax will be there for you through all the tough times to come."

Jane felt her throat thicken and a stinging behind her eyes. There were tough times coming. Probably. Eventually. No one really knew. But no matter what happened with his condition, there would be a time when Jane would have to deal with losing Jack. And having Dax beside her for that sounded amazing.

He couldn't fix everything that happened or went wrong, but he made things better. Facing things with him was infinitely better than facing them without him, no matter how it turned out.

"You totally used that wheelchair to get this win, didn't you?" Jane teased her dad, blinking back her tears.

Jack nodded. "Y-yes. This thing sh-should have some p-p-perks."

Jane laughed. He had a point. "Okay." She looked up at Dax. "I guess we have a grand prize to collect."

Everyone in the room applauded as Jane and Dax made their way to the stage. They hammed it up—it was Dax, so of course they did—with him raising their clasped hands high overhead as if they'd just been crowned the heavyweight champions and then dipping her back to give her a big, sweet kiss.

Jane was laughing when he righted her and accepted the huge basket of goodies and gift cards. She found her dad and Kelsey at the back of the room and could see, even from the several yards between them, that Jack was beaming.

He loved being in on the joke, and she could see that he'd had a great day.

Dax had been right. Getting Jack out had been a good thing. A great thing. And with Dax along, it had been much easier than other outings. He handled the chair and assisted Jack without even pausing in whatever funny story he was telling and didn't even blink when Jack tripped over his words. He'd thought ahead about how to avoid anything that might have been an obstacle, and he'd done it all with humor and a laid-back charm that made Jane once and for all sure she was madly in love with him.

With their big win in hand, they headed back for the car and back to Appleby. They dropped Jack off first. The girls kissed him goodbye and stepped into the hallway, when Jack said, "D-D-Dax."

Dax turned back. "Yeah?"

"S-St-Stay for a m-minute."

"Okay." He glanced at the girls. "Meet you at the car," he said to Jane.

"Uh, sure." She looked at her father. Oh boy, they were going to talk in private? "I'll walk Kelsey out."

Dax came strolling out ten minutes later.

Jane was leaning against her car the way she had been the day before in the Hot Cakes parking lot. She had her sunglasses on and her arms crossed. The perfect picture of nonchalance.

She hoped.

"Everything okay?" she asked.

"Totally." Dax gave her a smile, coming to stand directly in front of her.

"Was that all about me?"

Dax grinned and tucked his hands in the front pockets of his jeans. "The part about how much he liked me and knew I'd be good to you? Yes. The part where he asked me to help him into his chair? No. The part where I asked him to look up a couple of things for me and give me his thoughts? No." He gave a thoughtful, totally fake, frown. "So one-third of the conversation, yes. Which means, the majority of it, no."

Jane's frown was real. There were lots of things she wanted to know more about there. Like what Dax wanted her dad to look up for him. Jack had access to a computer in the community room and certainly knew how to Google things. But why would Dax ask him to look something up? Something like what? But the thing she was most focused on was that second one. "He asked you to help him into his chair?"

"He did."

"That's pretty... amazing."

"Is it?"

"He sometimes lets me help him, when he's feeling strong enough that it's not a lot for me to do. He never lets Kelsey or Cassie help him. He's almost always already in his wheelchair when we get here. He doesn't like people to see him weak or incapable."

Dax nodded but didn't say anything.

"Did you have to give him a lot of help?"

He took a breath but then nodded again as he blew it out. "He said he's tired from the outing. I had to lift him and did a lot of the work getting him into the chair."

"Wow, but he let you."

"Yeah. I didn't realize that was a big deal. I'm humbled."

"He trusts you."

"That's awesome." Dax seemed very pleased.

Jane just stood looking at Dax for a long moment. Her dad did not have great taste in women, that was for sure. But as she thought about his friends and the men he chose to spend time with, she had to admit he did well there.

"Your dad is a good guy," Dax said.

"So are you."

"You think so?"

"I do."

"That means a lot to me."

He said it so sincerely that Jane felt a little hitch in her breathing. "I'm glad." She waited a beat then said, "Dax?"

"Yeah?"

"Get in the car. The whipped cream is melting, and we have a long drive to your hotel."

Heat flickered through his eyes, and he gave her a sexy little smile, but he simply rounded the back of the car and got into the passenger seat.

———

He didn't dare touch her.

During the forty-five-minute drive from Appleby to his hotel he didn't touch her, though his palm itched with the desire to run up and down her thigh.

He'd never seen her in a dress, and the one she'd worn today left her shoulders bare and hit above her knees showing lots of smooth, creamy skin. That plus all the fork licking and laughing today had him wound tight.

He wanted to lace her fingers with his. Or rest a hand on the back of her neck. Something. Some kind of contact. But he couldn't. If he touched her, he'd be demanding she pull the car over and they'd have sex in her front seat again.

This time if he had her naked, he was keeping her that way for a solid twenty-four hours. She wasn't leaving his hotel room until Monday morning when she had to leave to go to work. Unless he could talk her into playing hooky and calling in sick.

He knew the chances of that with this woman were probably a thousand to one. But there *was* a chance.

So he kept his hands to himself during the drive. And as they walked into the hotel and across the lobby toward the bank of elevators. And as they rode up in the elevator without touching. And as they walked down the hallway to the suite without touching.

He waved his key card in front of the sensor and pushed the door open for her, standing back so she didn't even brush against him.

But the second he stepped into the room, set the pie down on the table just to his left, and the door thudded shut, he pressed her against the wall and kissed her.

He slid his hands up to the tie at the back of her neck holding the dress up. He pulled it loose and tugged the bodice of the dress down.

Her fingers went to the front of his shirt and began tearing at the buttons as he filled his hands with her breasts. He teased the tips with his thumbs, and Jane's fingers worked faster on his shirt.

Finally, the last button came undone, and she spread it open, running her hands over his chest and abs as he plucked at her nipples. They were kissing and gasping and moaning until she pushed him back slightly.

"Your pants are in the way again." She pushed her dress over her hips.

"You're right."

They both kicked their shoes off, and he tore open his jeans, shoving them and his boxers out of the way as she skimmed her tiny blue panties off.

When they were both naked, they came back together, their mouths hungry. Dax pressed her into the wall again, his hands roaming. He palmed her breasts, plucking and pinching, before gliding to her hips where he squeezed, then around to her ass where he cupped her, bringing her up against his aching cock.

Her hands were just as busy. She ran them all over his back, to his ass, then around and over his ribs and abs, before taking his cock in hand, squeezing and stroking.

"Fuck, you feel so damned good. I don't know where to start," he told her gruffly. He wanted every inch of her. He wanted to explore. He wanted to count freckles and catalog ticklish spots and memorize creases and curves, but he also just wanted to hoist her up against the wall and plunge deep.

"We have all night and all tomorrow," she told him breathlessly.

He pulled back and stared into her eyes. "You promise?"

"Promise."

"You're not leaving? You're staying here with me?"

"Definitely."

"I haven't even told you what I have planned."

"It doesn't matter. This is where I want to be," she said.

She gave him a playful smile that was full of something that nearly sent him to his knees.

Not lust. Not heat. Not naughtiness. That was all there too, but that wasn't what he latched on to.

It was the trust and affection that made him feel like he was a king.

She was looking at him as if she liked him. Just *liked* him. Wanted to be here. Was completely enjoying herself and knew the next several hours were going to be fun no matter what they did.

This was what he lived for. What he thought he lived for anyway. What he chased. Giving other people a good time. Making them happy. Being a temporary reprieve from the shit show that the real world could be.

But Jane was looking at him as if he were a hell of a good time before he'd done a thing to earn it. Sure, the day had been fun. He knew he'd made her happy today. But in his experience, the fun was usually about the moment. The Ping-Pong game, lip-syncing into a toilet brush, the session at Comic-Con, a dessert tasting, the time in bed. But then it was over, and he'd have to work to make the next time fun again.

Jane seemed to be anticipating all the fun they could have this weekend before it even started.

"Okay, then." He gave her what he knew was a wicked grin. "Then I do know where to start."

Without looking, he reached toward the pie on the table to his left. He took a handful of whatever he first came into contact with—cream topping and strawberry filling—and lifted it.

Her eyes widened, but she did nothing to stop him as he moved toward her breast.

She sucked in a sharp breath as he smeared it over her right breast and nipple, then down, over her ribs and stomach to her mound.

He went to his knees, his sticky hand gripping her ass, and pulled her toward his mouth. Then he proceeded to lick the sweet mess from her, starting at the bottom and moving up.

She was gripping the hair at the back of his head by the time he'd licked it all from her clit and the sweet folds on either side. He ran his finger over the area to be sure he got it all and found plenty more sticky sweetness, that wasn't strawberry pie, to tease his tongue. Then he ran his tongue and fingers over her stomach, up her torso, and to her breast. He licked and sucked making sure he left no trace of pie behind. She was panting and had whimpered his name a few times by the time he let her nipple go and sealed his mouth over hers, letting her taste the strawberry goodness from his tongue.

He slid two fingers deep into her as he kissed her, taking her to the edge of her first orgasm, then he pulled back so he could watch her come.

"Open your eyes, Jane," he said gruffly, rubbing over her clit.

She let her head fall back against the wall and her gorgeous blue eyes found his.

"Come for me," he urged. "I need you slick and hot and ready."

"Oh God," she gasped, gripping the forearm that was bunching as he worked her toward her orgasm.

"I need you ready to take me, Jane," he told her roughly. "I want you so fucking bad, and I need this sweet pussy soft and wet."

"I'm so ready," she promised.

"I need you to come."

"I want you *now*." She tried to pull him closer, tugging on his arm.

But he wanted her one orgasm ahead. He shook his head and pulled his fingers from her body.

"No!" she protested, gripping his arm harder.

He grinned at her clear frustration. "Guess we'll have to pull out the big guns."

"Yes. The *big* guns," she said, reaching for his cock.

He dodged her hand with a grin though. "Oh no. The rules say we don't move on to level three until you complete level two."

"This is a game?"

"Are you having fun?"

"I *was*." She pouted.

He leaned and plucked the big red strawberry off the middle of the pie. He held it up. "Well then, we need to use all the tools we've got to get you past level two."

"I already made it past level one?" she asked.

"You're naked," he said, nodding. "That's level one."

She huffed out a little laugh in spite of herself. "And level two is an orgasm."

He shook his head. "The orgasm is how you complete the level. Level two is my hands and mouth on you. No cock involved."

She nodded thoughtfully. "Okay. So then I don't think cock in pussy is really level three."

"No?"

He wasn't going to last long if she actually got into this and played along, he realized. He had fun making sure other people had fun. But rarely did they actually concentrate on *his* fun in return.

"I really think level three would be a non-pussy orgasm for you. So my hands and mouth on you."

He cleared his throat as heat slammed through him.

"And then"—she put her hand on his chest, rubbing back and forth—"missionary position would be level four. Then like cowgirl or reverse cowgirl would be level five. All fours would be level six. Shower sex would be level seven. And you tying me to the bed with your neckties would be level ei—"

Dax took her mouth hungrily. God, he was so fucking in love with her. As she wrapped her arms around him and kissed him back, he trailed the strawberry up and down her side. He felt the way her skin erupted in goose bumps in reaction. He pulled back just enough that he could rub it over her nipple. She shivered.

He pulled away from her mouth to dip his head and suck on that hardened tip as he trailed the strawberry down her body.

He let her nipple go with a little pop and looked up at her as he sank to his knees. "So clearly we're on the same team. If the mission is to complete all the levels and the way to do that is with orgasms."

She nodded, her eyes dark, her fingers sinking into his hair. "Yep. Same team for sure."

"So what's our opposition?"

"Time, I guess," she said with a smile. "We need to get through as many levels as possible before I have to go to work on Monday morning."

"Okay, then." He grasped one of her thighs and lifted it, draping her knee over his shoulder, loving her little gasp of surprise. "Then we need focus and determination and team-work." He sucked on the end of the strawberry, then drew it over her clit. He looked up at her as she let her breath out with a little hiss. "And strawberries."

"Sure. Whatever tools and accessories and magical amulets we can get," she agreed.

Well, in *Warrior of Easton*, the warriors collected diamonds on their quests.

Dax was very aware that he was getting closer all the time to getting Jane a diamond as a matter of fact.

But for the time being, he was more than willing to make do with the strawberry and his tongue and fingers and several dirty words and phrases.

She came hard only a few short minutes later, and he carried her to the bed, triumphantly.

"Level two, down," he said, tossing her onto the mattress.

She immediately turned on her stomach and crawled to the edge. "I'm ready to do my part for level three."

And she did.

Oh, she did.

By Monday morning they had conquered levels one through eleven and had a plan to knock out levels twelve through fifteen over the course of the next week.

———

"Hey!"

Jane turned at the sound of Max calling to her. She grinned as he jogged to catch up with her halfway across the parking lots.

"I'm so pissed off at you both," Max said as he came up beside her. He put his hand on his chest and took a deep breath. "And now I've had to run too?"

Jane rolled her eyes. Max led a spin class at the gym four days a week. Because there was no one else in Appleby who would have ever thought of getting up in front of a room full of other people on bikes and calling it a "class." And truly it was a total of four stationary bikes with Max at the front blasting music from his phone and calling out encouraging things like, "You've got this! Work it, ladies!" and "Oh yeah, feel that burn!"

But he really didn't like running.

"You're pissed at me?" she asked as he fell into step with her.

"I am. You spend your lunch breaks making googly eyes at Dax and then beat it out of here at the end of the day to get naked by five thirty and then spend your whole night fucking his brains out," Max said.

Jane gave a surprised snort-laugh. "I am *not* naked by five thirty."

Max lifted a brow in a very skeptical look.

"I have to eat first," she said. "Need to fuel up for the night of fucking his brains out." She grinned widely. She couldn't help it. She was happy. So, so happy.

Now Max snorted. "That's my girl."

"But I'm sorry I haven't been around as much this week." Dax was in the Hot Cakes break room most of each morning— not before ten or so, of course, but from about ten to one— chatting and hanging out and then eating lunch with her before he took off to work on some project he had going on now that he wasn't a Hot Cakes owner. "Everything okay?"

"Oh, I'm fine, except that I've had *no* information about how great the man is in bed or how huge he is or what kinds of gifts the hot millionaire buys his fuck buddy," Max said, propping his hip against the side of her car as she unlocked it. He grinned. "This is the kind of best friend information I require and have been denied and I'm not happy about it. At all."

Jane tossed her bag onto the car seat and then gave her friend a grin. "He's amazing in bed. I seriously think he's the best lover in the *world*. The orgasms are plentiful, and I still feel them the next day. He's *huge*. Like, porn star huge. And he buys me all the cake, pie, and cookies I can handle. And does very naughty things with them before I get to eat them. But I definitely get to eat them. I've probably gained five pounds this week." She paused. "Then again, we're definitely burning a lot of calories, so it's probably all good."

Max gave a happy sigh. "Even if you're lying to me, thank you. You are a really good friend."

She laughed. "You're so welcome."

"But truly," he said, sobering slightly and studying her. "You seem really happy."

"I am," she told him sincerely. "He's amazing. And everything is so good. My dad has never been happier. He's been letting Dax visit him and even let his sister and one of his buddies stop by. I thought my aunt was going to cry. Kelsey got a B on her last chemistry test. Cassie hasn't called me even once this week. Kelsey and Aspen have only fought twice this week and one of them was just a little tiff over what time they were leaving to go to some pizza party."

"Wait." Max held up a hand. He shook his head. "I don't even know where to start."

Jane smiled. Max knew everything about her family so he knew this was huge.

"I knew Kels was working on her chemistry," Max said.

"You did?"

"Yeah, she was in the break room after school the other day."

"She was?" Jane asked, surprised. "With Dax?"

"No, with Ben."

Ben was one of the food scientists on staff. "Oh. She was studying?"

"He was tutoring her. He's a chemist, you know," Max said with a little smirk. "And he's got three kids. He was really good about explaining things to her. And the cappuccino probably helped."

"I never even thought of that." She didn't mean the cappuccino.

"Dax did." Max didn't mean the cappuccino either.

She nodded. Of course he had.

"And Kelsey and Aspen are going to parties together?" Max reiterated.

"It's the fucking twilight zone," Jane said with a nod, her thoughts suddenly spinning.

"And we attribute this all to Dax?"

"We do," she said. Then she thought about that. She really did attribute that all to Dax. Things had gotten better because of him. Like magically. Which was amazing. Wasn't it? She frowned. "I mean, he got all the balls rolling anyway."

"When are you proposing to him?" Max asked with a chuckle.

Jane forced a smile. But her chest tightened at the same time. It wasn't that she was thinking about proposing, of course. They weren't going to get married. Married was forever. And there was no way this was forever.

Which, obviously, brought up the question *how long is this going to last?* And worse, *what happens when it's over?*

Her heart started thumping harder, and she pulled in a deep breath.

She was in love with him. She thought maybe Dax was feeling some pretty strong things for her too. But small-town Iowa and a woman who worked in a factory and hanging out with a teenager and a guy in a nursing home... how long would all that interest Dax?

He was a creator. He was larger than life. He traveled the world. He made things happen. He *lived* to make things happen. Big things. Bold things. Things a lot bigger than Appleby, Iowa could sustain. Sure, he'd been happy to make some changes at Hot Cakes and to help Aiden and Ollie and his other partners get things off the ground. But he'd given it up easily enough too. Hot Cakes had been a little project for him that he'd been able to move on from without any trouble.

He was already working on something new. He'd been busy every afternoon this week.

He'd made a huge difference in her life, for sure. But in the overall scheme of things, these issues weren't all that big. Or bold. He'd gotten her sister and stepsister to stop fighting so much. He'd found a way to better Kelsey's chemistry grade, and helped with her dad's depression. He and Jane had definitely been having a lot of fun with cake frosting and, well, every room and horizontal surface in her house. But what happened when they got through all the "levels"?

What happened next?

There would be something new for him to move on to no doubt.

And where did that leave them? Did Kelsey go back to not caring about her grades? Did Jack get depressed again? Did Jane go back to juggling all the balls by herself... kind of badly? *She* hadn't been able to get Kelsey and Aspen to see one single thing they had in common. *She* hadn't thought of Ben as a chemistry tutor even though she saw him, literally, five days a week. *She* hadn't even considered taking Jack out to a dessert tasting. Or any other event.

Suddenly her heart was racing.

Everything was going to suck when Dax got tired of Appleby. Of her crazy life. Of them. And it wasn't just her who was going to suffer.

Max was frowning and reaching for her. "Whoa. You okay?"

She shook her head.

"Breathe, baby. Breathe," Max said, grasping both of her upper arms.

She did. Kind of. It was shaky, but oxygen did go into her lungs.

"What the hell, Janey?" Max asked. "You were smiling and looking all lovey dovey—not to mention smug as hell about all the chocolate-covered orgasms—and then suddenly you looked like you were about to pass out."

She nodded and swallowed. "I'm..."

"Having a panic attack," Max said.

She nodded again. "I think so." Her eyes went wide. "Why am I having a panic attack? She gripped Max's forearms. "Why am I panicking? Shit happens all the time. I know that! I'm used to that! Why am I panicking?"

"Fuck if I know," Max told her. But he gave her a little shake. "You're in love with a millionaire who makes you incredibly happy, dishes out orgasms the way we dish up fudge coating, and has made your whole family better. Why aren't you—"

He broke off as Jane started breathing rapidly again, and her fingers dug into his arms.

She felt like her head was spinning.

"Holy shit, Jane, pull yourself together."

She wasn't sure Max was going to win any empathy awards or should be teaching any seminars on getting friends through panic attacks, but she did manage to suck in a breath.

"What is going on?" He was staring at her like he'd never seen her before.

That was fair. She was never like this. She had her shit *handled*, dammit. She was always ready for the next crisis, the next curveball, the next wrench in the plan. She expected it. She just took it as it came. What the *hell* was going on here?

"It was..." She cleared her throat. "The proposal thing."

Max frowned. "I was kidding. Jesus, you don't have to propose to the guy tonight."

She dragged in another breath. "No. I know. It's not that. It just hit me, I guess. Proposal means long term. Forever." She bit her bottom lip and blinked hard. "This isn't forever with Dax."

Max's frown deepened. "It's not?"

"Of course it's not!" she snapped.

She breathed deep again and let go of Max. He let go of her too but watched her as if he was pretty sure she was going to crumple at his feet at any moment.

"Okay, why not?" he asked.

"He's a millionaire playboy who is pseudo-famous—or maybe even *pretty* famous—because he really does have *tons* of fans. People want his autograph. They wear t-shirts he designed and dress up as characters he created and stand in line for hours just to get a selfie with him. It's *nuts*. And he jets around the world and drives a crazy car and wears a *hat* that cost more than my *rent*. More than *three months* of my rent actually. He thinks nothing of buying a business for millions of dollars and then selling it a week later so he can have sex with some girl he just met. He buys Ping-Pong tables as a way to fix all problems. The *idea* of setting up his laptop on my kitchen table to work made him crazy. He has to be in the middle of the action and *with* people all the time and *doing* stuff. Big stuff. He will never be able to be happy in Appleby, not long term, and if I try to keep him here and just settle in and think that he's going to fix all my problems and get used to everything being good, when he leaves it's going to be... devastating."

Jane was aware that she'd been talking nonstop, and very quickly. But Max just let her rant. His eyebrows were nearly in his hairline when she finished, but he listened, taking it all in. He didn't interrupt or argue or even shake his head.

When she was done, Max just stood there watching as Jane took deep, shaky breaths, blinked back tears, and thought about everything she'd just said.

Yeah. That was pretty much the sum of it.

She'd been floating on a sugar-orgasm-no-angsty-phone-call high for the last several days. But everything she'd just said was true and... it sucked.

This couldn't last.

Everyone in her life already expected and needed so much from her, and she felt like she was falling short most of the time. How could she be enough for a guy like Dax?

"So Dax isn't your Prince Charming," Max finally commented.

Jane frowned. "What?"

Max shrugged. "You work so hard, literally cleaning your stepmother's house, and it kind of made you seem like Cinderella with Dax as your Prince Charming, coming in to whisk you away from it all. But he's actually been your fairy godmother... well, father. He's made all these wonderful things happen, given you a little time off from your real life."

Oh. Wow. Jane swallowed hard. "He's given me a temporary reprieve," she said softly.

That was what Dax did. So very well.

"Yeah," Max agreed, unaware of just what that all meant. "But you're thinking your coach is about to turn back into a pumpkin."

Jane sighed and let her head fall forward. That was actually a really great analogy. "The clock always strikes midnight eventually."

"Yeah. I guess so." Max sounded a little sad.

Jane lifted her head and met her friend's eyes.

"Of course, the story doesn't end after midnight," Max said, clearly trying to be supportive.

"No," she admitted. "But it's not the fairy godmother who comes after Cinderella."

Max just nodded. Then he reached out and pulled her into a hug.

She let him squeeze her, appreciating the comfort.

When he let her go she gave him a smile. "Sorry about the freak-out."

"I guess you were due," he said. "I've never seen you do that. Not with all the stuff you have going on. You keep it pretty cool."

She nodded. "I think this just snuck up on me. I let my guard down. I'm usually better at remembering that the next mess is just around the corner."

"You are my favorite cynic," Max told her. He kissed her

forehead then pulled her car door open for her. "See you tomorrow?"

"For sure."

"If you need to get drunk tonight, I'll be at Granny's."

"I'll keep that in mind."

13

As she drove out of the parking lot and headed for Sunny Orchard, she thought about just heading straight for Granny's afterward. She might be better off with tequila with Max tonight. That, after all, was a much more stable long-term plan than whatever game she and Dax would play tonight.

She walked through the doors of the nursing home, her heart still beating faster than the walk from the parking lot should have caused. She hadn't been for a run all week because she'd been up late with Dax and because rolling out of bed was a lot harder with him lying next to her. Still, she wasn't that out of shape.

No, the increased heart rate was still about realizing she was in big trouble. But it wasn't totally her fault she hadn't seen what was happening. After all, Cinderella's benefactor had been a fairy god*mother*. A nice older matronly woman if she remembered correctly. Even in the Anne Hathaway version, *Ella Enchanted*, the fairy godmother had been the, albeit gorgeous, but very female Vivica A. Fox. That Jane had assumed the handsome and charming Dax was the *prince* in this story was a fair mistake.

And by the way, where the hell *was* her prince in this little analogy, then? Was she only going to get a platonic prince in Max or something? She stopped just outside of her dad's room and took a breath. Maybe her prince was her dad. Maybe this was a reverse Cinderella story, and her dad was the one getting the makeover—of his attitude and outlook—so he could find his happiness. Maybe Dax was *Jack's* fairy godfather, and Jane was just... one of the mice that turned into a coachman for the night. Or something. The metaphor was a little fuzzy there.

She pasted on a smile and ducked into her father's room. "Hi—"

But he wasn't there.

She frowned. His wheelchair was parked in the corner of the room, but Jack was absent. She knew he didn't have any appointments today. She hadn't seen him out in the lobby area. Of course, she'd been very distracted by her thoughts about Dax when she'd come through. She pivoted and headed back for the front.

But no, he wasn't in the lobby or in the dining room or in the community room. She approached the front desk. Taylor, the girl who manned the desk after school and on weekends, was there.

"Hi, Taylor, have you seen my dad?"

Taylor looked up. "Hi, Jane. Yeah, he's in Dax's office."

Jane nodded. "Oh okay." She started to turn away. "I'll just —" She swung back. "Who's office?"

"Dax's." Taylor pointed down the hall. "It's by Ken's office."

Ken was the nursing home director. "Dax who?" Jane asked. Dax was an uncommon name. At least in Appleby. And she knew everyone who had offices in this nursing home. She'd made a point of that. So she already knew what Taylor was going to say, but Jane needed a little time to process.

"Dax Marshall. The new owner."

Okay, that hadn't been enough time. Evidently. Because as

Taylor's words hit Jane's ears, she felt a wave of shock course through her that actually made her feel numb.

"The new... what?" Jane asked, aware that her voice sounded weird.

Taylor gave her a look that confirmed she sounded weird. "Owner."

"Right." Jane nodded. "So Dax is the new... owner. He bought this place?"

Taylor shrugged. "I guess. I got a raise, and we have a cappuccino machine now, so I'm cool with whatever happened."

Of course she'd gotten a raise. That alone probably would have convinced Jane that Dax really had bought the place, but the moment Taylor said the words cappuccino machine, Jane knew it was all true.

"I don't suppose there's a new Ping-Pong table somewhere?" Jane asked, trying to calm her breathing.

Her heart was pounding again, but this didn't feel like panic. This felt like anger.

Taylor gave her a huge grin. "There is. How did you know? They put it in the rec room."

"Lucky guess," Jane muttered.

So this was his new project.

He'd given up snack cakes, gotten bored, and bought a nursing home. That made sense.

At least in Dax Marshall's world, it did.

"By Ken's office, you said?" she asked Taylor.

"Yep. Just down the short hallway behind Ken's office, actually."

"Thanks."

Jane started in that direction, trying to get her emotions under control. Dax was a good guy. He made people happy. It was his singular goal in life, in fact. He had good intentions here, she was sure.

But she couldn't quite calm her heart rate or the thick, heavy, rough rope of stress that had twisted and pulled itself into a massive knot in her gut.

This was her father. This wasn't just a way to kill some time while Dax was hanging out in Appleby.

She heard her father's stilted speech as she passed Ken's office. She couldn't make out what he'd said, but she heard Dax's answering laugh. Then she heard another voice. It was Ken, the facility director, but even more important was what he said.

"What about birds?" Ken asked. "We can start with an aviary. I've seen those in other places."

"The article specifically mentions rabbits and guinea pigs," Dax said with a shrug.

"And d-d-dogs," Jack added.

"Definitely dogs," Dax said. "We're absolutely doing dogs."

"There's just a lot to think about," Ken hedged.

"Ken, people go out to shelters and adopt dogs on a whim every single day. Rabbits and guinea pigs too, I'm sure. I don't really think there is that much to think about."

Jane rolled her eyes. Thinking things through wasn't exactly Dax's strong suit.

"And who will be taking care of the animals?" Ken asked. "The nursing and housekeeping staff are already—"

"M-me," Jack said.

"And others," Dax said. "That's the point. Residents take care of them."

"But—"

"They're dogs and rabbits and guinea pigs," Dax said. "They're not nuclear reactors. And most of our residents have had pets in the past according to the survey. For those with dementia and memory issues, the research shows caretaking tasks come back to them almost miraculously. And those who don't have those issues are fine."

"So what about the goats and the chickens?" Ken asked, his voice a little weaker.

Goats and chickens? Jane shook her head. What was going on?

"Same thing," Dax said. "The residents involved with the farm program will have experience. It will come back to them. They'll tend the gardens and take care of the animals. But of course, we'll hire someone to oversee everything."

"The llama too?"

Okay, that was enough.

Jane stepped through the doorway. "Hi, guys."

They all looked over. Ken looked relieved. "Hi, Jane." He got to his feet quickly.

"I don't want to interrupt," she lied. She completely wanted to interrupt this meeting. She wanted to know what the hell was going on.

She looked at her dad, but Jack was just smiling at her much as he did whenever she came to visit. Maybe even a little brighter than usual.

Everything had been a little brighter this past week.

Because of Dax.

She felt that heavy, ropey stress knot pull tight in her stomach even as her heart fluttered a little. Everything really had been better because of him. It had been shockingly easy to fall under the everything-is-going-to-be-so-great spell.

She finally looked at Dax. He looked happy to see her too even if a touch sheepish around the edges.

Yeah, when had he been planning to tell her his big news anyway?

"You're not interrupting. I clearly have some reading to do," Ken said, skirting around her. "Come on in."

Oh, she was going to come on in. She waited until Ken had disappeared into his office and then she shut the door. She crossed her arms and regarded the two most important men in her life. Who had been conspiring behind her back.

"So you two have been busy."

Her father didn't look the least bit sheepish. He grinned widely and picked up a paper from Dax's desk. Dax's desk. In Dax's office. In the nursing home. Because he now owned the place.

She took a deep breath.

Jack waved the papers at her. "A f-farm!"

She shook her head. "I don't know what you're talking about."

"W-w-we're going to h-have a f-f-f-" Jack looked at Dax.

"We're going to have a farm," Dax said. He smiled at her from behind the desk.

His desk. In his office. She couldn't do that again. Every time she *really* thought about what she'd just learned, she got all worked up.

"How about we start at the beginning," she said. Calmly. She was proud of herself. "I understand you bought Sunny Orchard."

Dax nodded. "Yep. It was finalized yesterday."

The guy moved amazingly fast. Then again, he had an amazing amount of money and a number of powerful contacts, she assumed, and hell, maybe the company that had owned the nursing home had been happy to let it go.

"Why?" she asked simply.

"Well, mostly because I wanted to start this farm, and in spite of my very generous donation of time, money, and knowledge, they said no."

"So you just bought the whole place?" she asked, feeling her chest tightening. "Just so you could start a *farm*?"

"Not just any farm."

Jack waved the papers he held again. Jane took them and scanned over them. "What is this?"

"It's a program introduced in Europe and brought over here for dementia and Alzheimer's patients," Dax said. "It's a working farm. The residents live there and take care of the garden and the small farm animals. It keeps them active physically and mentally because it taps into tasks they've done all their lives. It gives them a sense of purpose which also keeps them to be calmer. And it's been studied and shown to actually slow some of the progression of the disease." Dax glanced at Jack. "Jack and I were talking, and I talked to some therapists and physicians, and they agreed that even for patients whose memory isn't affected, it would keep them active and productive and could help with things like depression and overall happiness. They would not only be participating in activities that are familiar, but by contributing things to the facility like vegetables and eggs and milk, they would feel important."

Jack nodded, grinning widely, and Jane felt her heart trip.

"And we can go even further," Dax went on. "We can get some of the residents into the kitchen, canning, and baking with some of our produce. Making salads. Egg dishes. And we've even talked about taking some things to the farmer's market."

Jane shook her head. He was... something. He was definitely a big thinker. It was hardly her fault she'd gotten all caught up in him and wanting to be near him and his energy and ability to take the simplest thing and make it more.

But this was her *father*. This was people's home. This was their life.

This wasn't a game or a whim or a crazy idea that may or may not work out.

"So this is what you had Dad researching after the bridal fair?" she asked, looking at Jack.

Jack nodded, clearly pleased.

"Yep. I gave him the name of the care facility out in New

Jersey that's doing this now and asked him to find out everything he could."

"You did that?" she asked her father.

Jack nodded. "U-used the c-c-computer."

"Wow."

"Jack's farming experience has been really helpful," Dax said, smiling at her dad. "I know you're probably shocked to find out, but I don't know much about it."

She rolled her eyes but Jack laughed.

"You've been working on this a lot," she said.

"It's been a busy week," Dax agreed. He was watching her now as if waiting for her to say more.

"It's a pretty big secret to keep," she said casually. Kind of.

She was sure Dax could see the tension in her face. Jack was studying the pages again and probably missed it, but Dax's gaze was firmly fixed on hers.

"I was planning to surprise you on Saturday with everything," he said. "*We* were." He glanced at Jack.

Jack looked up with another big grin. She swore she hadn't seen him this smiley in... too long. She felt her throat tighten. Damn Dax. He was getting Jack smiling. Which had been so great at the bridal fair. For that one afternoon. They could have done that again. Gone out somewhere. Taken him to a movie. Or hell, to a farm or a petting zoo or whatever if he was missing being around animals. They could have done the temporary make-things-good-for-right-now thing periodically to help with his depression.

Dax didn't have to buy the whole fucking nursing home and promise Jack a pony. Which he really might have, for all she knew. She wouldn't be at all surprised if there was something in the literature about how great horses were. She knew therapists used horses with little kids. Why would adults really be that different? And if Dax had read...

She sighed.

"G-g-goats!" Jack said.

She arched her eyebrows. "What?"

"Goats!" Jack said again, this time on the first try.

She looked at Dax. "What about goats?"

He laughed. "We were going to take you out to see the baby goats and then tell you all our plans."

"L-l-l—" Jack tried.

Jane looked at Dax. "Do I even want to know what that is?"

He was completely unabashed when he said, "And the llama."

"The *llama*?"

"We're going to have a llama too."

Jane blew out a breath. "Sure. That makes total sense."

"Well, in fairness, the farm already has a llama. More than one. And I think they're actually alpacas."

Jane frowned. "What are you talking about? You already have the farm?"

"We're going to be using some space on Dallas Ryan's farm. Do you know him?"

"Dallas? Of course I know him." Dallas had been a year or two younger than Jane in high school. He and his brother and a couple of friends ran a huge alpaca farm a few miles outside of town. They had plenty of other animals too, and she thought they grew alfalfa for hay if not other grains for feed. "You've talked to Dallas about this?"

"Yeah, they think it's great. The residents will still live here, but we'll transport them out to our corner of the farm. We'll have a greenhouse for the garden so we can use it year-round and a small barnyard and barn," Dax said. "Dallas and his guys will help us out with the care of the animals as needed, but our residents will do as much as they can. I'm helping them out by renting the space and helping with some upgrades to the build-ings and the road."

Jane couldn't believe how much they'd gotten done in such a short time. "Wow."

"We're going to be busy. With that and the new building project." He motioned to the wall behind her.

Jane turned with trepidation. Sure enough. Architecture plans were hung on the wall detailing a complete remodel of the facility they were now in.

She rubbed the middle of her forehead.

"This is a new advancement in nursing home care as well," Dax started. "Each wing becomes its own little community. There is a kitchen and living space in each, with the rooms surrounding the common area. There will be dedicated staff and smaller numbers of patients per staff members and—"

"Sounds good." It did. Of course it did. But it was all making her feel even more restless and worried. Dax, the gaming guru, was going to oversee a nursing home? "I um... just stopped by to say hi." She smiled at her dad.

She had to admit knowing he was here, hanging out with Dax, being kept busy, researching and offering ideas and input, and getting excited about something was pretty amazing. If it could be this way every day, she'd feel so much... lighter. Knowing he was happy and not sitting in his room by himself and was engaging and feeling valued made tears prick at the backs of her eyes.

And then what would happen when Dax moved on to something else? When this project was done and he was ready for a new challenge? Or worse, when this didn't work out as planned and he shifted focus? What would that do to Jack?

She swallowed hard. "I'm going to head out since you guys seem to have a lot to do." She crossed to where Jack was sitting and gave him a tight hug and a kiss on the cheek. She stepped back and looked at him for a long moment. "You look good, Dad."

He smiled and put his hand over his heart.

"I love you too," she told him, her voice thick.

She glanced at Dax, who was already up and out of his chair, on his way to the door.

"I'll walk you out," he said.

She nodded. She knew he'd want to know what their plans were for later. That wasn't what their conversation was going to be about, however.

J ane was not excited about the goats. Or the llamas.

He wasn't sure what was going on, but Dax had to figure it out. It was driving him nuts.

He'd planned to surprise her on Saturday, not just with farm animals, but with his whole plan for staying in Appleby long term and really, truly making a difference. Doing something important. Something meaningful. Something that would impact her family directly. Something he was really excited about and feeling great about.

He was going to make her father's life at Sunny Orchard better, dammit. Lots of other people's too. He actually felt a strange tugging in his gut that told him this was where he wanted and needed to be, what he needed to be doing, that was bigger than Jack. But it was pretty fucking awesome that he got to directly make things better for one of the most important people in Jane's life.

Or so he'd thought.

Until she'd walked in and looked like she'd just sucked on a lemon when they'd told her about the goats.

They didn't talk as they walked down the hall, through the lobby, out the doors, and across the parking lots. They didn't touch either.

Dax was wound tight and feeling annoyed before they even got to her car.

More specifically, he was feeling something familiar. Something he fucking hated.

He was feeling the way he felt when he'd just told his father about something new he'd done and was waiting for his father's reaction.

And knowing it would be disapproving.

"What the hell is going on?" he asked before she could say anything.

She sighed and turned to face him. "You bought the nursing home."

"I did." He felt defensive. He *hated* that.

"That's a little... much."

Much. It was a little much? "Have you met me?" he asked.

She actually snorted. "Yeah. That's fair."

"Why is this bad?" he pressed. He just wanted to get to whatever was the problem here. He realized he was projecting some here. But he was definitely getting the same vibe from Jane that he got from his father when he'd done something big and unexpected that his dad didn't quite understand. Or trust.

Jane took a deep breath. She did not rush to insist that it wasn't bad. Dax's gut clenched.

"You are making my dad really excited about this," she said.

Dax nodded.

"You're getting him involved. Getting him invested."

"Right."

"In something you just thought up a few days ago."

Dax clenched his jaw.

She cocked her head. "I assume anyway? Considering you set foot inside a nursing home for the first time ever last week? I assume this stuff about getting nursing home residents involved in farming and remodeling facilities into smaller living communities is new to you?"

"It is," Dax admitted.

"So it's nothing you've ever done before. Nothing you have any experience in."

"No," he said tightly.

She nodded. "I'm concerned, is all."

"About?"

"It not working out."

"Why wouldn't it work out? It's worked out in other places. We have no barriers to making it work here."

It looked to him like perhaps Jane was clenching her jaw a little as well. "How long did those other places work on the farm idea before it was successful?"

He frowned. "I don't know. How long would it take? You get the animals and plants, and you take the residents out there and have them take care of it all. That doesn't seem like a months-long endeavor."

Jane took a deep breath. "They need a little more than just 'taking them out there,' don't you think? They need assistance with things like handling tools safely and lifting and carrying things like buckets and feed bags. What if they can't manage navigating the uneven barnyard with their wheelchairs and walkers and canes? What if they can't properly latch the gates and the animals get out?"

He frowned at her. His chest was tight. In part because she was right. Those things were all considerations. But also because she was so focused on all the things that could go wrong. Why couldn't she see the good he was trying to do here? "Why are you focusing on the negatives? What about the sense of accomplishment they'll feel? The physical activity they'll be getting?"

"Because *you* have to think of those things!" she exclaimed. "If you're in charge here, you are responsible for their safety and well-being!"

"That's what I'm trying to do here! I want to improve their well-being!"

She swallowed. "I believe your intentions are good. I believe your intentions are always good. But you go from wanting to make a guy smile to... llamas! It's one thing if you're just a friend of one of the residents and you want to take him out to do some new things. But you're *in charge* here. You have to think about things like how to safely implement these things. You have to think beyond getting some goats and tomato plants!" Her cheeks were pink and her eyes bright, and her voice had risen as she'd been talking. "And you shouldn't be getting their hopes up about things. You shouldn't be promising my dad things you might not be able to do!"

Dax scowled at her and stepped closer. "I *will* do this. I told Jack I'd do this and I will."

She crossed her arms, and Dax wondered if it was a subconscious move to keep him from getting too close. "Fine. Maybe you will succeed in taking them out to see goats and llamas a few times."

"It's more than that." It was a lot more than that and he wanted her to know all about it. He wanted her to believe in what the program could do. He wanted her to be excited about it. But she had to be willing to listen to the possibilities. "This program has already shown great success in other places, Jane. And with the right people on board, *we* could go past what's already been done. Who knows what kinds of outcomes we could have? We could really study the psychological effects, the physical effects, even the effects on the community."

"This is one little nursing home in one little town in Iowa," she said. "It's hardly a place where cutting-edge research happens."

"The small-town setting is one of the best things we have going," he argued. "It will make it even easier to tap into resources and get people involved and to measure the effects of our residents continuing to be a true part of the community. Too often nursing home residents get forgotten, but if the farm initiative works at getting them out and working at something they love, there are other opportunities we could explore."

"You will need so much funding and staffing and so many permissions and—"

"We can deal with all that," he cut in.

"Doing this will take time."

"I've got time."

"Do you?" She lifted her chin. "You have time to hang out in this little town that has one bar and a nonexistent gaming conference scene?"

Wow, she was really putting up every possible obstacle. "I'll *make* a gaming conference scene if I need one."

"Right. There's never been anything that you couldn't make happen if you wanted it," she said, the sarcasm thick.

"There hasn't," he told her honestly. Her doubts were starting to piss him off.

"Fine. So you'll have a gaming conference here." She rolled her eyes though. "And you'll take my dad out to see the goats a couple of times a week, and you'll pay to remodel the nursing home. And then what?"

"Then I'll figure out what else needs to be done," he said stubbornly. Dammit, the "see the goats" thing was starting to really grate. It was *more* than that.

She threw up her hands. "This isn't a game, Dax!"

He felt that like a punch to the chest. "I know."

"These aren't snack cakes that can get a little squished in the packaging or that can come out a little misshapen and get sold for half price in the warehouse," she went on. "These are *people*. This is their home. And their health."

"I know that," he said, his voice gruffer now. This was a much bigger deal than anything he'd done before. He got that. He really did. That's why he wanted it.

Dammit, he wanted her to believe in him. More, he wanted her to see that he could make things better *for her*. That he could come into her life and improve absolutely *everything*. Jane was independent and confident and knew who she was and what she wanted. She didn't *need* him. But he wanted her to *want* him and to see that maybe she could live without him, but that living *with* him was better. Happier. More fun. Easier. *Something*.

Looking at her looking at him like he was nuts and screwing everything up, Dax realized the driving force behind all this was the same thing it had always been for him—he wanted to make life happier for the people around him. But now it was so much bigger. So much more important.

So much worse if he failed.

He loved her. He wanted her to want him in lifelong terms. Not for a meet-up at the bar for pizza or for hot weekend getaways in swanky hotels or for silly Saturday afternoons at dessert tastings. He wanted all of it. The hard stuff too. The stuff with the factory. The stuff with her sister. The stuff with her dad.

He'd only dabbled in it so far. He'd improved it all. A little. Temporarily.

But what Jack had said at the bridal fair was true—things were going to get harder ahead. And Dax wanted to be there for that. To make it better for Jane somehow. He didn't know what that would look like. Or even if he'd really be able to pull it off. But he was ready to do more than buy Ping-Pong tables and sweets. He wanted to do something real, something that would matter.

But what had he done upon buying the nursing home?

He'd bought a Ping-Pong table, and he had a jar of gummy bears on his desk here too.

She thought this, the first really big, serious thing he'd maybe ever done, was a lark. A whim. Something he'd just jumped into.

And she was right.

He'd read about it and the next day started researching the use of animals in eldercare. And goats. He'd been thrilled to learn about the alpaca farm outside of town, and he'd driven there immediately to meet the guys who ran it.

"You don't think I'll follow through on this?" he finally asked her.

She took a deep breath. "I know you care about my dad, and I appreciate you trying and getting him smiling and into something that's got him out of his room and looking forward. But that's what scares me. I know you're into giving people little escapes from real life and that's amazing. I'm a big fan actually. But I don't think my dad thinks this will be temporary. And I just don't know how serious this really is for you."

Now Dax felt like the punch had landed in his gut.

Right. She was a fan of his temporary escapes from the real world. She understood why those were important. She'd finally opened up and let him do that for her. And that was what she thought he was good for.

"So I need to stick with my strengths—fun breaks, recess, gummy bears."

She looked sad. "A week ago you owned a snack cake company." She shrugged. "You went in with these big plans, but instead of implementing any of them, you brought in TVs and cappuccinos. And then you gave it all up for sex."

Ouch. When she put it like that, he sounded like a real asshole. "I passed those plans on to the others though. Piper is working with Whitney and Aiden on a lot of it."

Jane nodded. "That's great. But do you think Piper and Aiden and Whitney will come over here and take things over when you get bored?"

Ouch, again.

But he hadn't gotten bored at Hot Cakes. Or given it all up for sex.

He'd fallen in love.

He just hadn't realized it at the time.

He needed to show her. He needed to stick with this. He needed to put in the time and the work and prove to her that he was in this for the long haul.

He could do that. Probably.

He wasn't good at being patient. He wasn't good at not getting what he wanted right when he wanted it—and he wanted *her* right now—but he could put in this work.

"And now I own a nursing home," he said.

She nodded. "All of a sudden."

He suddenly owned a nursing home. Which she, and everyone, had every reason to think he'd give up as soon as something more fun came along. It looked like he was just fucking around. As usual.

"Right. All of a sudden. Because that's how I do things."

She sighed. "You're a good guy, Dax."

"Who's a ton of fun," he added.

She nodded.

He reached for her car door and pulled it open. She looked at it then back at him, finally swallowing and sliding in behind the wheel.

He thought about just shutting it. Letting her drive off. Letting her believe what she was going to believe until he could prove otherwise.

But at the last second, he gripped the car door, sucked in a deep breath, and crouched next to her seat.

He needed to tell her this. At least once.

In case he *couldn't* pull this off.

In case he couldn't actually do something that wasn't temporary and just a good time.

"I'm also a guy who's in love with you."

Jane opened her mouth. Closed her mouth. Frowned. Then opened it again. "What?"

"I'm in love with you. But I've never been in love before, and my default mode is over the top, and you're not into gummy bears or Ping-Pong, so I bought a nursing home."

"You're *in love* with me?"

"Yeah."

"Are you *sure*?"

He laughed, but his chest and gut still hurt. He nodded. "Yeah. I'm sure."

"Wow." She was just staring at him.

"So yeah." There really wasn't anything else to say. He needed to figure out what he was going to do with Sunny Orchard. How to make Jane happy. How to be the one who made her happy. More than temporarily.

He started to stretch to his feet, but partway up he leaned in and kissed the top of her head.

Then he turned and headed back into the nursing home.

She didn't stop him. Or follow him back in.

14

Most people didn't believe you could work up a sweat playing Ping-Pong.

That's because most people played Ping-Pong for fun.

Not manically as a way of working off pent-up frustration and self-loathing.

Okay, loathing was strong. He didn't *loathe* himself. But he was disgusted with himself, and adding a new level to *Warriors*, including hacking more appendages off more monsters, hadn't helped. Nor had running—he *did* loathe running. Nor had visiting an alpaca farm.

Not that visiting an alpaca farm was supposed to help work off any kind of aggression, but he'd expected it to calm him. To make him happy. And it had.

It had also made him even more certain that he wanted to take the Sunny Orchard residents to visit the alpacas on a regular basis. He wanted to go with them too. He wanted to see them interacting with the animals. He wanted to see the cognitive—yes, he'd learned that word from his recent reading—and physical changes occur. And yeah, he wanted to play with the alpacas too.

That's where it all got mixed up with his self-disgust.

Why couldn't he just let it go? Why couldn't he just recognize that the best thing for everyone would be for someone else to be the administrator at Sunny Orchard and he could just own the place?

Over the past two days, as he'd texted and called Jane with no return messages or calls, he'd been trying to convince himself to hire someone else to be in charge of... well, everything. Someone else to do the programming and implement the new ideas. Someone with experience in the field. Someone who had contacts with other people in the field.

His argument with himself went something like this —"Bring in someone who's worked in eldercare for years."

"But if they've worked in it for years, maybe they're not the right person for *new* ideas."

"But they know better than you do what kind of outcomes to expect."

"But don't we want to expect *more* than what everyone's used to?"

"What if you're expecting too much?"

"If you shoot for the moon, even if you miss, you'll land among the stars."

"You read that on an inspirational poster when you were fifteen."

"Still counts."

"You're ridiculous."

"You're an asshole."

"Yeah, well you still know nothing about running a nursing home."

Which was true.

Dax whacked the little white ball harder. It bounced back at him as if intent on revenge for the pummeling. He hit it again. And again. And again. It wasn't really helping his frustration, but it did prove he wasn't drunk enough to have impaired his hand-eye coordination. At least there was that.

Also, he couldn't get fired for drinking at work. Because he didn't work at Hot Cakes anymore.

"Oh my God, you're even weird when you're depressed?" Grant asked from the Hot Cakes break room doorway.

Dax looked over. Grant, Ollie, and Aiden were watching him.

"How can you tell if he's depressed?" Aiden asked. "He's playing Ping-Pong and eating gummy bears. That's what he does when he's happy."

Ollie pointed at the table. "He's playing Ping-Pong alone."

Dax had shoved the Ping-Pong table in the Hot Cakes break room up against a wall. Ollie was right—that in itself was a sign things were wonky in Dax Marshall's world. He never wanted to do anything alone.

"And those aren't regular gummy bears," Ollie said, pointing to the jar on the table to one side.

The guys came closer, and Aiden grinned when he noticed the bears were swimming in clear liquid.

"Vodka-soaked gummy bears?" he asked Dax.

Dax shrugged. "I tried straight vodka, but yuck." Typical. He liked the fruit-flavored vodkas, and the cotton-candy vodka he'd tried once had been delicious but straight vodka wasn't his thing. Of course, he was basically a child in a man's body, so that tracked.

Aiden pulled a bear out with a thumb and finger and tossed it into his mouth. He shrugged. "I don't think they've been in there long enough. Don't they take a few hours at least to soak up the vodka?"

"Three days to be perfect," Ollie confirmed.

Dax crossed to the jar and picked up the large spoon next to it. He dipped the spoon in as if it were a bowl of cereal and took a bite.

Aiden nodded. "Got it."

"So gummy bears and Ping-Pong whether you're happy or pissed or brokenhearted, huh?" Grant said.

"Guess so." Thing was, until now, none of them had seen him brokenhearted. He'd never *been* brokenhearted. Happy and pissed, sure. But he'd never been in love, so no one had ever been able to break his heart.

"We need to talk," Grant told him. "How drunk are you?"

"Not drunk enough." The gummy bears had only been in the vodka for about an hour and eating them with a spoon still let him taste too much of the liquor.

"Then sit down."

Dax rounded the edge of the sofa and slumped into the overstuffed cushions. He tipped his head back into the cushion behind him. "I'm ready for my pep talk."

Grant took a seat on the coffee table directly in front of Dax. He snorted. "Pep talk?"

Dax lifted his head and frowned at Grant. "Yeah. My pep talk. Where you tell me I'll get over Jane."

Aiden snorted this time and took the chair perpendicular to where Dax sat. "You're not going to get over Jane."

Dax turned his frown on Aiden. "What?"

"Jane's awesome. She's one of those girls who, if you're lucky enough to get close to her, you don't get over. You fell for her and that's forever, man."

Dax sighed even as his heart turned over in his chest. That sounded accurate. "So is this a pep talk about how to get her back?"

"This is a talk about leaving Piper alone," Ollie said, sliding onto the arm of the sofa and leaning his elbows on his thighs.

Dax frowned. "What's wrong with Piper?"

"She's now obsessed with baby llamas for one thing," Ollie said.

"Alpacas," Dax corrected. Piper had been helping him with

research. Not only the farming program for people with dementia but other programs for eldercare facilities as well as state policies and any other issues he needed to be aware of.

Ollie nodded. "Whatever. And goats. And potbellied pigs. That's what she's spending her time researching."

"And by researching, Ollie means she's been making trips out to talk to Dallas and Justin. And enjoying those trips a lot," Aiden said.

Dallas Ryan and Justin Ross owned the farm. "So?" Dax asked.

"So Piper has... enjoyed getting to know those guys," Aiden said.

"Fuck off, Aiden," Ollie said.

Dax looked at Ollie. "Oh."

"There's no *oh*," Ollie said. "We just need her in the office doing Hot Cakes work. And Fluke work. Not oohing and ahhing over... stuff at the farm."

"And by 'stuff at the farm' you mean the goats and alpacas, not the guys taking care of the goats and alpacas?" Dax asked, suddenly feeling better. Giving his friends shit always made him feel better, and it was about fucking time Ollie noticed how amazing Piper was. Maybe seeing her flirting with other guys was what it was going to take.

"Piper doesn't dress appropriately for stomping around a *farm*," Ollie said with a frown. "It's ridiculous she's going out there."

Well, that wasn't entirely untrue, but there was no way Ollie was concerned about Piper's clothes. Okay, that might not be true. Piper looked sexy as hell in the dresses and skirts she wore. Ollie might very well be concerned about *that* and what Dallas and Justin thought of her dresses and skirts. But he wasn't worried about her shoes getting dirty.

In fact, Dax had images of the farmers he'd met tearing off

their flannels and tees to lay them down over the dirt so Piper could walk through the barnyard in her hot-pink pumps like a queen. With her two shirtless escorts checking out her curves in her pin-up dresses.

He grinned. He really did love that Ollie was annoyed by this.

"Oh, no worries," Aiden said. "She got some boots."

Ollie looked over at him. "What?"

"Piper got some boots. They're like rubber rain boots. But they're bright pink with black and white polka dots. And go up to her knees. They're pretty cute."

Of course they were.

Dax could see by Aiden's grin that he really liked that this was annoying Ollie too.

"Well, great," Dax said with a nod. "Then it's all fine."

Sure, because the biggest problem here had been that Piper didn't have appropriate footwear for the barnyard.

"*Anyway*," Grant said, pulling their attention back to him. And his eye roll. "Ollie has a point."

Dax frowned. "What?"

It wasn't that Grant had *never* said Ollie had a point, but it was rare. Ollie didn't make points. Ollie came up with crazy concepts. Then Dax turned them into more tangible ideas. Then Aiden turned those ideas into actionable points. Then Cam turned those points into paperwork. And finally Grant turned that paperwork into dollars. So no, Ollie didn't often make points.

"Piper is doing a lot of work on the farm plan and that's fine. But *you* haven't done anything with it for two days."

"I'm working through some things." And texting Jane. And then trying with everything in him to *keep* from texting Jane. And then texting Jane about how he was sorry he kept texting and bugging her and how he was going to leave her alone. And then texting her about how he really was going to leave her alone, but first he wanted to say one more time that he loved her. And then texting her that he knew he was pathetic with all the texting.

He could only hope she hadn't told Zoe about it. Or that at least Zoe hadn't told Aiden. Or that at least Aiden hadn't told the rest of the guys.

"You're playing Ping-Pong and drinking a ridiculous amount of cappuccino and moping," Grant said.

"That's how I work through things."

"Bullshit."

Dax's eyebrows went up. "It is."

"I've known you for nine years," Grant said. "It takes you, max, six hours to work through things. We're going on fifty-some hours now. You're moping and avoiding."

"I don't mope and avoid."

"Exactly. So get off your ass and do something."

Dax sat up straighter. "Hey, this isn't very supportive."

"You don't need us to be supportive," Grant said. "You're in love with her, and you're mad because she called you on some shit."

He frowned. "I think I like Ping-Pong better than this." He started to get up.

"But she was wrong."

Dax sat back down. "Go on."

"She panicked because you were your usual self," Grant said. "And your usual self does spontaneous things just because they sound fun."

Dax started to get up again. He knew this.

"At least, that's why she thinks you did it," Grant went on. "Because that's what *you* think you did."

Dax sighed and settled back into the cushions. Honestly, his head was swimming a little from the vodka, and he was too tired to keep getting up and down. The manic Ping-Pong game had something to do with that. But more, he hadn't been sleeping well since he'd walked away from Jane.

He'd been determined to give her space—other than the texting, of course—but staying away, and her radio silence, was killing him slowly.

And he'd probably mess up the staying-away-physically thing too if he could go to her and say he was sorry for buying the nursing home. But he couldn't quite say that with any sincerity. He was sorry it had upset her. But he wasn't sorry about the things he'd learned and the excitement he felt about the possibilities. Or the excitement he saw in the staff and the residents who were anticipating the changes.

He'd also go to her if he could and say he was going to be selling Sunny Orchard. But he hadn't quite gotten around to doing a single thing about selling it yet either. It had only been two days. That was one excuse. But the truth was, it was because he didn't want to sell it. He wanted to make it work.

"I do things just because they sound fun," he said to Grant. "That's true."

Grant shook his head. "You're missing a key part here. The things you do sound fun to you *because they make the people you care about happy.*"

Dax frowned.

"Painting your office yellow and furnishing it with beanbags sounded fun, not because you love beanbag chairs, but because every time I walk in there and sigh, it makes Aiden, Cam, and Ollie laugh," Grant said. "I mean, I believe you like beanbag chairs, but you insist on them because of the chain reaction they cause in your friends. Me being in a room with beanbag chairs makes everyone feel lighter."

Dax narrowed his eyes at Grant. "Even you?"

"Maybe," Grant hedged.

That was good enough for Dax. He grinned. "Go on."

"You might *do* a lot of over-the-top things and sponta-neously decide some new activity or trip or project sounds fun, but it's always about how those trips and projects will affect the people you care about. When it comes to people"—Grant pointed at Ollie, then Aiden, then himself—"you stick. Nine years, Dax. Lots of trips and projects and craziness, but we have been a *we* for nine years."

Dax felt his smile die as he stared at Grant. He hadn't been expecting that.

"And I think Jane is perfect for you," Grant went on. "She's had a tough time, and even if things with the nursing home work out and things with her sister get easier, everything she's been through has impacted her and will stay with her. She's someone you'll get to spend a lot of time making happy."

He blew out a breath. "God, I hope so," he said fervently.

Grant nodded. "You need someone who needs to be made happy every single day. And she needs someone fully committed to doing that."

Dax swallowed hard. He was definitely committed to doing that. He wanted to be that person for her. He typically looked for the good time, but with Jane he wanted to be there for it all. "So what do I do now?"

"Make sure she understands she's one of your people. Everything else will make sense to her in time," Grant said.

Dax stretched to his feet and clapped his hands. Then he wobbled a little. Maybe he'd had a couple of spoonfuls too many of the gummy bears.

Grant pushed him back onto the couch. "You're getting on a plane early tomorrow."

Dax frowned. Then nodded as he remembered. "I have a nursing home conference in Austin."

Grant nodded. "That's a good idea."

"Yeah?"

"Well, you don't know shit about running a nursing home, so yeah," Grant said.

"But I need to go talk to Jane."

"I'll go talk to her," Aiden said.

Grant shook his head. "*I'll* go talk to her."

"You will?" Dax asked.

"If anyone knows how crazy you can seem but can love you anyway, it's me."

Dax's eyes got wide as he sat up straight. "Did you just say you love me?"

"I did." Grant stretched to his feet.

"I love you too, Grant." Dax was grinning bigger than he had in two days. And it wasn't just because of the liquored-up gummy bears. He had amazing friends. He must be doing *something* right.

"Yeah, yeah." Grant smoothed the front of his tie and stepped around the edge of the couch.

"I love you too, Grant," Aiden echoed, with an equally big grin.

"Shut up, Aiden," Grant said as he headed for the door.

"I love you the most, Grant!" Ollie called.

"I already regret everything," Grant said then pulled the break room door shut behind him.

But they all knew he was lying.

Dax watched him go, unable to ease his frown. He looked at Aiden. "You really don't think I should go find Jane? Or call her at least?"

Aiden shook his head. "You need to *stop* calling and texting her."

Okay, so she'd told her friends about that. And Zoe had told Aiden.

"She's with Zoe and Josie every night," Aiden said.

That made him feel a little better. "I just need to wait for her?"

Aiden shrugged. "Yeah. I mean, you said everything you could say right? You told her you loved her. Nothing has changed on your end. You're going to get your shit together and learn about nursing homes and you're going to keep going with this and make it kick ass and show her you're sticking around. But that will take time. You just have to be patient."

"I'm not good at that."

Aiden laughed. "No kidding."

It came from having a lot of money from a young age. And being accidentally successful in everything he'd ever done. Dax knew that. But instant gratification was the norm for him, and he'd very rarely had it turn out badly.

Dax settled back against the cushions once again. "I'm not going to last long. I need a grand gesture."

Aiden shook his head. "Just let Grant talk to her. Go to the conference and just... let it work out."

Dax frowned. God, he missed her so damned much. What if it didn't work out? What if she really was the one woman he could never fully win over? "Is she okay?" he asked Aiden. "Is she angry? Sad? What?"

Aiden shrugged. "She's drowning herself in Zoe's bakery case."

Dax frowned. That didn't surprise him. At least she was with her friends. And he had to admit, he was glad she was at least a little upset. Jane being fine without him was a really real possibility.

"Wouldn't that be more like suffocating?" Ollie asked. "I mean, you have to pull liquid into your lungs to drown. Pie filling is kind of a liquid, I guess, but no way could you really breathe that into your lungs. Crumbs and icing and stuff could get stuck in your nose and throat, though, and block your airways. Which is suffocating. Besides, choking is absolutely the more common way to die from baked goods. No question."

It took him a second to notice both Dax and Aiden giving him strange looks.

"What?"

"This is why Piper goes out to an alpaca farm to flirt with other men," Aiden told him.

"She doesn't go out there to flirt with anyone," Ollie said. "She just likes alpacas. Evidently."

"Uh-huh."

Ollie rolled his eyes. "It has nothing to do with me."

"Okay." Aiden shrugged.

Ollie frowned. "It doesn't."

Aiden and Dax shared a glance. Ollie really didn't know Piper had a crush on him. It was maybe better they didn't point it out.

"I think she's concerned you'll actually forget to eat for days or you'll hook up with some woman who will take you for all your money, and you won't even realize it until you go to pay a parking ticket you got because you parked your car on the street for four days straight while you were in the middle of a project and sleeping at the office."

"Piper's like an older sister to me," Ollie said. But he shifted on the arm of the couch, clearly a little uncomfortable.

Maybe he was starting to catch on that there was more there.

"Piper is five years younger than you," Aiden pointed out.

"Well, she's... my assistant. And sweet. That's why she takes care of me."

Dax actually snorted. "Piper is not sweet." She was kind. She was empathetic. She was seemingly all seeing and all knowing. But she was no nonsense and a bit cynical and impossible to bullshit.

"I don't understand why she puts up with you," Aiden told Ollie in a way only a really true friend could.

"Well, Grant loves you," Dax said, pushing up from the couch. "And I pretty much do too."

"Grant never said that, and you're drunk," Ollie told him, also getting up.

"I could see it in his eyes," Dax assured him with a grin. "And I'm not that drunk."

"Yeah, well, I love you too," Ollie said. "And I'm sorry your girlfriend can find the same comfort in pie and cake that she can with you."

Dax sighed and slung an arm around Ollie's neck. "Thanks, Mr. Compassion." They started for the door.

"And Piper is not going out to that farm to flirt," Ollie said again.

"Right. Just like you're only worried about her going out there because of her shoes," Dax told him.

———

"That's it. I'm putting my foot down."

"Try to take this pie away from me, and lose a finger," Jane told Max as she shoved another bite of strawberry pie into her mouth.

"I'm serious. I've had it up to here," Max said, pulling out the chair opposite her at the table she'd claimed three days ago at Buttered Up.

"Leave me alone, Max. If I want to eat my feelings, I can. I'm a grown woman and immune to guilt and bullying."

"Oh, I don't care if you eat your feelings, honey," Max said. "I'm just sick of not being able to buy anything strawberry from this bakery. There hasn't been any strawberry pie, muffins, scones, or even a tart for three days."

"That's because we ran out of strawberries, and our supplier doesn't come until later today," Josie said. "Those are the last ones, and Jane made us swear to hide everything in the back when we said we were running low." She pointed at the two empty mason jars that had held strawberry pie and the one Jane now had her fork buried inside.

"You're a mess," Max told Jane.

"No shit." She took another bite.

Josie climbed up onto the ladder she'd pushed in front of the tall shelves that displayed old photos and memorabilia from the bakery's history. She held a feather duster.

Zoe remained behind the front counter waiting on the few customers still trickling in and out, but the morning rush was over. And now her friends could concentrate on Jane. Much to Jane's chagrin.

"I'm so glad you're here, Max," Josie said as she reached to whisk the duster over the picture frames and vintage cookie jars on the highest shelf.

Jane frowned at her. "I haven't been that bad."

"I don't like seeing you this sad," Josie said. "Especially when you could go fix it right now."

"I'm working through some things," Jane said grumpily.

She'd been doing everything grumpily since she'd watched Dax walk back into Sunny Orchard three days ago. And eating strawberry pie grumpily was difficult because it really was heaven on earth.

"What things?" Max asked, sitting back in the chair and looking at her as if she was pathetic.

Which, of course, she was.

"That Dax loves me," Jane said.

Max just sat, clearly waiting for more. "And?" he finally asked.

"I think he really meant it."

"Oh, for fuck's sake," Max said. "Of course he meant it. He bought a *nursing home* because of you."

Jane's eyes widened. "Right? I know. *That's* what I've been thinking about."

Max shook his head.

"Well, seriously," Jane went on. She even put her fork down. "When he told me he loved me, I asked if he was sure."

Max chuckled.

Jane frowned. She'd been serious when she'd asked. "And he said 'why else would I buy a nursing home?' and *that* is what I've been thinking about for two days. I mean, honestly, why else would he? For fun? I don't know if owning a nursing home is really fun. At least not on the scale with going to Comic-Con and the other stuff he's done. And then there's the farm thing. I mean, he could go out and hang out with Dallas and Justin and those guys any time if he suddenly thinks goats and llamas are fun. He doesn't need to own a nursing home so he has an excuse or something. And then there's my dad. I mean, I know Dax likes him and wants to make him happier, but he could go over there and visit him. Or take him on outings like we did the other day. He would *not* have to buy the nursing home just to make my dad happier. So I think maybe he really did buy it because he loves me, and somehow loving me made him think about how he could do something bigger and more meaningful and something more... permanent."

She dragged in a deep breath, very aware that she'd been ranting, but that had all been swirling around in her mind for two days now amid the sugar and caffeine and now just came tumbling out. She'd been desperately trying to figure out another reason for Dax's seemingly impulsive purchase, but she couldn't come up with anything else.

She watched Max. He seemed to just be waiting to be sure she was done.

Josie's sigh was audible. "I promise you I've told her he meant it when he said he loves her," she said to Max.

"I believe you." Max gave Jane a sympathetic look. "But she's never been in love before. She doesn't know what to do now that she believes it."

"Do you think she believes it?" Josie asked. She turned on the rung of the ladder partially so she could look down at them.

"I do. I think it's sunk in."

"But it shouldn't be this hard," Josie insisted. "She's in love with him too. He's been texting her almost nonstop. She needs to just go be with him already."

"Hello!" Jane said. "I'm still here."

"Josie's right," Max told her.

Josie gave her a smug look and turned back to dusting the shelves.

"You need to just go be with him," Max said.

"It's not that easy," Jane said. Grumpily.

"Of course it is," Josie said. "Falling in love should be the easiest thing."

"It's not easy when there are all these other people who are getting involved. It's not just sex and pie, you know. There's toilets and chemistry tests and wheelchairs and freaking llamas."

"I believe they're alpacas, actually."

Everyone turned toward the new voice. Including Josie. Who actually whipped around quickly. Which caused her to wobble on the ladder. Which caused her foot to slip off the rung. Which caused her to fall.

Fortunately, the new guy caught her on her way down.

Jane gasped and was halfway out of her chair when the man's arms went around Josie, sweeping her up, and eliciting a little squeak from her.

Everyone froze for a moment.

"Holy shit, that was smooth as hell," Max said.

"Josie, are you okay?" Jane asked at the same time.

But Josie didn't reply. She was staring at the man who held her. As he stared back at her.

"Um." Max shot Jane a look.

She shrugged at him then looked back at Josie and her savior. "Josie?"

Still nothing.

"Jocelyn Diane!" Jane said loudly.

That shook Josie out of her daze. She blinked and then looked at Jane.

The man seemed to snap out of it too. He swung Josie's feet to the floor, righting her.

Josie swept a hand down the front of her dress and apron and cleared her throat. "Yes. Yeah. I'm good. Fine."

"Wow." Jane looked at the man. "That was amazing. Great reflexes."

"Well, we've had some practice at this." He was looking at Josie when he said it.

Jane frowned. "What do you mean?"

"Uh, this is... uh..." Josie tucked her hair behind her ear, and Jane was very interested to see her friend was blushing. "This is the man who caught me the other night too."

Jane felt her mouth drop open. She looked at the man with wide eyes. "Really?"

"The other night?" Max asked.

"Josie slipped off a stool in here the other night and was saved by a handsome stranger," Jane said, her mouth curling. "Or so the story goes."

Josie's blush got darker as Jane spilled that she'd called him handsome.

"Maybe you need to keep your feet on the floor around here," Jane teased.

"Or maybe not," Max said with a grin. He extended his hand to the other man. "I'm Max."

"Grant Lorre." The man took Max's hand.

"Wait." Jane frowned. "Grant Lorre? As in Hot Cakes Grant Lorre?"

"Yes."

"As in our *boss*?" Jane asked, shooting Max a glance.

Max cleared his throat. "Oh shit. Sorry. We didn't recognize you, Mr. Lorre."

"I wouldn't expect you to," Grant said. He looked at Jane. "I'm actually here to talk to you. And not about Hot Cakes."

"Me?" Jane asked.

"It's about Dax."

"Oh." She sank back into her seat. Was she in trouble for fraternizing with him when he'd been her boss? They hadn't slept together, but their flirtation had probably been obvious.

"I'm going to... go"—Josie started for the kitchen—"do ... something... somewhere else."

It was clear Grant flustered her friend, and Jane couldn't wait to dig into that further with Josie and Zoe and a bottle of wine later. But Grant was here to talk to her about Dax. Which meant they might need two bottles of wine later.

"Yeah, I'm gonna head out," Max said, getting up. "Call me later if you need," he told Jane. Then he swiped the one uneaten strawberry muffin from in front of her. "Love you."

"Love you too," she said. Suddenly her stomach was twisting, making her regret all the baked goods she'd consumed.

After the door closed behind Max, it was just Jane and Grant left in the bakery. Besides George and Phil, two regulars. They came in after the rush, sat at the same two tables every morning, and read the paper. They didn't come in together, exactly, but, both widowers, they came in at the same time and stayed for the same amount of time every morning.

She focused on the man across the table. She had to admit she understood why Josie might be a little flustered after being in his arms. He was very good looking. Tall, broad shouldered, dark hair and eyes. He looked as comfortable in his suit as she felt in her yoga pants and the t-shirt that had been washed a million times and was soft as a baby's bottom.

But he had an intensity about him that made him not her type. Her type was, apparently, a charming goofball who was only intense about Ping-Pong and llamas. Wait, excuse her, alpacas.

"How is Dax?" she asked. God, she missed him. When she wasn't thinking about how crazy he was. Or how, if she went to see him she'd probably propose to him, and there was a good chance she'd come home to find a baby goat or an alpaca in her living room some night.

No, that wasn't true. Even when she thought about those things, she missed him.

"I'm guessing kind of miserable about now," Grant said, looking at his watch.

"Really?" Did she want him to be miserable? Maybe a little. *She* was miserable. And five pounds heavier than she'd been two days ago.

"Airplanes and hangovers don't mix well," Grant said. "Though, he should definitely know that by now, so I wouldn't give him too much sympathy."

"He's on an airplane?" Her heart thunked hard against her chest. Dammit, he'd gone back to Chicago. She'd chased him off.

No! She didn't want him to leave. He couldn't run Sunny Orchard from Chicago. That meant he'd probably sold it. Son of a bitch! "How is it that he's able to keep buying and selling major businesses so quickly and easily?" she demanded of Grant. "Shouldn't these things take a few days, at least? I couldn't sell my mountain bike for *three months,* and it was practically new—I do *not* like biking because biking *sucks*—and I was asking like a hundred bucks! That was a steal! How can he just change his mind and snap his fingers and everything just *poof* falls into place? And why didn't any of his friends stop him? Any of *you*?" She glared at Grant. "You *know* he would be great at this nursing home thing! Fun innovations, bold ideas, making people happy—those are his specialties! He needs to start doing something more permanent. To see that he can make people happy long term. That he's not just a temporary reprieve for people."

She stopped, realizing that not only had she been ranting again but this time it was at her boss. One of them, anyway. Having this many was starting to get annoying. Oh, and she'd pretty much just told *herself* that Dax needed to keep the nursing home.

Grant just waited until she was done, however.

When Jane pressed her lips together, he said, "I agree. Except for the part about biking. Biking is great. And that selling major businesses is fast and easy. It's not. But he hasn't even tried to sell the nursing home, so there's that. Which is also why we didn't try to talk him out of selling it."

She pulled in a deep breath. Okay, he wasn't selling it. That was good. But he was still on an airplane right now.

"Then why is he going back to Chicago?" Maybe he just needed to get more socks or something from his apartment.

"He's not going to Chicago. He's on his way to Texas. For a nursing home conference."

She took that in. "Oh." She frowned. "Oh." He was going to a conference. To learn. To network. To figure some things out. "Wow."

"And I fully expect that in a year, he'll be presenting at conferences like that one, teaching other people about how to implement programs like the ones he's going to be doing at Sunny Orchard."

She smiled at that. "You think so?"

"I do. Because of all the things you said." Grant leaned in. "Look, of all people, I get where you're coming from. The things

Dax does are short term, fun, frivolous. But that's all on purpose. Those things accomplish his goals. But this is... different. It's more than that. He doesn't want this to be short term, and he knows it will take time and there will be ups and downs."

"He does?" she asked.

Grant hesitated then nodded. "He probably does."

She laughed lightly.

"Listen, Dax is brilliant. And he's got a huge heart. He's a pain in the ass, but I've been lucky enough to be his friend for nine years. I could have taken a number of jobs and made a ton of money and hung out with people more like me. But I need Dax. I need them all, but sometimes I think I need Dax and Ollie the most. The dreamers. The guys who are willing to go big. The guys who are willing to make me ask 'what if?' once in a while." Grant smiled. "I like to play it safe. Thanks to those guys, I have adventures too."

"And it always works out?" Jane asked, her heart hammering.

"Definitely not," Grant said. "But we're still here. Nine years later. Laughing."

She nodded. "So I can trust him to put his heart into this and do his best?"

"Absolutely. And," Grant added, "when you get one of us on your side, you get all five of us. And we're a pretty formidable team."

Jane smiled and nodded again. "Seems that way." She felt lighter. Her stomach hurt a little, but it was definitely now because of overdoing the sugar and butter for two days. "I feel like I'm going to want to kill him from time to time," she admitted.

"Oh, you will," Grant agreed.

She laughed.

Grant got to his feet. "It was nice meeting you finally," he said.

"You too." She hesitated but then asked, "Hey, Grant?"

"Yeah?"

"I don't suppose... this is really unlike me to ask, but I think maybe this once I need to be a little over the top for Dax. I don't think people do that for him much, and I was thinking that might be good for me too."

"Okay." Grant looked amused.

"And, what the hell, I guess I might as well be a little bold and ask you... I don't suppose you would be able to help me get to Texas to where he is? Like today? Like soon?"

Grant smiled and nodded. "Yeah, I could do that."

Her heart flipped and she nodded. "And I also don't suppose you know where I could get a gigantic gummy bear?"

That surprised him a little more, evidently. But he nodded again. "Well, I *have* known Dax Marshall for nine years. I know more about gummy candy than any man should."

"So you could get me *and* a gigantic gummy bear to Texas in the next few hours?"

"Yes, I could."

She grinned and hopped up out of her chair. "Don't tell Aiden, but you're my favorite boss."

He chuckled and started for the bakery door. "I'll have Piper call you in a little bit."

"Great!" Jane felt happiness washing through her and reached for the rest of her unfinished strawberry pie. She was now celebrating after all. For just a second her brain—and stomach—asked, *are you sure about this?* But she refused to ever be in a position where she was sick of strawberry anything. She scooped up a big bite.

Just as Josie came through the swinging doors from the kitchen.

Her gaze landed on Grant who stopped at the door, looking over at her.

They both froze for a moment, and Jane felt her eyes widen watching them.

Then the kitchen door swung back and hit Josie in the butt, startling her and making her take an awkward step forward.

When she'd caught her balance, she looked up at Grant again.

"'Bye, Josie," he said, a slight smile curving his lips.

"Um, bye, Grant."

"Maybe I'll see you again. Soon."

Josie nodded slowly. "Do you like sweets?"

Grant's smile grew and he nodded. "I do. Though I'm very particular."

"We can do whatever you want. Special order," Josie said.

Jane put a hand over her mouth to stifle her giggle. She wasn't sure her friend even realized how flirtatious she sounded.

But Grant did. His grin grew almost wolfish. "I'll keep that in mind. For sure." Then he stepped through the door, pulling it shut behind him, the little bell above tinkling merrily.

Josie continued to stare at the door for almost ten seconds.

"You'll do whatever he wants, special order?" Jane finally demanded, allowing herself to laugh out loud.

"What?" Josie asked.

Zoe was laughing too. "Do you like sweets?" she asked, mimicking Josie's voice but batting her eyelashes. "You little hussy!" She swatted Josie playfully with the towel she held. "Willing to give Grant your sweets just because he caught you heroically in his arms not once, but twice."

Josie's cheeks were pink but she laughed. "That is *not* what I meant."

"Uh-huh."

"We run a *bakery*," Josie insisted. "He said he'd see me again. I'm sure he was talking about my cupcakes."

"I'm sure he was talking about your cupcakes too," Phil piped up from his table.

George nodded.

Jane, Josie, and Zoe all burst out laughing.

"Well, I have to say," Josie admitted. "The name Hot Cakes is taking on a whole new meaning with these guys in charge."

Jane couldn't agree more.

Comic-Con was four million times better than Nursing Home-Con.

This thing wasn't even called Nursing Home-Con. It wasn't even that cool. Dax left the conference room at the hotel with a thick packet of handouts, feeling like he was in way over his head. Which, of course, he was.

They'd been talking about financials and Medicare payments and the pros and cons of contracting therapy services versus hiring your own in-house staff. All. Damned. Day.

Not one mention of innovative activity programs. Not one hint of anything having to do with goats.

At least they were playing Frank in the lobby. He heard the intro to "I've Got the World on a String" overhead as he stepped into the atrium.

But he came up short as his gaze landed on the woman standing under the massive chandelier in the center of the marble floor.

She was dressed in a gray pinstriped suit that Frank would have loved. She also wore black heels and a very sharp felt fedora with a black silk band above the brim.

She also had gorgeous, long red hair. And had a gigantic red gummy bear tucked under one arm and a toilet brush in the other.

Dax wasn't sure what he loved most.

Then she started lip-syncing to the song. Into the toilet brush.

When she got to the first musical declaration of being in love and pointed the brush at him, Dax finally took a deep breath: a huge, relieved, happy-to-be-alive, madly-in-love breath.

This was good. So very, very good.

He looked around and spied a cream-and-gold upholstered armchair near a tall potted plant. He pulled the chair out, took a seat, and settled in to watch the show, propping an ankle on his other knee.

Jane's eyes widened, but she shook her head as if to say, "Of course."

And she kept lip-syncing.

She even had a little choreography. A few steps that looked like maybe she'd picked them up from Kelsey.

By the time she got to the last line of the song she was right in front of him, and she'd gone down on one knee and had the huge gummy bear extended as an offering.

He'd never been happier in his life.

He hadn't realized they'd attracted a crowd until the people gathered in the lobby started to applaud.

Jane was blushing hard. Public spectacles, grand gestures, calling attention to herself wasn't her style at all. But her gaze was locked on his.

"I wanted a life-sized gummy bear, but this was the biggest Grant could round up on short notice," she said. "It's strawberry though."

He smiled at that. "It better be."

"And if that's not enough, then this fedora is another of

Frank's. It's... I don't remember. But Grant has the paperwork. It's official."

He wanted her so badly. God, this woman was everything. She was generous and funny and down to earth and loving and *real* and everything he'd never known he needed.

"If it's not enough for what?" he asked. "Jesus, I'm so happy to see you. Candy and lip-syncing is the whipped cream and sprinkles on top of this freaking gorgeous, sweet pie that I don't even think I deserve."

"It's to say I'm sorry for doubting you," she said.

He stood swiftly, pulling her to her feet. "You had every reason to doubt me. I have no idea what I'm doing, Jane."

She shook her head. "That shouldn't matter. You've given me no reason to doubt you. You care about the things you do and the people you do them for. You find a way to get things done, and you have a whole team of people who will pull together to help you. I never should have thought for a second that this would be any different."

"This is your dad. And I can't fix it. It's serious."

"But you can make it better. You always make things better. Just being there and listening. And taking us out. And taking us to see llamas. And making sure we always eat dessert."

"Strawberry pie might not always be enough," he said, cupping her face.

"No. It won't be. But *you* being there will be. I love you, Dax."

"I love you too, so damned much." He pulled her in and kissed her. Not with heat, but with all the love and hope he felt because of her and that he wanted her to have because of him.

She wrapped one arm around him. The one with the toilet brush. The other still hugged the gummy bear.

Their crowd applauded again.

He pulled back after several long, sweet moments and grinned down at her. "I'm so happy you're here."

"Me too. I'll bet the robes and room service here are awesome."

"You took time off work?" he asked.

"I did. The three days while you're here."

"Wow. Now I *know* you love me," he said with a grin.

She nodded. "I do. So much."

"And now you can go to these Medicare seminars with me."

She laughed and shook her head, pulling back. "No way. This is *your* idea. I just make snack cakes. Llamas are all you."

She did so much more than make snack cakes. But he just sighed. "They're alpacas."

"Right. Whatever. Do you have a suite?" She started toward the elevators.

He was hot on her heels. Jane was here. She loved him. They were going to make this work.

"I do." He crowded her up against the wall of the elevator as soon as the doors swished shut.

"Wonderful." She kissed him. "The strawberry pie should already be up in the room."

He was instantly hot and hard. "I'm going to have to tip the housekeeping staff extra, aren't I? We're going to make a big mess."

She nodded with a grin. "I certainly hope so."

"And with all that in mind," he said, his eyes drifting up to the hat on her head. "On a scale from zero to ten, how weird would it be to ask you to wear this in bed?"

She lifted a brow. "A seven. But I matched my bra and panties to it because I knew you'd ask."

He laughed. "I love that you know me."

"I do." She kissed him quickly on the mouth. "And I'm telling you right now... this gummy bear isn't even allowed in the bedroom, so don't ask."

———

Thank you so much for reading Forking Around! I hope you loved Dax and Jane's story!

Grant and Josie's story is next in Making Whoopie!

This marriage of convenience is about to get sticky!

———

The Hot Cakes Series
Sugarcoated
Forking Around
Making Whoopie
Oh, Fudge (Christmas)
Semi-Sweet On You
Gimme S'more

———

If you love sexy, funny, small town romance and, well, hot kitchens and baked goods ;) you should also check out my
Billionaires in Blue Jeans series!
Triplet billionaire sisters find themselves in small town Kansas for a year running a pie shop...and falling in love!

Diamonds and Dirt Roads
High Heels and Haystacks
Cashmere and Camo

Find all my books at
www.ErinNicholas.com

———

And join in on all the FAN FUN!

Join my email list!

And be the first to hear about my news, sales, freebies, behind-the-scenes, and more!

Or for even more fun, join my **Super Fan page** on Facebook and chat with me and other super fans every day!
Just search for Erin Nicholas Super Fans!

ABOUT ERIN

Erin Nicholas is the New York Times and USA Today bestselling author of over thirty sexy contemporary romances. Her stories have been described as toe-curling, enchanting, steamy and fun. She loves to write about reluctant heroes, imperfect heroines and happily ever afters. She lives in the Midwest with her husband who only wants to read the sex scenes in her books, her kids who will never read the sex scenes in her books, and family and friends who say they're shocked by the sex scenes in her books (yeah, right!).

Find her and all her books at
www.ErinNicholas.com

And find her on Facebook, BookBub, and Instagram!